WORLD OF MONSTERS

BY
JOHN LEE SCHNEIDER

SEVERED PRESS
HOBART TASMANIA

WORLD OF MONSTERS

WWW.SEVEREDPRESS.COM

ISBN: 978-1-922551-92-4

"And they worshiped the dragon which gave power unto the beast: and they worshiped the beast, saying, Who is like unto the beast? Who is able to make war with him?"
Revelations 13:4

"Come not between the dragon, and his wrath."
William Shakespeare

CHAPTER 1

The monsters were back again.

Jonah shut his eyes. It had been a long time since they'd seen any of the giant beasts looming on the horizon, but it was a sight you never forgot.

First, the mountains seemed to come alive, followed by a rumble in the earth and the roar of living thunder.

In the cockpit beside him, Naomi began to cry, because she knew what always came next.

"Please," she whispered. "Not again."

But there was no denying it. As Jonah banked their small plane north, scanning the eastern skyline, the view remained the same as far as the eye could see.

It had been nearly twelve years since the world was destroyed, but it seemed that the Apocalypse never stopped. And no matter how far they ran, it always seemed to come back to find them.

Jonah and Naomi had been living in the mountains of Wyoming ever since the last outbreak. They had found themselves a nice, cozy little cabin. There was access to a river for fishing, and nearby, they discovered a small air-park, where Jonah had acquired their little plane.

In his previous life, Jonah had been a guide-pilot, taking hunting and fishing charters up into remote areas inaccessible by ground. He had met Naomi on the day that life had ended – 'KT-day' survivors called it – the day giant monsters from the prehistoric past, somehow resurrected, had risen up and smashed the world beneath their feet.

At the time, Jonah and Naomi were two strangers who simply happened to walk out of the same general store together, only to find a *Tyrannosaurus rex* waiting in the parking lot – just one of a legion of beasts that had suddenly and inexplicably reappeared, all at once, in every city, on every continent, wresting dominance of the Earth away from hands of humankind.

The story in the days that followed suggested genetic experiments gone awry, mimicking prophesied Biblical Armageddon.

From Jonah's viewpoint, he couldn't see where it mattered. He and Naomi had been running ever since, surviving together in a dangerous new world.

But their cabin in the mountains had been a safe haven for a long time. After a while, it even seemed that ecological equilibrium might actually try and reassert itself.

As survival dictated, the two of them established routines – gathering basic necessities – food and water, chopping wood for fire. The cabin they had found was well-built and fully-stocked. It was even fitted with an electric generator, allowing them many formerly-modern comforts, so long as they used them sparingly.

Likewise, the nearby air-park was outfitted with a handful of small aircraft – obviously catering similarly to Jonah's old hunting/fishing charter industry, and included a small helicopter that was still in working order, along with an amphibious Cessna bush plane designed for both ground and water-landings.

Naomi, herself, was learning to fly, and after only a few weeks, Jonah was finding she was already better at it that he was. Not that he was surprised – she was better at everything she tried.

Today, he had taken her out over the continental divide and the New Gulf below.

The landscape of North America had dramatically changed. Shortly after KT-day, an errant nuke had apparently landed in or near the San Andreas fault, initiating a series of seismic upheavals that had shifted tectonic plates across the entire continent. And either through happenstance or malicious intent, something similar seemed to have happened along nearly the full range of the Rocky Mountains.

Jonah didn't know the how or why of it, but long-dormant volcanoes had once again begun to erupt. The Rockies had always been considered one of the more potentially dangerous volcanic regions, and now something had awakened the dragon under the mountain. The North American continent was rocked with seismic upheaval on a scale that would have dwarfed Krakatoa.

What was once the United States had now been split down the middle, creating a chasm from Texas nearly all the way into Canada. Initially, a massive canyon several miles wide, in the intervening years, that gap had been filled-in by the ocean, creating a new waterway that ran right through the middle of the country. What had once been mountains bordering on open plains was now coastline.

It was actually a fairly spectacular view and one of the main selling points for Naomi when they'd first picked out their new home. She'd always wanted a house that overlooked the ocean.

They were learning how to live in the new world – first and foremost, by keeping to the highlands. That was something they'd picked-up in the early days, in the heavily-tyrannosaur-populated country back west. It turned out the resurrected beasts didn't like altitude. The Mesozoic-era was a hundred-and-fifty-million years of lush, sultry environment and the creatures that had evolved in it didn't like the arid highlands, so the mountains were mostly safe.

You also ran into fewer *T. rex* the further east you got. Jonah wasn't really sure why, but the tyrannosaurs in general seemed to have gravitated west. Of course, you still got carnosaurs – allosaurs, megalosaurs, BIG carcharodonts – not to mention the herd-beasts – massive monsters armed with an array of horns, spikes, plated armor, and some of the larger, long-necked sauropods were pushing a hundred tons or better.

But most of those beasts preferred the open plains, which in the immediate region, had now been split by an inland sea.

All in all, it had mostly been a good-life, if rustic and isolated, and really not that different from the way Jonah, himself, had lived before the fall.

Naomi, for her part, had seemed content enough – at least until just recently.

The flying lessons had been a distraction. It had been a hard year for her.

Just last month, Naomi had announced to Jonah that she was pregnant.

And then, just two weeks later, she had miscarried.

As it turned out, it wasn't her first.

It was one of those things she had never spoken of before – kept private in a closed-vault with the man who had been her husband in her previous life.

Lieutenant Lucas Walker had been an American hero, who had died fighting the Apocalypse, and he was the man Naomi had *chosen*, as opposed to being saddled with in the wake of the storm.

That previous miscarriage, she explained, was why she and Lucas never had kids. Furthermore, after losing this second pregnancy, she was now afraid she might be barren.

Jonah had known Naomi for nearly twelve years, and these were the sort of things that were still coming out. As she'd lain in bed that night, sick and nauseous in the aftermath, she confided to him that she'd actually always been a little bit afraid of being pregnant.

"As a little girl," she said with a half-bitter laugh, "I always said I *never* would. But *now*...?"

She trailed off, but Jonah understood well enough.

'*Now*' meant after the end of the world, and maybe the end of the human race.

Jonah, who himself had been a little dubious about the prospect of being a parent in this dangerous new world, had done his best to console her.

"Maybe it's for the best," he said, holding her hand. "I mean, medical considerations aside, what kind of life would there be for a kid?" He nodded to the Spartan accommodations around them. "We've got each other, but who would *they* have?"

"We're not the only people left," Naomi replied.

That was another sore spot. Naomi had occasionally ventured the idea of searching out other people – they had periodically encountered encampments of survivors, and in the past, met fellow travelers on the road.

In those instances, there had been two attempted robberies, both at gunpoint. That was not to mention the odd groups of post-Apocalypse crazies. In Jonah's view, these were all good reasons to maintain residence high in the mountains.

There had also been a rather harrowing experience with the surviving military – '*drafted*' they'd called it, although '*shanghaied*' might have been a better word, once they'd found out Jonah was a pilot, and found themselves in need.

They'd *both* been lucky to walk away from *that* one alive.

"We may not be the very last people on Earth," Jonah said, "but you've seen who else is out there."

Naomi had not answered. She knew perfectly well.

Nevertheless, in the last few weeks, she had been spacey and despondent – sleeping too much, incommunicative and listless.

Moreover, she'd reported having odd dreams.

This had actually dated back to just before she'd initially announced her pregnancy. They were vivid dreams that seemed more like memories – more than that, like *visions* – of a place she called 'the Valley'.

Jonah had chalked it off then and now to hormones, first from her pregnancy, and then from the emotional crash after her miscarriage. It was natural enough.

Still, Jonah was worried, because Naomi *did* have a tendency to fixate – once she got an idea in her head, she was hard to dissuade. After KT-day, she had talked him into a cross-country jaunt in search of her missing husband – a trip that had ended with them crashing Jonah's rickety old chopper in the North California mountains after being attacked by pterosaurs, which, as it turned out, went after helicopters like bats after bugs.

Jonah understood psychology well enough. He recognized that this 'Valley' was likely an idealized projection manifesting in her dreams.

For her part, Naomi acknowledged this was likely so. Still, the dreams persisted.

Jonah hoped it would pass. It wasn't inconceivable that Naomi would take it as a sign that they needed to seek out other people.

He also knew that if she decided to force the matter, he would eventually acquiesce to her wishes. Push came to shove, he could deny her nothing if he thought it would make her happy.

But he was also getting older – and tired. And he desperately did not want any more adventures.

Now, however, as he looked out on the horizon at the living mountains of marching behemoths, it seemed that he wasn't going to be given a choice.

The giants had returned – and these monolithic beasts were well-along into madness – the infection had clearly spread.

The prehistoric fauna that had invaded the world periodically *bloomed*.

They called it the Food of the Gods – as fanciful as it was literal – and it invariably killed the creatures it infected. But before it did, it caused the resurrected beasts to *grow*. And then it drove them mad in a rabies-like cycle of agony and death – only then to be consumed by other beasts, causing the infection to erupt again and again, leaving nothing but utter destruction and devastation in its wake.

A single infected sauropod was a two-thousand-foot beast that could single-handedly lay waste to a city – an army of them could devastate an entire region.

On KT-day, they had rampaged across the whole world.

Long ago, the surviving military had devised a strategy to keep the infection from spreading.

When the blooms appeared, they burned them out.

Even now, as always followed, Jonah saw the twin flares of a jet-fighter approaching on the horizon.

And as always, he knew it would be armed with nuclear fire, to be spread like napalm across the entire landscape.

Once, almost twelve years before, Naomi's husband, Lieutenant Lucas Walker, had delivered a payload just like that, stopping an impending bloom that threatened to wipe-out what was left of humanity.

Lieutenant Walker had fired his missiles only moments before his fighter had been destroyed by giant flying dragons.

Naomi had watched him die. It was the death of a hero.

The military had lost a lot of heroes after KT-day.

That was how Jonah had found himself briefly inducted into service.

Jonah had never wanted to be a hero, and had certainly never wanted to fly a fighter-jet – he was just the only one available that *could*.

So there he found himself, strapped-in behind the controls of an F-16, flying Hail-Mary into a swarm of giant flying monsters, with a nuclear missile of his own attached to his wing.

And just like Lieutenant Lucas Walker before him, he had fired his payload, laying down a storm of atomic death on a whole region, extinguishing yet another bloom before it had a chance to spread.

General Nathan Rhodes, last representative of grand old Uncle Sam, had told Jonah he was a hero.

Jonah swore he would never do it again.

He thought he had done his part – afterwards, he and Naomi had fled.

But now the war continued. The nuclear war-birds were flying once more.

And Jonah knew that once again, he and Naomi would have to run.

Naomi's tears were blinding her and she buried her face in her hands. Jonah turned the plane, heading west.

Behind them, the light of a nuclear explosion lit up the mountains and the sky, consuming the marching army of giant, rage-infected beasts, burning and cauterizing the infection in radioactive fire.

Jonah lay his hand on Naomi's shoulder, feeling her tremble as, in a heartbeat, the life they had lived for more than ten years was suddenly gone forever.

CHAPTER 2

"We're definitely blooming again, folks."

Major Hicks arced his F-16 over the New York City skyline, where Food of the Gods-infected monsters rampaged. Perhaps it was appropriate, for New York was where it all began.

In the last couple of days, outbreaks had been reported in several regions at once, all east of the New Gulf, from Montana and Wyoming to a pretty good-sized bloom down in Texas.

But the biggest bloom had sprouted up here in New York, which had been ground-zero on KT-day, where the first giants had hit.

There were no people here – the city had long been abandoned. Hicks was hoping General Rhodes would just let this one burn out.

But he had his doubts – not so long as Dr. Shrinker was advising him.

Hicks' radio crackled in his ear. Major Tom was calling in from the Mount.

"I've got confirmation of at least five different sites, just today," Tom said. "This is the most activity we've seen in years."

Tom paused a moment.

"You know what *that* means."

Hicks sighed. He did know. He liked Tom – 'Major Tom' Corbett, who had turned down promotion, just so he could keep his call-sign and nickname – but right now, Hicks was tempted to be angry with him, just for telling him what he already knew.

The Food of the Gods was spreading again. And that meant nukes.

By Hicks' measure, since the end of the world, there had been more nuclear detonations just on the North American continent alone than the entirety of the Cold War – many times over.

They had gotten the Maelstrom base on-line almost eight years ago – the last surviving nuclear-site in North America – and the nuclear option had been rerouted and simplified. Today, all launch-codes resided in the safe of General Nathan Rhodes, supreme commander of the post-American military forces, and the last bastion of the United States government.

The former checks and balances that functioned as nuclear security had now been reduced to a push-button launch directly from the General's office. Rhodes simply picked the location, programmed in the code, and launched the ICBM missiles directly from the silos out of Maelstrom.

There was, of course, practical necessity behind this – the technology that once existed as a fail-safe was long-gone. There had also been incidents of infiltration and sabotage. After KT-day, there had been several errant launches – something that should have been impossible, yet it had happened.

In the days that immediately followed, their nuclear arsenal had been abruptly reduced to a few fighter-jets – 'hand-delivered' payloads, as they called them – which were risky for a number of reasons, not the least of which was a sky-full of giant flying monsters, and a limited number of trained pilots.

These days, air-strikes were largely unnecessary, ever since the Maelstrom site had once again become operational, but Rhodes still insisted that his pilots remain active and trained – the General believed in maintaining options.

Today, their single hand-delivery air-mission was the one over Wyoming – a more remote location and a smaller bloom. The pilot was one of the young guys and the mission was specifically assigned as part of his training – a kid named Wedge, who came to the Mount as a teenage-refugee, and who Hicks had trained himself.

Most often, however, strikes were carried out via remote, right from Rhodes' office.

The command and capability for nuclear attack lay solely within the province of one man.

Hicks had known Rhodes a long time, and considered him an honorable soldier and a courageous leader, who he would – and *had* – follow through Hell.

But he was also of the opinion that being a singular nuclear power was too much for any one man.

Hicks believed he had seen Rhodes wobble under that weight just a little bit.

And worse, Rhodes' primary adviser was the Mount's resident mad-scientist, Doctor Victor Shriver – '*Dr. Shrinker*' to the rank and file.

Shriver's policy, as 'scientific adviser', was 'Nuke a bloom, burn a bud' – which meant that an active infection, such as had broken out in New York, was treated with a full-on nuclear strike. Any single infected beast, particularly one that had already died from the infection, was burned out with napalm in order to keep the carrion from being scavenged and spreading the infection all over again.

But there had been a lot of full-on blooms lately – and a lot of nuclear strikes.

And they always followed the same pattern – the initial sprout at some seemingly random location, and then the larger bloom, infecting every species in the region, from carnosaurs to ceratopsians to giant sauropods.

But eventually, the tyrannosaurs would congregate on the site.

Shriver, from the depths of his scientific intellect, claimed to have isolated the specific cause, but it was one Hicks could have told him almost from the beginning. It was the same reason most of the recent blooms had sprouted in the east.

Tyrannosaurs were the key. And by now, they knew well enough what they were after.

It was a certain little parrot-talking lizard.

They were diminutive, two-foot creatures that looked like miniature sickle-clawed dromaeosaur-theropods. Survivors in the aftermath of KT-day remembered them well – the wretched little beasts were seemingly everywhere, underfoot, like rats, and always found ghoulishly scavenging off human corpses – never touching any of the infected carcasses of giants.

But they were more than just foul little vermin – so much more.

As a group, they called themselves, 'Otto'. And they had destroyed the world.

A two-foot, cloned, parrot-talking lizard, responsible for it all.

According to Shriver, they weren't intelligent in traditional terms – as individuals, they appeared to be no more than scaly little myna-birds, repeating human phrases.

It was when two or three or more of them got together.

'Gestalt', Shriver called it.

And when they appeared in numbers, the larger beasts seemed to do their bidding.

That is, with the exception of tyrannosaurs.

For whatever reason, the *T. rex hated* those little bastards.

Hicks had seen a Tyrannosaurus walk through lava and munitions fire just to stomp a single one of the scaly little rats flat. And, God-forbid, if a *rex* were infected, it became a single-minded, unstoppable juggernaut that would root the little lizards out mercilessly, wherever they found them.

This also explained why most of the blooms in recent years had sprouted in the east. The west was tyrannosaur territory – *T. rex* and its tyrant-kin were scarce beyond the New Gulf.

Scarce, but not absent, because when the blooms sprouted, they were always there – and anywhere they sensed the presence of Otto, they followed.

This time it had been in New York.

In a way, it was its own tell – by initiating the bloom, the little lizards invariably marked their own presence.

Shriver had suggested this was symptomatic of their gestalt hive-mind. He compared them to a computer – each individual 'Otto' was like a single-chip, and together they formed a mass memory bank, able to perform complex functions. But just like a computer, they were practically stupid – they lacked the ability to truly think or to innovate.

The repeating blooms, Shriver explained, were like a repeating program, mindlessly acting out a single-minded function.

Otto, Shriver said, operated on one single goal, and that was the complete and total irradiation of the human race.

There were still humans on Earth, and as long as there were, Otto would never stop.

Ironically, it was these very efforts that invariably incited the wrath of the *T. rex.*

But with no ability to innovate, they kept reenacting the same program, no matter how many times it blew back on them.

Shriver called it the organic equivalent of a computer attempting to solve a problem with inadequate software.

Hicks would have called it the very definition of insanity – after a thousand times, to keep expecting a different outcome.

And the constantly-repeating result was the destruction of entire regions.

In a way, that same inability to innovate was rather like Shriver himself.

Major Tom had once remarked to Shriver that his 'Nuke a bloom' policy was destroying ecosystems across the entire continent.

Shriver had replied that he was fine with it.

"It's necessary," Shriver said, "in order to starve the unnatural wildlife. In effect, it is the ecology itself that has become the enemy. We have to wipe the slate clean."

And *that* was the scientific mind guiding policy these days.

"Myopic focus," Major Tom had said to Hicks as they left Rhodes' office on that particular day. "It's a substitute for intelligence. No different than that damned parrot-talking lizard. Preoccupation with a single goal, with no concept of collateral damage. Or even practical results."

Tom had shaken his head in frustration.

"And what's worse, he's only a secondhand expert. The son-of-a-bitch doesn't even really know what he's talking about."

Unfortunately, on that particular front, Hicks knew they were fairly limited in their options.

In terms of 'experts', on the subject of Otto, or the resurrected prehistoric fauna in general, there were really only two. The first was the scientist who had created them, a geneticist named Nolan Hinkle, who was now nearly twelve years dead.

The other was his daughter, Shanna, supposedly an even greater genius than her father – herself a product of genetic research, born genetically perfect.

Rumors persisted that Shanna still lived, dwelling somewhere out west, in an idyllic place called the Valley.

Hicks had met her once briefly, many years ago, just before the fall of the old world, bare weeks before KT-day. He didn't know how smart she was, but he would have been happily willing to testify to 'genetically-perfect' – she was perhaps the most beautiful woman Hicks had ever seen.

It was almost impossible to describe. She had a quality that seemed almost to transcend physical beauty.

She *shined*.

Shriver had some of Shanna's notes – '*cliff-notes*' Major Tom called them – regarding both Otto and the Food of the Gods.

As far as the little lizard was concerned, Shanna's theory was that he operated as kind of a composite 'id', left to act out on its own, with no moral checks or restraints, its every action was pure escalation of destruction.

And as for the Food of the Gods, that was all apparently over Shriver's pay-grade. In her notes, taken mere days before KT-day, Shanna claimed to be within weeks of a cure – a cure that included both the elimination of the progressive madness, as well as the chemical's transmissibility – but Shriver had been stuck on that last page for almost twelve years.

Hicks' radio crackled once again, as Major Tom reported in.

"I've got confirmation," he said. "Rhodes says to withdraw to safe distance. He's sending in missiles."

Hicks sighed.

"On Shriver's recommendation?"

Major Tom returned his sigh.

"That's affirmative."

That was also a repeating pattern.

"I'm beginning to hate that son of a bitch," Hicks replied.

He tapped his own headset, bringing up Lieutenant Wedge in Wyoming, who was waiting on orders for his own first nuclear drop.

For Wedge, it was a graduation and Hicks could hear excitement in the young man's voice, like an eager puppy.

"Wedge here, sir."

"Word is given," Hicks replied. "Let it fly."

"You got it, sir," Wedge replied.

Hicks shut his eyes. When he opened them, he could already see the flares of the incoming ICBMs headed for New York. He turned his plane west, leaving the city behind.

Behind him, the desolate abandoned skyline waited, all-unknowing – once a buzzing Metropolis, the very center of the modern world, it had been ground-zero on KT-day, and was now long-since a desolate ghost-town, notable only for its remaining giant tombstones – towers of concrete and steel that once seemed to reach for the stars.

There was a blinding glare of light as the missile struck home, and New York City was finally destroyed once and for all.

"Strike confirmed," Hicks reported. "Target destroyed."

Without another look back, lest he be damned and turned to salt, Hicks headed for home.

CHAPTER 3

Two-thousand miles away, on the other side of the continent, Shanna was returning home.

She often thought of her father as she looked down into the Valley.

Her annual pilgrimage into the mountains always brought her back to this particular crest of hillside, which gave her an expansive view as the land sloped away.

She steered her old pickup along the edge of the unkempt mountain road. The brush was overgrown and the scenic beauty below belied the passage of human civilization as if it were nothing but a brief ecological daydream.

The oft-repeated words of her father, the late semi-legendary Professor Nolan Hinkle, echoed in Shanna's ear.

"The Earth is resilient," he had told her. "It is humankind that was not meant to last."

Shanna often wondered what her father would have thought of this new world, had he lived long enough to see it. He had been right about so many things.

It had been less than a dozen years since KT-day, but already the footprints of humanity had grown light. What once were farmlands, was now open wilderness, and even the paved-over landscape of the cities and towns had rolled with the movements of the Earth, splitting roads, grinding the terrain back into earth and rock.

Once upon a time, there would have been people along her journey. No longer. In fact, the Valley ahead represented one of only a few enclaves of her own species that Shanna knew for sure still existed in the entire world.

That was only one reason why she was looking forward to getting home.

Human contact was something Shanna had never taken for granted, which was a factor of the isolated life she had lived as a child – the life her father had given her – but it was a double irony that her father was also very much responsible for the life she lived today.

And while growing-up on a tropical island had its appeal, hers was an isle populated by monsters – monsters created by her own father.

'Monster Island' had long been the subject of urban legend. For Shanna, it had been home.

A top-secret research facility, originally populated by two scientists, a husband and wife team, Nolan and his wife Elizabeth, who was a brilliant genetic scientist in her own right – the two of them living isolated and alone.

Alone, that is, until the day that, into this sequestered, controlled environment, they had brought a little girl.

And what a special little girl she was.

Just *how* special would not become fully clear until much later.

Nolan Hinkle was a pioneer in genetic engineering, a serendipitous confluence of aptitude and intellect, perhaps perilously close to the border of rationality.

It was Albert Einstein who admitted that logic collapsed at the sub-atomic scale.

This is the level where DNA research began.

And of course, it was common knowledge that Hinkle's efforts at genetic engineering went far and beyond the rational.

Case in point was his daughter, Shanna, for it was through her that he established the breakthrough that allowed all the rest of it to go forward.

For many years, one of the tripping points in genetic research in regards to cloning was that the offspring picked up and exacerbated the genetic flaws from the parent. But it was within Shanna's genes that Hinkle developed and perfected his 'purification process'.

Conceptually, a sort of prenatal super-vitamin, the solution was administered early in the first trimester of Elizabeth's' pregnancy.

The result was that Shanna was literally born genetically perfect.

A simple look at her confirmed it – the long, clean limbs and bright, even features – so different from that of her dumpy parents – genetically perfect with an IQ that possibly surpassed that of both her mother and father together.

Combined with a physical health and lightness of spirit, Nolan Hinkle himself, described his daughter as, "what God really meant."

With a little help from a test-tube.

And it was on top of Shanna's genes that the foundation for all the rest of Hinkle's work was built. It was from her very genetic code that the final extract for the purification process was derived, and it was thereafter applied to every other creature on the island.

As such, a little bit of Shanna, a smidgen of her DNA – her very essence – was spliced into every one of them.

If Nolan Hinkle was Creation's tool, then his daughter, Shanna, was the lever on which it turned.

The possibilities had seemed limitless. Within their grasp was the power to not only eliminate the extinction of species, but to eradicate birth-defects, disease, world-hunger – to maximize human potential.

These were just some of the blessings Shanna's parents had tried to bring to the world.

But then, a number of things had gone very wrong.

First and foremost, Elizabeth Hinkle had died.

Shanna herself had been very young, and didn't fully understand the circumstances, but there had been some kind of an accident. All she knew was that her father had been brokenhearted.

In retrospect, Shanna suspected that his wife's death might have compromised her father's dubious grip on rationality.

Nolan Hinkle had, after all, stared into the mechanics of Creation, the recipes for God's cookbook, and perhaps had already been driven just a little bit mad.

And perhaps it was this little slip that allowed the rest of it all to happen.

Certainly, there was no malicious intent.

Nolan Hinkle would have happily given his gifts to all the world. Could he be blamed if those gifts had been perverted and abused?

Who knows what great good might have come, were it not for a single aberrant creation?

A tiny little creature called Otto, who Shanna herself had once much-loved as a family pet.

Otto was the second thing that had gone drastically wrong.

The third was the Food of the Gods.

Otto was an early experiment in intelligence, immediately in the wake of Shanna's own birth. The little creature's genetic ground-note had been an animal called Troodon, a smallish relative of the sickle-clawed Velociraptor – an abortive attempt to force cognitive reason into an organism that had not yet evolved past the soul of a reptile.

The Food of the Gods...?

Well... that was something different.

As her father had said at the time, it could change the world forever.

And change the world it did – it ended it.

With his typical whimsy, Nolan Hinkle had christened it the 'Food of the Gods'. And it quite literally was.

It was no coincidence that almost all the creatures on Hinkle's island represented giants of their lines, the titans of each evolutionary branch, pressured by evolution and environment to *grow*.

But now here was the chemical equivalent of evolution.

It took Hinkle years to isolate the gene, an extract of the pituitary gland, and years more to synthesize it.

But he did it. And the Food of the Gods came into the world for the first time. As dreams coalesce into order, so a vision becomes reality.

Of course, there *were* a few pesky little bugs.

For one, the chemical only worked on genetically engineered animals – something about the cloning process and the resulting 'flexibility' of the DNA.

This would have been acceptable if not for other problems. As Hinkle tactfully put it, the extract had a 'derisive effect' on the affected animals' temperament – they became "cantankerous and aggressive."

In truth, the *'derisive effect'* was much like rabies – progressive and degenerative. A timid, eight-pound lab rabbit became quite formidable at four-feet and two hundred pounds.

That was to say nothing of an already hundred-ton sauropod.

The final problem, however, was the clincher – the deterioration inevitably proved fatal.

Over a period of weeks and progressively escalating madness, the chemically-produced giants inevitably died.

No doubt, Hinkle would have eventually solved all these troubling glitches. After all, he was a genius and thought of little else. Alas, he never had the opportunity.

Because Otto let it out.

To be fair, Shanna knew her father had always regarded Otto as a bit of a failure – not much more than a yapping, lizard-like puppy, chirping out myna-bird-type expressions, always chasing about at their heels, following them around the island like an ever-present mascot.

But damned if Otto didn't turn out to be a lot more than that.

And damned if the scaly little rat hadn't had the run of Hinkle's lab for years – *and* had taken to cloning himself, apparently in quite large numbers.

And apparently, for a period of years he – *they* – had been sneaking critters of *all kinds* off the island, to all four corners of the world.

Then he had infected them with the Food of the Gods.

The Age of Monsters came with shocking suddenness. Humanity fought back with bombs and planes.

Mostly with desperation.

Definitely in futility.

The rampage eventually spread worldwide.

There were still people left in the world who knew what Nolan Hinkle had done. Some blamed him for it – probably even hated him. But whatever he had meant to the rest of the world, he had been Shanna's father, and she had loved him dearly. And she also knew that he would have never wanted to harm a soul. Were you supposed to hate Einstein for the atomic bomb?

Shanna supposed some people did. But with people now so few and far between, hatred was, by and large, something Shanna happened to think the species couldn't really afford.

It was a subject Shanna had worked over in her mind a thousand times – a permanently unresolved itch – and she pushed it out of her head with practiced effort. Even the weight of conscience must be shifted from time to time, and there was nothing you could do but live the life you were given.

Shanna steered the old pickup out onto the main road. She had been making this trek for years now, almost as long as they had lived in the Valley, so she knew to expect an escort. And sure enough, Shanna soon saw her greeting party waiting up ahead.

She coasted the old truck to a stop, set the brake and stepped out. Smiling, she leaned on the horn.

The massive shape that lay stretched across the road started awake, kicking once, snorting and grunting, as if in reaction to a dream, head popping up like a suddenly alert dog – staring down from some twenty feet high.

Tyrannosaurus rex was not an uncommon sight in the new world, particularly in the Valley. This particular female was known in the area as Trix, and Shanna guessed her to be over forty-feet from nose-to-tail and nearly eight tons.

Trix' five-foot skull split into a mouthful of serrated, spiked teeth nearly the size of bowling pins, and a drooling tongue lolled out as the giant head dipped in Shanna's direction. The gaping, tooth-studded maw yawned towards her...

... and the giant tongue nearly knocked her over in an extremely wet, sloppy kiss.

CHAPTER 4

"Hey, girl. Did you miss me?"

Shanna laughed with real love as she patted the big rex on her rough, scaled nose. Shanna had a way with all the creatures, but the *T. rex* were special. One of the first of her father's creations in the wake of the purification element perfected in her own DNA, the rex were *closer* somehow.

The steel muscles of the mighty beast's neck flexed as Trix lowered her head down to where Shanna could climb aboard. Abandoning her truck, Shanna scrambled up the scaly hide, mounting herself, as if on horseback, across the big female's broad neck.

Asked why she called her 'Trix', Shanna said the name just sort of popped into her head. "She just *looks* like a Trix."

The big rex stood, raising Shanna's own head above the tree-line and she could now see all the way out to the lake.

It had been more than ten years since they had first come to the Valley. Shanna would have called it time well-spent. It was certainly not the worst of lives. Who was to say which was the better world? After all, the last one had ended badly.

That was not to say there weren't still inherent dangers. Simple travel through the mountains was an adventure all its own. Some roadways survived, but they took you through routes that had been perilous even when they were still being maintained. And while Shanna's own community still utilized the localized roads, almost all the surrounding countryside was now grown-over. The modern ecology was heavy and jungle-like, much of it Mesozoic.

More importantly, beyond her Valley, was beyond the protection of the *T. rex*.

And while Shanna had a way with most of the big saurians, the more primitive theropods were notoriously chancy, and the larger the species, the more temperamental they seemed.

In particular, the giant carcharodonts, the allosaurian counterparts to the *T. rex*, were flat-out dangerous.

Even worse were the human-sized sickle-claws, who were simple bone-deep evil. The big carnosaurs were all but nonexistent in the region, due to the persecution of the tyrannosaurs, but the sickle-claws were small enough to occasionally slip past, and they ran periodic raids. The Valley lost a few members beneath their wicked claws every year. Venturing outside of tyrannosaur-territory was venturing into theirs.

That was why Shanna didn't make her twice-yearly trek up into the mountains entirely unaccompanied. She patted Trix comfortingly on the back of her massive, spike-toothed head. For Shanna, there was not a safer spot in the world than right here in the crook of the big female's neck. The *T. rex* pack were certainly protection enough in the Valley.

Up in the mountains, of course, west of the Cascades into Idaho, was the rest of her 'extended family', as she discreetly referred to them, for the benefit of her human Valley neighbors.

To a first-timer, Caesar's tribe could be a little intimidating, so Shanna chose not to overemphasize their presence or their precise nature. They had settled up in the rugged peaks of the Bitterroot mountains high in the Idaho Rockies, and they would escort Shanna from the Oregon Cascades the rest of the way. And all along, she would be pampered with the best fruits – and occasional grub – they could find.

For her trip through the mountains, two or three members of the tribe, always including Caesar himself, would also escort her most of the way back. The only stretch where she was entirely alone was while she hiked to where she always left her truck.

When asked why her mountain-folk didn't simply accompany her all the way to the Valley, Shanna would explain that they didn't get along at all well with the *T. rex*.

"Once you've seen an eight-ton gorilla square-off with a *Tyrannosaurus rex*," she explained, "you wouldn't do it again either."

That was usually enough to discourage further conversation.

It was a dangerous world, for sure. Shanna wouldn't argue. On the other hand, she couldn't help but note a few ironic constants.

In one era, thousands of people were killed every year by metallic beasts called automobiles. These days, it was genetically-engineered monsters.

A truism, Shanna thought, was that no matter where you were in society, there would always be something there to bite you.

Best not to complain, lest the fates remind you how things can always get worse.

The Valley itself had started with a bare handful of settlers – refugees running from the Apocalypse just like all the rest. But over time, that number had grown.

Shanna shut her eyes and, for just a moment, she let herself feel their lives.

That was another unforeseen side-effect of the purification process – Shanna *felt* things.

Growing up, it was mostly just sort of an empathy with nature and the creatures that shared her island – the tyrannosaurs and giant apes in particular – but almost never with other people.

She sometimes got snippets from her father – a sense of his moods and emotional weather – something she attributed to their familial relation. But she never felt anything from any of the military or sometime scientific visitors to her island.

Then she had met a young man named Cameron, who was part of an investigative journalist crew that had managed to infiltrate the security of their island. And for the first time in her short, sequestered life, Shanna was able to look into the heart of another human being.

It wasn't long after that she became pregnant, and then *everything* changed.

Whatever was within her – her *shine* – suddenly seemed to amplify, as if the world around her had suddenly come into tune with her perceptions.

People around her felt it as well, whether they knew it or not – they gravitated towards her, as if simply being in her presence made them *feel* good.

That was more of a blessing in a post-Apocalypse world than one might imagine.

Cameron described her as a sunlamp, and all the rest of them were plants – an empathic photosynthesis.

This became even more evident once they had set up residence in the Valley, and other survivors begin to filter in, as if drawn by her light.

There had originally been only thirteen who had first come in with her at the very beginning. Cameron called them Shanna's first disciples – a random assortment of human beings who, after KT-day, had just become an endangered species.

First among these disciples was a charter pilot-slash-crop-duster – a long-time friend of Cameron's, dubiously nicknamed 'Maverick' – and every bit the reckless daredevil that the name implied – along with his stern and stoic father, who everyone called by the formal 'Mr. Wilson'.

One of Shanna's closest friends was Doctor Rosa Holland, who became the Valley's first physician, and had, in fact, helped midwife Shanna's own pregnancy.

Of course, the adrenaline-addicted Maverick proved to be her most regular customer, and she had stitched or bandaged him up on an almost weekly basis during all the intervening years since they'd first settled in the Valley – a long-term relationship that had left no love-lost between them, at least on Rosa's end – Maverick, himself, was all *about* love.

Rosa had once told Shanna she believed Maverick banged himself up just for the opportunity to hit on her. She had slapped his face more than once since they'd first met – it had almost become a running joke between them.

Over time, Maverick had assigned Rosa a number of affectionate nicknames – 'the spinster' and 'old maid'. Rosa, for her part, thought he was a 'Neanderthal pig', the 'exception that proved Darwin's law', a 'missing link', and she was fine with his weekly visits to her infirmary, as they allowed her the opportunity to see him in pain.

Of course, not all of Shanna's 'disciples' had started out as such. Five more of that first group of refugees had been soldiers.

Among the more initially reluctant settlers, Wilkes and Garner had originally been assigned guards, transporting Shanna and her friends to the Mount as prisoners, but their chopper had crash-landed in the mountains after being attacked by pterosaurs. Cooper, Johnson and Bradbury had been part of an abortive rescue attempt that had not gone much better. Now all five of them were among Shanna's most steadfastly-loyal, and had all pledged that they would kill or die for her.

Then there was the one who had come in with her and then moved on. Mark Bakker, the young loner of the group, had left the Valley, continuing on all the way to the coast, having come west simply because, in the old world, it had once been his home.

And then there was the couple that lived on the hill – the highest slope in the Valley and the furthest out of town, deliberately away from all the rest.

Shanna always passed their house first when she came down out of the mountains. Now, with a grunt from Trix, Shanna paused, looking down on the open field below.

Loping across the open meadow was Big Red – a young male rex, so-named because of the crimson-tint to his skin. A product of one of Trix' earliest broods, Big Red was still young, but he was already the largest *T. rex* in the territory.

The young boy perched on the big rex' neck appeared no larger than a sparrow on an elephant's back.

Lucas was the boy's name, and he was the youngest member of the original party that had first come into the Valley, no more than six-months old at the time. Now, he had just turned eleven, and was just cresting into adolescence, showing the first signs of the straight stature, and broadening of the shoulders, as he perched like an Indian riding unsaddled across Big Red's mighty back.

Shanna stopped to watch.

A remarkable young man, she thought – the *T. rex* were looked upon with no little trepidation by most of those that lived in the Valley, despite Shanna's placating influence.

Lucas' parents were the last of the original settlers that had come in with Shanna herself. His mother, Allison, came from rough circumstances that to this day, she had never divulged. She had been traveling with a man named Bud, and while Shanna was never quite certain if he was Lucas' blood-father or if he had come on late, he had adapted the role unreservedly.

Something in Allison's past life had scarred her. The old world was more than a decade gone, yet she still seemed to hide, as if it might yet come back to haunt her.

The three of them lived on the hill, away from town. They kept to themselves, grew crops, raised livestock, including a troop of small ceratopsians, producing eggs.

Lucas was the Valley's first son, born six months after KT-day – perhaps the first-born child anywhere in the new world.

Shanna's own daughter, Leanne, was the first birth in the Valley.

And Leanne...?

Well, she was a handful. One year younger than Lucas, and eyeing her own journey into her tween-age years.

Shanna paused on the thought. The old world was gone, and now the new generation was beginning to grow up without its memory – only stories of what had been told about before.

She looked down at Lucas on the field, riding Big Red like a mustang, the young tyrannosaur charging like a greyhound from one end of the field to the other, with all the boundless energy of youth.

Shanna had started to smile when suddenly a chill seemed to blow through her like an icy wind.

It was late spring and the weather was warm, but Shanna's breath suddenly caught in her throat and her hand grabbed at her chest as if with a heart palpitation.

Below her, Trix grunted.

Out in the field, Big Red trotted to a stop.

Both tyrannosaurs turned and looked to the east.

Shanna caught her breath as she followed their gaze. That icy chill was a sensation she had felt before – and quite often just lately.

She knew what it was.

It was a sense of mass death – and of burning.

She had first felt it post-pregnancy – the first time a nuke had been deployed to wipe out an outbreak of the Food of the Gods.

This time it was far away, but it was more than one.

In the same way she felt a bond with the new wildlife, she likewise felt their fear and pain when they died.

Trix grunted again. In the field below, Lucas was patting Big Red's side, puzzled as the big rex snorted and kicked.

The *T. rex* felt it too.

Presently, the sensation began to recede, like a layer of melting frost. Trix snorted, as if shaking away a headache.

Shanna frowned. She knew the Valley wasn't the only establishment of humanity left. She knew about the Mount.

Just as she knew that sometimes, in some places, the Food of the Gods still bloomed.

But there was nothing she could do about any of it. She kicked her heels at Trix' shoulders and the big rex began to trot forward once again. Cameron would be waiting for her at home.

Her mood, however, had darkened – the zest had just gone out of the day.

Thus preoccupied, Shanna neglected to notice the presence of a strange truck parked high on the slope, not quite hidden by the brush.

Just above the house on the hill.

CHAPTER 5

Human settlements in the Northwest were not restricted just to Shanna's Valley – her... *aura*... was further reaching than that. From the mountains to the coast, her light shined.

The coast had always been a fishing community and it was once again. Humans were like any animal – they went where the food was.

Mark Bakker had come in with Shanna's first party, and he was the first to arrive at the coast. Today, he was captain of the biggest boat on the water.

All fishing these days was done out of the largest vessels possible – and for very good reason.

Fishing had always been hard, dangerous work, but in the new world, it had taken on an entirely new dimension. The first thing they discovered were sharks.

Sharks were always prevalent along the West Coast, wherever you found seals. But up in the Northwest, they had never been the problem they were in the surfing communities of southern California, because the water was mostly too damn cold for swimming. But surfers who'd tried it had been attacked.

Megalodons, however, added a whole new wrinkle.

These giant predators instinctively targeted surface prey just like their smaller Great White cousins, except that Megs were evolved to be whale hunters. Their natural prey was roughly the size of an average fishing boat, and just like white sharks attacked surfers resembling seals, the first boats that ventured out on the water got hit.

It was really quite a sight to see a seventy-foot Megalodon blast from the water with an entire fishing trawler in its jaws.

The obvious solution had been 'get a bigger boat'. However, there was still the problem of infected-giants – in which case, there was simply no boat big enough.

The Food of the Gods had filtered out over time, but the real solution again came from the simple presence of Shanna herself, in the form of yet another otherwise terrifying prehistoric sea monster.

Pliosaurs were giant ocean-going reptiles, resembling a fifty-foot seal, armed with the jaws of a crocodile. Megs were less of a danger when pliosaurs were around, and the big reptiles were naturally less aggressive to boats because they were fish-eaters, rather than surface hunters like Megs – *and*, in fact, predated on juvenile Megalodons.

Besides, being territorial like crocodiles, the pliosaurs had an orca-like effect on the Megs, and tended to drive them from the area.

And while Shanna's pacifying aura had zilch effect on fish, the temperament of pliosaurs seemed rather like the local *T. rex*.

So once again, Shanna's influence prevailed.

But it was not Shanna that brought Mark back to the Northwest – he came because, once upon a time, it had been his home.

Mark had been not-quite twenty-one when everything first started. And six-months before KT-day, he had gotten an early preview of what the world had waiting in the wings.

Born a fisherman's son, Mark had worked on the boats since he had been twelve years old. It was hard, dangerous, dirty work, but his father had insisted he learn – teach a man to fish and blah-de-blah, bullshit-bullshit-bullshit.

His family had always been fishermen and Mark's father assumed Mark himself would aspire little further. Not many locally-grown boys actually *left* the coast.

Nonetheless, after high school, he'd managed to gain acceptance to one of the state schools and Mark had hauled stakes. Once he'd left the coast, he'd intended never to return.

He'd gotten a job on a cruise-liner, traveling the world with the ritzy first-class crowd. And along the way, he had met an attractive passenger – a young woman named Sally, an upper-class princess in her own right, who had a taste for working-class roughnecks. His future was looking bright.

But then the world had gone and ended.

Funny how things worked out.

The first thing that happened was that the cruise-liner had sunk – which was actually a fairly common-occurrence in an industry that ran its ships close to the tropical coasts and near jagged shallow reefs. Of course, everything would have *still* been fine, except that all the passengers had actually made it to shore.

At the time, Mark had never heard of 'Otto', and was only passingly familiar with urban legends like 'Monster Island' and 'Area 51', but it turned out that this small stretch of the Central American coast was the site of a grow-operation the world had yet to dream of.

Eventually, Mark would hear the story from Shanna herself – how a little lizard named Otto, a genetically-engineered failure of an experiment in reptilian intelligence, had been smuggling creatures off her island for years, establishing breeding populations in remote areas worldwide.

But at the time, all Mark knew was that first night, as a hundred ship-wrecked castaways had camped on the beach, monsters out of a prehistoric nightmare had walked out of the jungle and killed them all.

Sally and Mark had been the only survivors – and when they'd eventually been 'rescued', they had been taken into custody.

As it turned out, similar incidents had started to occur in isolated areas all over the world. The powers-that-be, in the person of a man named General Nathan Rhodes, had determined that the two of them had become both security risks and intelligence assets.

Rhodes had called it 'protective custody'. Mark called it captivity.

Although, in retrospect, it had probably saved their lives. Because when KT-day had hit, they had been safely sequestered away on a remote military base, far from the cities, while the rest of the world had been summarily destroyed.

But the Apocalypse had eventually found them out as well, just a few short months later, when the Food of the Gods had sent an avalanche of monsters to stomp their base flat.

And it had to be *that* night – the first time Mark and Sally had been separated in over a year, after she had taken ill, and was moved to the infirmary.

After it was all over, Mark had climbed out of the wreckage to see what was left of the compound, and that was nothing.

He had stared at the devastation, absorbing the mind-numbing reality that Sally was now gone.

It was over. He had failed her. And he would simply have to live with that.

In all the time since, he still had not quite forgiven himself.

And so, having now officially lost everything, and with no other purpose, Mark had headed for home.

Of course, in the new world, nothing was ever quite so simple as that.

Just making it across the country had proved an odyssey all on its own.

The first thing he'd done after escaping the demolished military base was to stumble into a rex-nest, and had barely escaped being eaten by dog-sized yearlings, the last of which had collapsed nearly at his feet as he'd unloaded his pistol on the lot of them.

Their mother, however, a five-ton female, had not been happy. Mark had discovered the innate stubbornness of a tyrannosaur as that damned beast had chased him relentlessly for the next six weeks and nearly six-hundred miles – and she would have gotten him too, ironically, if not for yet another psychotic female who had tried to *feed* him to her.

Mark supposed 'dragon-worship' was just the sort of nuttiness that *had* to happen next.

Danger came in many forms in this strange new world, and this time it had been in the face of a young lady named Lily – a spritely, sexy woodland nymph, who Mark had spent one night with, before she and her troop of 'sisters' – a pack of pagan Amazons who called themselves the 'Coven' – had decided to placate their new gods by offering him up as a sacrifice to the 'dragon' that was chasing him.

Fortunately for Mark, this group of hellcats had underestimated 'Big Rexy's' eagerness in the matter. The mamma rex had demolished most of a nearby military base while hunting him down, drawing reprisal in the form of troops and attack choppers, who interrupted the sacrificial ceremony with guns and black-hawk choppers.

The outraged Coven had fired back with their own guns and all hell had broken loose.

In the ensuing chaos, Rexy had taken a bad-step over a cliff, and the Coven, including Lily, had been taken into custody – *protective* custody, of course – much as Mark once had been.

Mark, himself, had run like hell. But before he had gone, he had stumbled across the mamma rex, lying broken and suffering, but still alive, at the bottom of the cliff.

Truth to tell, he'd actually felt badly for the giant beast. He hadn't meant to despoil her nest, and perfectly understood the mother's rage.

In an ill-advised moment of compassion, he had decided to put the poor creature out of its misery with a gunshot to the head – an effort that backfired badly as the sole witness to the act was the mamma rex' last-surviving hatchling.

That sneaky little SOB had picked up the chase where his mother had left off, and 'Junior' proved to be almost worse than his mother.

T. rex were remarkably light-footed, but a five-ton female you could at least see coming. *This* little sucker would suddenly be right up on you, jumping out of the bushes, snapping miniature jaws that could take your hand off like a wire-cutter.

All this was before he even *met* the giant gorillas.

By the time he'd stumbled onto Shanna's party traveling through the Rocky Mountains, he'd been happy to join up – they had a helicopter and he was anxious to get the hell-and-gone for home.

Further irony was that the West turned out to be tyrannosaur-territory. And as it turned-out, the *T. rex* just *loved* Shanna.

And like a lost-dog, Junior had tailed him all the way to the Valley, more dogged than the crocodile that had eventually gotten Captain Hook.

That by itself was reason enough for Mark to abandon the Valley in favor of the coast.

Worse than his mother, Mark had thought – of course, he'd thought that before the little sonofabitch had grown up. These days, Junior stood over twenty feet tall and more than forty feet long.

Accordingly, Mark stayed clear of the Valley. No matter *how* well-behaved the *T. rex* were around Shanna, Mark felt better with the Coastal Mountains between them.

He had stayed there ever since.

Over the years, the fishing community had grown as well. It seemed to be where all the misfits ended up – those that responded to Shanna's glow, and perhaps appreciated the more congenial temperament of the local dragon population, but tending to come from rough stock.

Mark supposed he was one of them.

He had been a young man when it had all started, but now he had aged beyond his years. At this stage, the thought of growing old alone was a preference.

Perhaps he wasn't exactly happy, but at least his life had established a semblance of equilibrium.

He'd been born and raised a fisherman's son.

In the new world, he was a fisherman once again.

CHAPTER 6

Sally could see the unending war was taking its toll on General Rhodes.

She was sitting in his office when Major Hicks reported back, confirming the nuclear strike on New York, and then the successive hits on the other four blooms sprouting all over the country.

Rhodes never faltered but Sally could tell it was beginning to weigh on him. As his personal assistant, she saw him every day, and she had watched the lines of age sink into his face like cracks in stone.

He remained stout and straight, like a support pedestal on an ancient tower, but eventually even stone must crumble to dust.

Rhodes stood from his desk, turning towards the window, staring out at the world from the highest point on the Mount. It was the peak of the mountain that the facility had been built upon, and it looked down to where the New Gulf had filled the canyons below.

Sally glanced at the others in the room. Beside her, Major Tom looked tired.

And sitting deliberately opposite the two of them, Dr. Shrinker – *Shriver*, Sally corrected herself – was looking at the General expectantly.

Finally, Rhodes sighed, turning to Sally and Major Tom.

"You two can go," he said. "I think we're done for the day."

He remained standing as Sally and Tom rose from their chairs.

Shriver remained silent, waiting for them to leave.

Tom glanced at the doctor distastefully as he followed Sally out to the elevator.

"Wonder what *he's* got in mind," Tom muttered.

Sally didn't answer, but she had a good idea. There were usually only two things on Shriver's mind – the Arc Project and the Food of the Gods – and both always circled their way back to finding Shanna and the Valley.

Tom tapped the elevator button.

"Going down to the commons?" Tom asked amiably. His wife worked at the med-unit, which was on the same floor as the daycare where Sally would be headed to pick up her daughter, one level above the civilian-living quarters – what everyone who lived there called the Caverns – but it was all part of the Arc Project – Shriver's plan to repopulate the human race.

Sally liked Tom. Everyone alive today had a survival story, but Tom's had to top the list.

When KT-day had struck, he had been operating a one-man space-station in orbit, and he had been trapped in space for over a year. He had only managed to finally return to Earth via the escape-pods once the International Space Station came into range of his orbit.

Ironically, his time in space was how he met his wife. He had been able to receive radio waves, people broadcasting from the planet surface below – and in particular, a young survivor out of Alaska named Kristie.

She had been his picture on a desert island – the psychological fix that allowed him to cope with his isolation – and he had fallen in love with her before she ever even knew he existed.

Tom had once told Sally that the scariest moment in his life was when he finally met Kristie face-to-face. How could she possibly know what she had meant to him?

Of course, it helped that his constant surveillance allowed him to arrange an air-rescue team to save her from a troop of sickle-claws that had her cornered and surrounded.

The elevator dinged as it reached the top floor.

As the door slid open, there was a woman waiting inside.

Tall, slender, with deadly sultry eyes, she smiled thinly as she saw Sally and Tom waiting. Tom nodded back neutrally, stepping aside to let her pass.

The woman's name was Michelle and she had been a fixture nearly as long as Sally herself. She rarely spoke, but she showed-up at the end of every day, waiting patiently for Rhodes to finish his business.

"The General is still in a meeting with Dr. Shriver," Sally said.

Michelle nodded as she stepped past them, heading towards Rhodes' office. Sally glanced at Tom who shrugged as they stepped into the elevator together. As the door shut, Tom whistled through his lips.

"That woman gives me the creeps," he said.

Sally nodded. He wasn't alone there.

She wasn't sure whether to classify Michelle as Rhodes' consort or mistress or bodyguard. Sally had never once seen any PDA between them, yet she was always in the background, ready at his side – and never in the office until the end of the day. *That* was Sally's domain. Rhodes kept his private-life private – an act of compartmentalization that was utter and absolute.

Michelle herself was cold and emotionless, like a dancer at a downtown bar. Sally had no idea how old she was, but she never seemed to age. And by all appearances, she was steadfastly loyal.

But Sally had not forgotten where Michelle came from.

People all went crazy in their own ways, and before she'd come to the Mount, Michelle had been living with a little tribe up in the mountains.

Once, they might have been called pagans or witches – or Satanists, even. But after KT-day, they became dragon-worshipers.

They called themselves the Coven, and the first thing they did on arrival was sabotage the security of the Mount, and would have brought the whole place down had it not been for Michelle herself, who had sold them out at the last minute.

Rhodes apparently took this as a selling point.

But Sally thought she understood her perfectly well.

What Michelle really respected was power. An amoral alley-cat, she was utterly self-serving. So long as she perceived Rhodes as the highest authority on the planet, she would be unquestioningly loyal.

But Sally wondered what might happen to that steadfast loyalty on the day that someone bigger and badder happened to come along. As far as Sally was concerned, the fact that she had turned on her Coven sisters at the drop of a dime only suggested fidelity until the moment it became congenial to stick a knife in your back.

Rhodes, for his part, seemed fine with that dynamic, as though the possibility of someone bigger and badder had never occurred to him.

The elevator kicked a little on its tracks, prompting a small screech from Sally. Tom smiled, although she knew his time stuck in a small capsule in space had left him a bit claustrophobic as well.

Since the last seismic upheaval, the Mount had been restructured. Originally, it had been built deep into the mountain, with the intent of being resistant to nuclear strikes. No one had ever considered giant, rage-infected monsters, and they certainly had not anticipated a tectonic plate-shift capable of splitting the continent in half.

The lower levels had been crushed and buried, along with most of the concurrent civilian population. What was left of the original facility bordered on a sheer cliff that looked down into what was now the New Gulf.

No one was sure how deep the waterway was, but it was wide-enough to accommodate an aircraft carrier – one of the few that had survived KT-day – allowing them a runway for jets.

The top-deck of the Mount was built over a lava cap that formed a flat-plateau, and was outfitted with a helipad. Rhodes' administrative office was located in the hollowed-out cavern a hundred feet below – what civilians at the Mount called the 'Dark Tower'.

Dr. Shriver's lab had also been relocated on this level after his lower-basement facility had been lost in the collapse.

Beneath the administrative floor was the detention-level, and several hundred feet below that was an open hangar, which utilized the largest natural cavern in the mountain. On its east wing, the hangar opened out over the cliff, designed to accommodate the larger cargo choppers, and was utilized for storage and maintenance.

On its opposite end, the cavern narrowed into a smaller opening that emptied out onto the western slope of the mountain, which was where most of the land-based vehicles operated out of. The infrastructure for the remaining levels had been built around this natural fissure in the mountain, as well as the labyrinth of tunnels below.

The upper and lower levels of the Mount were joined by a winding staircase on the south side, and an elevator system on the north. Both access routes utilized hollowed-out lava-vents and both led directly down to the hangar, with the staircase continuing on down into the Caverns and the lower-basement levels underneath.

The elevator, built into the north side, bottomed out at the hangar-level, where the vent shaft became compressed rock, and so a secondary elevator was built on the south side, adjacent to the stairwell, providing access to the maintenance and residential levels, and allowing the transfer of heavy equipment to each floor.

Power at the Mount was facilitated through a combination of hydro and thermal energy. Seismic activity had brought plasma levels closer to the surface – another reason they could no longer access the older, lower levels, with the heat being prohibitive.

The civilian living quarters were located adjacent and below the main hangar, making wider use of the natural interior catacomb-network of caves, which was where the 'Caverns' community got its nickname.

This was the area where Shriver had reinstituted the Arc Project, with its primary goal being the repopulation of the human race. And while the day-to-day operations in the nursery/daycare center were mostly handled by civilian nannies, the regimented production of human offspring was overseen by Shriver himself.

Before the seismic upheaval that had collapsed half the Mount, the population had been two-hundred soldiers, with a civilian population of exactly three-hundred – almost all women and children, as per Dr. Shriver's Arc Project guidelines.

Currently, the civilian headcount was about half that. Nearly all of the original community had been killed in the collapse, and this time, the repopulation had been slower. In the immediate wake of KT-day, refugees had come running. Afterwards, it was more of a slow filter.

The reason, of course, was clear enough – there weren't that many humans left.

On the other hand, their resources also weren't what they used to be. As 'science-adviser', Shriver had implemented further restrictions.

Therefore, as the population of the Mount grew, some people were farmed out to a handful of other bases. The Maelstrom base received the bulk of the outgoing soldiers, along with their largest outside air base located in Idaho. And because the surrounding terrain of the Mount was not suitable for crops, they also had food-grow operations scattered about, that took in a larger portion of civilian workers.

Between all these facilities and bases, the American population, all-told, was around two-thousand human beings, officially documented as still-living on the continent, notwithstanding undeclared or non-military encampments and settlements. It was assumed that surviving pockets of humans existed elsewhere, in other countries, but these areas had been hit much harder on KT-day, and had fared much worse in the subsequent exchange of nuclear arms that followed – there had been almost no communication from anywhere overseas.

But at the Mount, the Arc Project continued. The current census reflected a melting-pot of military and civilian as the children born after KT-day began to grow, and who were now almost all the sons and daughters of soldiers living on the Mount.

Sally's own daughter, Dawn, was ten years old, and was one of the few exceptions – she had actually never known her father. Sally had been pregnant when she first came to the Mount, and she had last seen her child's father, a young man named Mark, who had been the love of her life, disappearing into the prehistoric wilderness, all unknowing, as he left her behind.

It was ironic – Sally and Mark had been together over a year, and only separated for one night after Sally had fallen sick – morning sickness, as it turned out.

And that just happened to be the night Food of the Gods-infected giants had finally found them, destroying the military base where they had been stationed.

Mark never knew Sally had survived. And she herself hadn't yet even learned she was pregnant.

Dawn was the first child born at the Mount, more than a year-and-a-half after KT-day, and she had grown-up knowing nothing else. Raised in the nursery, schooled in the daycare, she had barely ever even been outside.

It broke Sally's heart a little bit every day, when she picked her daughter up, to take her back to their little honeycomb quarters – lavish by the standards of civilians as Sally was allowed an apartment on the officer's floor.

The elevator door dinged as they reached the hangar. A buzz of activity greeted them as the doors slid open. The hangar was usually a busy place, and eyes turned in their direction as the elevator to the upper floors indicated VIP personnel. Sally was still chagrined to think of herself that way, but she supposed it was true. She was assistant to the General – for all intents and purposes, an adviser to the King.

Eyes followed her and Tom as they made their way across the hangar to the secondary elevator to take them down to the civilian levels – the Caverns. The Arc Project.

When the elevator opened into the Caverns, the commons area outside the daycare was crowded as parents filtered in to pick up their children at the end of the day.

Major Tom smiled as Kristie separated from the crowd. He met her with a hug and a twirl, followed by a big kiss, like a couple meeting at an airport after a long separation.

Kristie laughed, nodding a greeting to Sally, who returned a smile.

Tom indicated the elevator behind them. "Hold the door?" he asked.

"You two go ahead."

"Okay. See you tomorrow."

Tom whisked Kristie off her feet, stepping back over the threshold as the door closed behind them with a ding.

Sally grinned as she turned back into the crowd to look for Dawn.

The grin faded as she saw her daughter standing separate from the rest of the milling children, along with another girl, both of them looking scuffed.

Sally sighed. The other girl's name was Sabrina, and there had been trouble between them before. And the boy sitting beside them, looking nervous as his mother talked to the daycare worker, was likely the subject of this most recent spat.

The boy's name was Justin, and his mother, Kathryn, was a fiery-tempered woman that Sally, herself, considered a bit of a wildcard. Sally wasn't sure they were exactly friends, so much as parents-in-law, ever since their two kids had, as Kathryn put it, become 'puppy-lovers', dating back to a card Justin had given Dawn last Valentine's Day – something which apparently didn't sit well with Sabrina.

Sabrina was also born at the Mount, not long after Dawn herself, and at ten years old, she already wore make-up and would bat her eyes at you like a vaudevillian stage-actress.

"Some girls just started out as tramps," Kathryn had once remarked to Sally. "Knowing her mother, that one never had a chance."

Sally had nodded. She knew Sabrina's mother, and didn't much care for her either.

Lily was her name, and she had just turned nineteen when she had given birth to Sabrina. Supposedly, the father was the soldier she was currently married to – Captain Stevens, master and commander of the lone aircraft-carrier stationed in the gulf below, but who had been a smitten, love-struck young Corporal at the time Sabrina was born. But based on the timing, Sally suspected Lily had already been pregnant when she first came to the Mount.

As if the thought had summoned her, Lily appeared among the crowd of parents arriving to pick up their children for the day. When she saw Sally and Kathryn standing there, she blanched.

Seeing her mother, Sabrina pulled away from the daycare worker, who let her go with a shrug, glancing helplessly at Sally and Kathryn.

"Let me guess," Kathryn said, "she's the one that started it."

Sabrina ran over to her mother, pointing accusingly back in their direction. Sally couldn't hear the words, but Lily quickly scooped her up and hurried back into the crowd.

That was another thing that bothered her – in the ten-plus years that she'd known her, Lily had never once looked Sally in the eye.

Sally knelt beside Dawn, who was looking morose. There was a mouse developing under her right eye.

"She punched me," Dawn said, fighting tears.

"I tried to stop her," Justin interjected. He had a welt under his own eye. "She hit me too."

The daycare lady shook her head. "I'm sorry. I broke it up as fast as I could."

"It's okay," Kathryn said. "Not your fault."

She glared over her shoulder in Lily's direction.

Kathryn, who had been a social worker in the old world and hated all things military as a matter-of-course, had scowled.

"You know," she said, "my grandmother was a Wiccan, but *that* bitch is just a slut."

Kathryn nodded curtly to Sally.

"Maybe you can have the General send her out to one of the food farms."

"I'll take it under advisement," Sally replied.

Kathryn took Justin by the arm as she stalked away in a huff.

Sally sighed, taking Dawn's own hand, turning back into the rush of milling parents. As she did so, she caught Lily glancing back furtively in her direction, even as she made an effort to disappear into the crowd.

Today, Lily was in the company of another woman who Sally knew all too well – a woman named Ginger, also a daycare worker, who worked at the nursery with the littler kids.

Ginger was a bit older, and had no children of her own. She compensated by being mother to everyone – Granny Goodness.

The two of them were the last remaining members of Michelle's Coven 'sisters' who still remained at the Mount.

It was a small loss, as far as Sally was concerned. When the group of them had nearly brought the Mount down, they had nearly taken the human race with it.

Lily worked maid service. And while cleaning Shriver's lab – under supervision, no less – she had become infatuated with one of the little parrot-talking lizard-ghouls called Otto that Shriver kept on the site, and she had let the little creature out of his cage, bringing him back to show her sisters.

It was that little indiscretion that had allowed Otto the opportunity to compromise the security of the Mount – up to and including their nuclear options. If not for Michelle turning-coat at the last minute, that could have easily been the end of everything right then and there.

Ironically, because every member of the Coven – besides Lily herself who was pregnant in the infirmary – had, as a result, been locked-up in the detention level when the quakes had hit, collapsing the then-commons area of the Mount, they were almost the only civilians who had survived.

And because they were women – and, per Dr. Shrinker, all of viable age – they were pardoned.

There were priorities – the Arc Project needed breeding stock.

Not that it mattered in the end. For better or worse, the members of the Coven had chosen not to accept that role, and shortly thereafter, they had left the Mount – or 'escaped' as Shriver phrased it – after hijacking an RV truck, and driving over a guard on the way out.

Besides Michelle, Lily and Ginger were the only ones who remained behind – Lily, by then, being a new mother.

And Ginger...

Well, Ginger had since stayed on to act as sort of a crazy aunt to Sabrina. She was well-known in the Caverns as an eccentric, prone to quoting wild lore and arcane teachings.

Rhodes had kept an eye on the two of them, particularly in regards to Ginger, and anyone who might be listening to her preaching, or any following that might gather around her.

"Their right to practice religion," Rhodes had told Sally, "may be considered to be on suspension."

There were few freedoms from the old world that were still observed on the Mount.

Perhaps that was necessity – survival was paramount, which was likely why Rhodes continued to listen to Shriver after all these years. In dire times, perhaps a totalitarian state was the only option.

Still, there were rumors of another place. Somewhere out west. A semi-mythical sanctuary where things were different.

It was a place called the Valley.

One of the people who believed in it was Shriver himself. It was, in fact, his obsession.

Rumors insisted this was where Shanna, daughter of the infamous Professor Nolan Hinkle, who had brought down Armageddon on them all, had finally settled down.

Shriver had pestered Rhodes for years to root out this supposed Shangri-La – he had used words like sedition and insurrection.

For whatever reason, this was one area where Rhodes had chosen not to heed Shriver's recommendations.

"Our priorities," Rhodes had told Sally, "are not going to be rooting out surviving human encampments."

For her part, Sally knew very well why Shriver wanted to find the Valley. And that was Shanna herself. Shriver had said so. For one, she was rumored to be a genius, the sole living heir to Professor Hinkle's work and legacy – possibly the key to curing the continuing plague of the Food of the Gods.

Also, she was rumored to be genetically perfect.

That was something that would be an invaluable asset to Shriver's Arc Project.

A little genetic manipulation in the human race might go a long way.

And while she'd never said so, Sally happened to be another who believed in the Valley.

The reason being, she *knew* it was there – she could *feel* it.

Somewhere out west.

And the last thing she wanted was for Shriver to find it. Because she had no doubt what would happen if he ever did.

Perhaps Rhodes himself felt the same way. Sally suspected the General himself was not enamored by the police-state that he'd allowed his own Mount to become.

As long as there were rumors of a better place – somewhere – there was always hope.

And as she held her daughter tight, Sally knew that hope as much as anything kept dreams of the future alive.

CHAPTER 7

Caesar had been making his way back from the Valley when he heard the truck engine approach.

He had left Shanna several miles behind after accompanying her home from her bi-annual trip to visit him and his tribe.

Like the *T. rex*, the great apes shared a bond with Shanna as one of Nolan Hinkle's first creations. But the tyrannosaurs were her guard dogs, and they had a tendency to bite, so Caesar was happy enough to keep out of their way.

Caesar was the leader of the tribe of great apes that dwelled high up in the Idaho Rockies. As a mature silverback male, he stood twenty-three feet tall when reared to his full height and weighed over eight tons.

His tribe had grown over the years. Currently, his mate, Zira, was pregnant with their third child. His lieutenants, Cornelius and Dr. Zaius, both had offspring of their own. And dwelling up in the mountains left them mostly clear from conflict with the saurians, even living outside Shanna's Valley.

There was, however, still the issue of encroaching humans. Not all the two-foots had followed Shanna's aura to her Valley, and those that hadn't tended towards a darker persuasion.

So Caesar was on guard when he heard the approaching truck engine.

He had been following an old logging road that led over the pass, and it was one that looked like it had seen recent maintenance – a sure sign of human habitation. He hoped it wasn't a budding settlement or he might have to relocate his own tribe. Humans could be intolerant and dangerous, especially in numbers.

Caesar grumbled as he rubbed his great hands over the hairless patches marking a pair of old bullet wounds scarring his arm and shoulder.

A military-style RV came into view on the road ahead and the big ape shuffled into the side brush out of sight.

He sat impassively as they passed. There was an old fueling station a quarter-mile up the road, and as Caesar watched, the truck pulled over and the humans got out.

Despite the appearance of the vehicle, however, the passengers were clearly not military. They actually had the appearance of beatniks, garbed in black and adorned in bones and beads.

They were all females, Caesar noted, and they puttered quickly around the old gas-pumps with obvious ritual. This was apparently a site they had utilized before. Instead of fussing with the old public filling station, they went right to the storage tanks and attached a siphon hose.

The whole process took less than five minutes, and they carefully resealed the storage tank.

Then one of them, evidently the leader, turned to the woods, placing her finger to her lips, and let out a loud, piercing whistle.

There was a rustling in the brush.

Caesar's heavy brows curled and his broad lips drew back over his thick, sharp canines in a snarl.

Out of the bushes hopped a troop of mid-sized sickle-claws.

For a moment, Caesar had an impulse to move forward out of his hiding before the truck-full of human females were torn apart.

But then the leader who had whistled stepped forward, and as Caesar watched, astonished, she extended her hand and the sickle-claws hopped right up to her, sniffing at her like a dog.

Caesar was frankly amazed. He had never seen this behavior from sickle-claws before – not even around Shanna. In his experience, the clawed beasts were pure and simple bone-deep evil.

Which, he thought, suggested something about this troop of human females.

And that, he decided, was something best to be avoided.

The big ape turned, intending to do just that, when a telltale stench prickled his sinuses, and he made an about-face, staring back at the scene down the road.

It was a foul psychic stench that he recognized well but had not sensed in a long time.

From out of the truck, a troop of smaller lizards appeared – in appearance, they were not much different than the larger sickle-claws.

Otto.

The little creatures hopped up on the truck's hood, hooting and chirping like birds.

That explained the sickle-claws' obedience.

Now Caesar moved forward.

One thing that the *T. rex* and the great apes had in common was a zero-tolerance policy for *those* little bastards.

But before he got twenty yards, the truck started up and pulled back onto the road, with the Ottos riding up top and the sickle-claws bounding along behind.

Caesar trotted to a stop, watching as they dipped over the hill.

The big ape frowned.

They were headed west, in the general direction of the Valley.

He wondered if they were foolish enough to attempt the tyrannosaur-territory there. *T. rex* noses could detect a sickle-claw a mile away. And if they sensed the presence of Otto, they would root them out like a bear digging for termites in an old log.

Caesar paused a moment, wondering if he should follow.

The truck, however, was already out of sight. There was no way he could catch up to them on the open road.

Still, he was troubled. Now he found himself concerned about his own tribe in his absence, especially if sickle-claws were prowling about – let alone Otto.

Caesar stepped up his pace as he resumed his northeast path back over the mountain. He still had a long way to go.

He had put another hour and almost ten more miles behind him when he felt a sudden chill.

Caesar stopped in his tracks.

A low growl escaped him as he now turned and looked to the east.

Much as Shanna had herself, Caesar felt the same sense of burning and death emanating like a cold wind.

The big ape stood staring, indecisive. The sensation was far away, but it was not the first time he'd felt such things in recent weeks.

Things were getting bad again. As he glanced back to where Otto and the strange troop of human females had disappeared, he wondered what deviltry might be afoot.

Again, he thought of his tribe, his mate and young ones, and in the wake of the cold psychic wind, he found he wanted to be near them again.

With a grunt, he stepped up into a fast trot, heading for home.

CHAPTER 8

Leanne hid in the bushes as she watched Lucas from the hillside.

Her mother had just gotten home an hour before from her sojourn in the mountains, and she had sent Leanne off to the town market. Leanne had side-tracked past Lucas' farm, which wasn't exactly on the way, but she had already been headed this direction.

She didn't tell her mother where she was going – she knew what Shanna would say, and nothing irritated Leanne more than being told she had a crush on Lucas.

Leanne could not fairly be called spoiled – not in this difficult and dangerous new world – but she could be a bit imperious. She was well aware of her mother's role in the community, and her own resulting place as well.

It might be better said that she fit the role of a princess – not in the global-nation's sense, but more evocative of one of those old-time 'kingdoms' that might encompass a single region or town – or valley.

Leanne was ten years old, and in as big a hurry to grow-up as any little girl ever was. By all outward appearances, she was full of uncorked energy and unbridled confidence. Yet, the truth was that this outer facade masked a strong sense of self-doubt.

And perhaps one reason was actually *because* of who her mother was to the people of the Valley – that, and the things Shanna could *do*.

Case in point, she had come riding home on Trix, the senior female *T. rex* in the Valley – the pack leader. Shanna had a way with them. They responded to her like dogs.

Leanne herself was actually a bit afraid of the tyrannosaurs, and they didn't respond to her in the same way at all.

That was really the source of her fascination with Lucas – he could ride the *T. rex*. No other person in the Valley besides Shanna herself had even dared *try* it – not even her father's daredevil pilot-friend, Maverick.

Leanne could see Lucas now, down in the field, mounted across Big Red's shoulders – the biggest rex in the entire territory.

She watched him with a mixture of jealousy and awe, and she was absolutely adamant that it had *nothing* to do with *any* kind of crush!

That was also why she hid from Lucas, just to make sure *he* didn't think so either.

Truthfully, she thought of him as a bit of an oafish show-off, always trying to impress. Once, when she'd come across him fishing over at the lake, he had shot a bird out of the air with his bow. It was just a little songbird, just to show her that he could. Leanne had been horrified.

Lucas, of course, had been crestfallen at her reaction, and then he had made it worse by offering to make her a necklace out of the feathers.

On the other hand, even her mother was impressed by his way with the *T. rex*.

Some people judged your character by whether or not their dog liked you. It was quite another thing to be able to jump on the back of a Tyrannosaurus.

Which left Leanne all the more frustrated that she couldn't do it herself.

Down below, Big Red had slowed to a trot as they approached a small grove of trees on the opposite side of the open field not far from the lake. Leanne could see Lucas pat the big tyrannosaur on his thick, scaly neck, and Big Red bent his head low, allowing him to dismount – from there, the two of them walked in tandem.

Leanne struggled to see as they were now moving out of sight.

Making sure not to reveal her presence, she began to circle the hillside, hunting for a vantage with a better view.

As she reached the crest just above the grove, she peered below – and in doing so, tripped herself up and went tumbling down the slope.

Leanne let out a screech as branches and shrubs broke beneath her, leaving her scratched and scuffed in a heap as she rolled to a stop just beyond the grove.

Fighting tears, she struggled to catch her wind, a second before she looked up to find a pair of snorting nostrils and a mouthful of twelve-inch teeth hovering just above her.

Leanne found her breath and let out a scream.

Big Red cocked his head, staring down at her, and a moment later, Lucas appeared beside him.

His eyes wide with concern, Lucas rushed over to where she had fallen.

"It's okay," he said. "He won't hurt you."

Leanne cowered, staring up at the massive rex.

Lucas knelt beside her.

"Really," he said. "It's okay. He knows who you are."

He turned to Big Red, holding up his hand.

The enormous tyrannosaur stooped its gigantic head and Lucas patted the scaly snout before turning to Leanne, motioning her to come forward.

Frozen and breathless, Leanne lay still until Lucas reached out and took her hand, pulling at her gently.

Leanne's heart hammered as he brought her hand up to touch Big Red on his gnarled muzzle. The skin was rough as stone. The big tyrannosaur let out a rumbling breath and Leanne nearly swooned.

"See?" Lucas said. "He likes you."

Leanne was not so sure. The big rex blinked down at her like a bird eyeing a grub.

Lucas let her hand go and Leanne sat back, staring up, still unable to speak. Big Red reared back on his haunches, a low growl emanating from his throat.

"That's a *T. rex* purr," Lucas said, smiling.

Leanne's legs were shaky as he helped her to her feet, scarcely aware of the assorted scrapes and bruises she'd gained in her tumble down the hill.

Big Red was the largest rex in the Valley, even though Shanna said he was not yet even fully grown. He had actually been the runt of the litter, and quite picked-on as a hatchling. If Lucas himself hadn't rescued him, he likely would have died young from a broken leg.

But things were changed now that he had grown.

"You wanna see something?" Lucas asked.

Leanne looked at him dubiously. That had been what he'd said before he shot the bird out of the air with his bow.

But now he took her by the hand, and with Big Red in attentive tow, he led her towards the grove of trees.

Nestled within the circle of brush, was Big Red's mate, Sue. After Trix, Sue was the largest female in the territory. She was curled around a nest full of eggs.

Big Red's first brood.

His courtship with Sue had been quite a day in the Valley – the day that the big red rex earned his right to respect.

A fight between *T. rex* was the sort of thing that drew everyone's attention, and mating season was always good for a scrap or two. But this year, it had boiled over into something new – a changing of the guard.

It was Big Red's first mating season, and he and an older, cocky young buck named Junior had fought it out over Sue's affections – a fight Big Red had convincingly won – and this had led to a conflict with Rudy, a full-grown male, who fancied himself the Valley's heir-apparent dominant ruler.

Big Red had long been the persecuted outcast because of his red-skin – and since *T. rex* social structure was heavily-based on dominance and hierarchy, by challenging for a mate, let alone winning, he was also contesting his established place at the back of the line. Rudy wasn't prepared to tolerate that.

When the two of them had gone at it, the entire Valley had been shaken. Even Shanna had stayed clear – something that had frightened Leanne nearly as much as the battle itself.

Shanna had held her daughter close.

"Sometimes," she said, "you just have to let these things resolve themselves. It's nature."

Rudy was a particularly aggressive male. In his youth, he had been the leader of the local gang of teenage male toughs, who ran in their own pack, separate from the more social females. In his maturity, he had taken the solitary position of dominant rogue, assuming kingship and mating rights with the local pack of females – a position he had defended against all comers for more than ten years.

Nevertheless, Big Red had defeated him. And in this instance, something new had happened in *T. rex* culture, because Big Red didn't kill him – doubtless due to the influence of Shanna.

Rudy had retreated to the outskirts of the Valley. Junior and the other young males had followed, and the roving gang now patrolled the outlying areas of the territory, leaving the main Valley to Big Red – the new rogue.

And the rogue walked alone.

At least, until mating season. Tyrannosaurs were the only large theropod known to pair-bond. Big Red hovered over Sue and his nest protectively, as Lucas led Leanne in close.

Sue's voice was a low, suspicious rumble as Leanne looked wide-eyed at the circle of foot-long eggs. She leaned forward, fascinated.

"Don't touch them," Lucas cautioned.

Leanne was about to object – "I wasn't *gonna!*" – when she was suddenly startled by a scream.

Both *T. rex'* heads popped up at the sound, and Lucas stood bolt-upright.

The scream had come from his parents' house.

A moment later, there was the sound of gunshots.

In a flash, Lucas was on his feet, sprinting for home.

CHAPTER 9

Allison had been watching her son and his pet *T. rex* from the ridge above her house when she saw Leanne come bouncing down the hill.

That little girl had been coming around a lot just lately, often stopping on the ridge just to watch Lucas and Big Red. Allison found herself a bit chagrined. Leanne was Shanna's daughter and all, but she still found herself inexplicably bothered. Perhaps it was just her being an overprotective mother, resisting her son's first attention from girls.

Allison had mentioned Leanne's name to Lucas, who had been very stand-offish and evasive – clear signs of a crush.

While she wondered what might develop as they grew older, personally, Allison thought the girl was actually more interested in her son's pet tyrannosaur than in Lucas himself. Once upon a time, in the old world, it would have been a fancy car.

Once upon a time, she herself had been a young girl fascinated by just such things.

For Allison's part, her son's pet rex had taken more than a little getting used to. It had frankly scared her to death when Lucas had first brought it home, still a miniature juvenile and lame of leg, asking, "Can we *keep* him?"

Allison smiled a little, remembering the look on Bud's face when he'd come home from the fields that day to find a pint-sized *Tyrannosaurus rex* stretched out on the floor of his kitchen.

But it was an amazing thing – Lucas and his pet rex seemed inseparable. Allison had actually grown to trust it, even occasionally feeding the big tyrannosaur herself by hand.

Bud had never quite warmed up to it, but he didn't object, or at least, didn't overtly stand in the way, even after the thing began to *grow*.

Down below, Lucas was fussing over Leanne where she had fallen, with Big Red hovering over the both of them like a giant red dog.

Allison sighed. Her boy was growing up. She could already tell he was going to be a handsome man, and even in the sparsely-populated Valley, he was bound to attract attention. She supposed she should be grateful it was from the local princess.

Still, the old world had taught a lot of lessons of what happened when commoners mixed with royalty.

Allison's own background was 'common', to say the least, and she had learned a lot of those lessons personally – primary among them was that status and bearing did not always mean virtue. In fact, it was often quite the opposite.

Not that she believed that of Shanna, or else she wouldn't have followed her to this Valley, but the scars of her old-life ran deep.

Lost in her thoughts, Allison was startled out of her reverie by the retort of a breaking branch – a deliberate sound, like a rap on a window-sill.

When she turned, she saw an RV truck parked along the old road that ran along the edge of the woods at the crest of the ridge.

Allison frowned. There weren't that many working vehicles in the Valley. Mr. Wilson had opened up a little shop in town, restoring and renovating old machinery, including cars and trucks, primarily for farm and hauling operations, and Allison recognized most of them by their owners. This vehicle was strange and new.

Then she saw a slim figure standing among the trees, a short distance away.

A woman. Dressed in black, adorned with animal bones and feathers, her garments marked with arcane symbols. And even though it had been many years, Allison still recognized her face.

Allison's blood ran cold.

Today, it seemed, indiscretions of the past had finally come due.

The woman's voice drifted across the empty woods.

"Hello, Allison. It's been a long time."

Allison's hand drifted to her pocket, where she always carried her pistol.

"Hello, Christine," she replied.

The woman separated from the trees, not quite out in the open.

That was how they operated – ninja-style tricks. Allison was suddenly consciously mindful of her surroundings. If she was being shown one thing, something else was likely going on somewhere behind her.

She was also suddenly keenly aware of her son out in the field.

Christine smiled – that shark-like smile of hers. When Allison had known her, back in the old world, she had been one of the Coven's primary enforcers. Her and a crazy, psychotic bitch named Michelle.

In all the years since, even after the end of the world, Allison had always dreamed it would be one of those two that finally came for her someday.

"Imagine," Christine said, "how surprised we were to find *you* here. You betrayed us. No one leaves the sisterhood."

Christine's smile widened.

"But the Coven always takes care of its own."

Allison knew that all too well.

She reached for her pistol, whipping it out of her pocket, cocking it and flipping off the safety in the same move.

But when she brought the gun up, aimed and ready, Christine had vanished, ducking somewhere into the surrounding foliage.

Ninja-style tricks, Allison thought, looking around.

She glanced up at the truck still parked on the hill.

Then she turned and began running back towards her house.

Out on the field, Lucas and Leanne had disappeared into the grove of trees.

Down below, her house was silent and dead.

Allison burst in through the back door.

Lying on the floor was Bud.

He had been torn apart and was slathered in blood.

Standing over him, was a pack of sickle-claws, their claws and teeth dripping red.

Allison screamed.

She unloaded her pistol as they came for her.

CHAPTER 10

Lucas sprinted for his house like a jackrabbit, leaving Leanne trailing behind. Big Red thundered in his footsteps – the ground shook as the big rex broke into a run.

The moment they got to the front door, three sickle-claws burst out, claws splayed.

Leanne skidded to an abrupt stop. The hook-clawed devils were her single worst fear – the one creature that even her mother was frightened of.

But Lucas charged forward with a mad yell, unslinging his bow in mid-run, fitting an arrow in the string and firing even as the first of the raptors leaped.

The shaft caught the beast dead in the chest, the shot fired as direct and straight as the arrow that had killed the little songbird. The sickle-claw let out a screech, tumbling into the dust, twitching.

A second dromaeosaur leaped as Lucas was fitting another arrow, but this one proved unnecessary as Big Red arrived a step behind, chomping the creature in two in mid leap.

Lucas fired his arrow, dropping the third, even as two more of the deadly clawed beasts darted out of the house...

... and ran right into Sue as she charged up behind Lucas and her mate. Sue's five-foot jaws snagged the first sickle-claw's leg as it attempted to dart past, amputating the limb at a stroke, and the smaller theropod flopped to the ground, only to be squashed into the dirt under the big female's giant foot.

Lucas fired a final arrow at the last of them, skewering the creature in the ribs as it turned to escape.

The entire exchange had taken less than twenty seconds.

Without missing a beat, Lucas ran up the steps of his house, where the front door was left standing open, knocked askew on its hinges.

But as he reached the doorway, he stopped.

Leanne ran up behind him and she heard Lucas' breath leave his chest in a strangled sob.

With the door hanging open, you could clearly see inside.

His parents lay in the middle of the living room floor.

Lucas was trying to talk.

"M-m-m... Mom...," he choked. "Dad..."

Leanne took one look and then turned away, horrified.

Lucas dropped to his knees, and buried his face in his hands.

Over his shoulder, Big Red's voice rumbled out in a low moan. Beside him, Sue growled softly.

"Lucas...?" Leanne began, helpless, not knowing what to say.

Crouched on his front steps, unable to look anymore, Lucas began to sob.

And none of them saw several skulking figures, all dressed in black, hidden in the grove of trees surrounding Sue's nest and her unguarded eggs.

CHAPTER 11

Lucas' parents weren't the only ones killed that day. The sickle-claws staged several raids across the entire Valley in one of the boldest mass attacks in years.

Two people were hit just outside of town – a farmer and his wife, found torn to pieces and partly eaten – along with a pair of fishermen, in separate assaults out by the lake, who had both been badly mauled, but survived the initial attack by virtue of their own sidearms. The first man, Rosa managed to save, albeit with more stitches than she'd ever given anyone in the Valley besides Maverick. The second man eventually died of his wounds.

Shanna had sent Cameron and Maverick out with Garner and Wilkes, the Valley's senior ex-military men, to patrol the area, but by then, Trix and her pack had already chased the renegade dromaeosaurs down.

It was hard to tell how many of them there had actually been after the rex females got through with them, but Shanna was at least confident their tyrannosaur noses had rooted the last of the evil beasts out.

Shanna had come out of her house to find Leanne hysterical and in tears, and had gone up the hill to find Lucas sitting over the bodies of his parents, with Big Red and Sue standing guard.

It wasn't until shortly thereafter that they learned there were more than just human casualties – a discovery announced by sudden bellowing roars, first by Sue, and then Big Red himself, when they found that their nest had been pillaged and their eggs scattered and smashed.

There was something simple and basic about a mother's grief, and in an animal, it was utter and unaffected. Shanna felt the pain wafting off of Sue like a personal loss as the big female moaned and wailed over her lost brood, even as Big Red postured and growled helplessly.

Shanna was bothered by the strategic nature of the assaults. It was beyond the sickle-claws' mental capacity, and it stank of the influence of a certain scaly little lizard lurking behind it.

Otto had not, to Shanna's knowledge, dared enter the Valley in years, but you never knew. Those damned little bastards were so hard to predict beyond the sheer nihilism of it. You never knew whether there was a plan, or simply destructive escalation.

Scratch that – there was *always* a plan, and there was *always* escalation – you just never knew *what*.

Neither had she sensed the little lizard's presence. He – *they* – had been learning to hide from her, but not when she was focused and looking – not after she knew they were there. There was always that psychic-stench of sulfur.

Shanna wondered if it was possible they were learning to control the sickle-claws from a greater distance these days.

Or was it something else? *Someone* else?

They had found tire tracks in the woods up behind Lucas' house, leading onto one of the old mountain roads. Shanna had asked around, and no one in the Valley, with its limited number of operating vehicles, could account for them.

Shanna insisted on keeping a stepped-up guard around the community, and Cameron had complied unquestioningly. Garner and Wilkes rounded up Cooper, Johnson, and Bradbury, all the rest of the local ex-military, and along with Cameron and Maverick, they had set about making daily patrols along the perimeter of the Valley.

Cameron had long-learned that when Shanna had one of her 'feelings', it was best to pay attention.

Then there was Lucas.

The boy had not cried as much as Shanna would have expected, and she found him out in the field the next day, after Cameron and Maverick had removed the bodies of his parents.

He was going through his daily chores, working on the crops, tending to the livestock. Big Red was attentively hovering a short distance away.

Shanna knew the boy was in shock, but he seemed to at least be functional. He was certainly not the only orphan in the Valley. She would make sure to keep tabs on him going forward.

Leanne was also badly shaken, and had been staying uncharacteristically close to home. Shanna took quiet note that there were no more secret trips to Lucas' farm – it seemed she suddenly didn't want to be around him anymore.

Shanna supposed that was natural enough. She didn't know what Lucas thought about it, but she felt her own heart break just a little.

They maintained their patrols, but there were no further incidents with sickle-claws for the rest of the summer, or the remainder of that year.

Still, Shanna remained vigilant, watching the hills – and checking in on Lucas regularly.

And so time went on. Life in the Valley continued.

Eight years passed.

CHAPTER 12

Time, it seemed, did not heal *all* wounds.

Naomi woke with a scream.

Lying beside her, Jonah started awake, his heart pounding in his chest. Then he realized Naomi had been dreaming.

It was not the first time.

For most of the intervening years since they had been driven out of the mountains of Wyoming – ever since Naomi's last miscarriage – things had been better.

But then, just in recent weeks, her dreams had been coming back in force.

Jonah found himself wondering if perhaps she might be pregnant again, if maybe this was a sign.

Last time, however, there had been dreams about a whimsical Valley. This time, they had taken a darker turn – these were full-blown nightmares.

Nightmares about a dragon.

Naomi trembled in bed next to him and Jonah held her, stroking her soothingly, whispering that everything was alright.

He sincerely hoped that everything really was.

They had resettled further west this time, up in the mountains of Montana – again, always keeping to the higher altitudes.

Starting over once again.

Their lodgings were actually fairly grand. Montana was a state that was mostly highlands. It was sparsely populated, but it had once been a popular spot for people who liked the outdoors, and there were a lot of recreational areas in the mountains, as well as vacation homes, all outfitted with provisions for the weather, emergency generators, solar panels – they practically had their pick. They had toured the abandoned houses like a young couple window-shopping in a street-of-dreams neighborhood.

When Cameron had first landed their rickety old Cessna near one of the ski resorts, and Naomi had gotten a look at the houses on the hills, she had laughed and told him that she would have made him leave Wyoming years ago, if she'd had a brochure for *this* place.

Jonah was grateful for the lift in her spirits. He desperately wanted her to be happy. And just as desperately, he wanted to finally settle down somewhere for good.

In the eight years since Wyoming, Jonah was beginning to go gray.

Naomi, who was several years younger, was only barely showing her very first streaks, and was holding up her looks quite well. But tonight, as she lay next to him, her eyes were undercut with shadows, and Jonah could see what she might look like as an old woman.

And as he himself was cresting middle-age, it occurred to him, for the first time, what it might be like for her when he was gone.

She had still talked periodically about the Valley – always with that odd, spacey look in her eyes, as if she was seeing something far away. But she had brought it up more often just recently, especially since the dreams had begun again.

And more and more, she talked about it as if it were a real place.

Jonah was worried about her – about these dreams – visions or whatever – he was concerned they might be some kind of delusion.

He worried even more that she might actually be picking up on something real.

Worse, it seemed to be catching – he was almost beginning to believe in the Valley himself. There were times when they lay in bed together where he thought he felt snippets from her dreams – always when they touched.

Her preoccupation with the Valley was like a flower bending towards the light.

But Naomi's impulse to follow that light was countered by Jonah's own impulse to protect her – to keep her safe.

Of course, always ready to question his own motives, he wondered if that was really what he was doing.

Or was he just keeping her to himself?

Still to that day, he had never in his heart believed he deserved her. He knew very well that they had wound up together because he had been the only one there.

Perhaps the thought of other people – beyond the backwoods crazies and military police-states – was in some way a threat?

He hoped he wasn't that small.

For her part, Naomi had her own doubts. It was not too hard to convince her to play it safe. After all, the last time they'd sought out other survivors, they had gotten a good look at a nuclear explosion. You didn't get to walk away from too many of those.

Although, in their case, it happened more often than you might think.

As they lay there together, Jonah wondered if he was being selfish.

He also wondered again if she might be pregnant.

And if so, what then?

Beside him, Naomi's trembling had finally stopped as the dream's images faded and she began to calm, drifting once again into sleep. Her eyelids fluttered.

And as he touched her, caressing her, holding her close, once again, he thought he felt a little bristle of static, as if she were a conduit connecting a circuit.

In the past, it had been a warm sensation like a magnetic attraction, pulling to the west.

But now, as Naomi again moaned in her sleep, Jonah felt a chill – like a mental scent of sulfur and brimstone.

The scent of a dragon.

Coming from the east.

CHAPTER 13

Caesar was having dreams of his own.

He had been feeling edgy for a while now. It was nothing specific – just a general sense of uneasiness.

The tribe had been restless as well. The youngsters had been owlish and prone to spats. His mate, Zira, had been henpeckish and hectoring.

Cornelius and Dr. Zaius actually brought the matter to his attention. They all felt it.

It had already been a bad year, filled with bad omens. Among other things, it seemed that there were humans encroaching once again.

Just the other day, while out scouting the hills, Caesar had spotted another truck-full of human females, garbed similar to those that had been traveling in the company of the sickle-claws and Otto several seasons before.

These women had not been accompanied by dromaeosaurs this time, nor Otto, near as Caesar could tell. They had the appearance of scouts, possibly seeking out new territory.

This particular band had been headed north, and in that direction lay a military encampment – something else Caesar had learned to avoid.

He remembered, as well, that it had also been shortly after the last time that he'd encountered that troop of human females that he'd felt the turmoil emanating from the east, accompanied by distress from Shanna herself, and pain in the rex.

In retrospect, he wondered if he should have at least made an effort to chase them down. Nothing good could possibly come from any human trafficking with dromaeosaurs, and particularly not with Otto.

But in the end, Caesar's instinct was always to avoid conflict when possible. He was an ape first – perhaps nearly as intelligent as a human, but still an animal.

Besides, he knew he couldn't have caught up to them on the road in their truck, nor had he seen them in the area in the years since.

Now, however, it seemed they were prowling about once more.

He wondered if it was related to the dreams. Or why those dreams had suddenly been worse after Shanna had left from her seasonal visit this year, as if the warm glow of her presence had blocked the ambient chill.

Or possibly had cloaked a dark presence.

Either way, Caesar had woken up today feeling troubled, and the first thing he had done was stand and look to the east, at the rising sun – the star of the morning.

Beside him, Zira had groaned in her sleep, and when she'd awoke, cantankerous and testy, she had also stood and looked to the east.

From where came the Morningstar – what humans called the Devil.

Or the Dragon.

CHAPTER 14

Shanna had long been aware of an unseen presence.

It was disturbingly reminiscent to that familiar psychic sulfur stench that she associated with a certain parrot-talking lizard – yet, it was also pointedly different.

For one thing, it was stronger, but at the same time, it was also muted, like pain from a wound blocked with anesthetic. In fact, she had first noticed it as a numb spot – something she could *almost* ignore.

In retrospect, she dated it back to the sickle-claw raid that had taken Lucas' parents several years before.

And for some reason, she also associated it specifically with the despoiled rex nest on that same day.

That was another thing – after that series of attacks, the sickle-claw raids in the Valley seemed to drop off dramatically, and in the time since, they had become rare to all but non-existent – almost to the point of luring one into non-vigilance.

Almost. Shanna never forgot they were out there.

Because shortly thereafter was the first time she had sensed that barely-detectable presence, like an after-thought – just a vapor of brimstone.

Barely-there, that is, until just recently.

Just that morning, Shanna had woken from her own dream, and for the first time, that dark presence had suddenly clicked to full-awareness in her mind, like a door had been opened from outside, and someone – or some*thing* – had been looking in.

It was like having God staring in at your thoughts.

Or more likely, the Devil, because the feeling had left her cold. And for a brief moment, her own thoughts started to reflect back, looking out at the invader. In another second, she would see into the intruding mind as well.

Then the door had abruptly shut and Shanna had sat awake, blinking in the dark.

Two thousand miles away, on the opposite end of the continent, the little creature called Otto blinked back.

And as by rote, it spoke aloud in the voice of its creator – a kindly, if perhaps slightly mad genius – always the same phrase, no matter how many times it was cloned, they always said the same thing.

"I am Otto."

In truth, they weren't genuinely intelligent, at least as humans understood the concept. Individuals were practically no smarter than the parrot-talking lizard they appeared to be. But when several of them got together – three seemed to be the magic number – than you began to see evidence of measured action.

Dr. Shriver had variously compared them to a gestalt hive-mind, or an aberrant computer program running simulations, and acting them out in the real world – an organic artificial intelligence.

They were known in the new world, and had even attracted worshipers, much as snakes and crocodiles had at various times over the course of human history.

The group of followers that called themselves the Coven had even compared them to a magic spell – which, by the laws of black magic, was like a living thing that you were never supposed to leave unguarded, or else it would begin to act on its own, building upon itself like a snowball.

Currently, the enigmatic little lizards' numbers were concentrated in the east, opposite the continental split from the Valley. And it was no coincidence that in the bubbling cauldron of seemingly random action and faulty logic, that was also where most of the conflict with the military had occurred – including the vast majority of the post KT-day blooms, that had managed to destroy vast swaths of territory, not only with the Food of the Gods, but the responsive nuclear strikes as well.

There were two primary and very practical reasons Otto had migrated east – the first was because the west was tyrannosaur-territory.

The second was a related factor – and that was Shanna's Valley.

And while tyrannosaurs were clearly their biggest problem, it was Shanna who was the crux.

In point of fact, Otto had been trying to kill her for years, even before KT-day. Most sickle-claw raids in the Valley had actually been assassination attempts.

The protection of the *T. rex*, however, was a formidable obstacle.

Otto couldn't even safely enter the territory, and couldn't come anywhere near the Valley without being sniffed out by either those tyrannosaur noses, or being given away by their own psychic stench, let alone in sufficient numbers to adequately manage a pack of sickle-claws.

That was where their human worshipers, that group of mammalian females who called themselves the Coven, came in handy as familiars.

At secondhand, within reasonable range, the sickle-claws were manageable for their female human-handlers, as were some of the more primitive large theropods. And while it wasn't practical to send a big carcharodont into the Valley against the similar-sized but more powerful

T. rex, guerrilla-style raids with the smaller, sneakier dromaeosaurs were a viable option.

But their last major raid in the Valley had not been aimed at Shanna – the rex brood was the bounty Otto had sought that day.

Among the shattered remains of the nest, it would not have been obvious that several of the eggs had not simply been smashed, but stolen.

After all, DNA for the purposes of cloning is best obtained from embryonic tissue.

And after nearly a decade of running the same repetitive program over and over, the organic gestalt hive-mind had finally produced an idea, and attempted to try something new.

Tyrannosaurs had long been singled-out as their biggest problem.

So now they took the DNA from one of the stolen eggs and combined their own genes with that of a rex.

The experiment proved to be an unanticipated success.

Much like the first time they had destroyed the world.

No matter how exact the science, the chaos factor always seemed to rule the day.

Unexpected differences in their hybrid-creation manifested early on.

There were physical differences, obviously, but that had been part of the point, because one primary advantage commanded by the *T. rex* was purely and simply size – and the rex-gene had proved the dominant influence, which had also been the point.

Their creature grew quickly, which was partially a deliberate result of Otto's own genetic-machinations, but also due to the efforts of Professor Nolan Hinkle himself, who had engineered his creations to mature significantly faster than they had in nature. During the Mesozoic, a tyrannosaur reached sexual maturity as a teen, and full physical adulthood in their twenties, much like a human, but the modern-day, reconstructed *T. rex* matured at about half that.

But at just over eight-years old, Otto's tyrannosaur-hybrid progeny was already reaching full adulthood.

He had the form of a powerful rogue male rex, but with the well-developed forelimbs and grasping claws of a dromaeosaur, while still retaining the powerful tyrannosaur skull and jaws. He was slightly more slender in build than a true *T. rex*, but was still a massive beast, standing over twenty-five feet tall.

But the differences were far more than physical.

For one thing, he developed true language, markedly distinct from the parrot-like mimicry of his genetic parent.

More importantly – and more concerning – was the fact that, while their creation seemed able to tap into their gestalt mind, he was *not* one of them.

Their creature called itself 'Draco', absorbing the term from human literature, plucked out of their group memory banks.

He existed separate and distinct. And he very much had a mind of his own.

Shanna's influence was undoubtedly a factor. As a by-product of the purification element that was at their cloned genetic core, all the recreated creatures in the modern world carried a bit of Shanna in their DNA, Otto included. It was where they got their 'shine'.

The conception of Draco, with Otto's own DNA, combined with that of a rex, more than doubled that percentage.

In Otto, it manifested in the instinctive 'id' that was their gestalt group consciousness – it was why the closely-related sickle-claws responded to them like trained troops, but they only had limited control over the larger beasts, such as the carnosaurs and herd animals. They could activate simple impulses – anger, fear, sloth – they could get them to walk where they wanted to – but not much more.

Their creation was different.

Sickle-claws, for example, responded to him at distance, with fine-tuning that far exceeded Otto's own influence.

More significantly was the reaction demonstrated by the larger beasts after the last active bloom.

Initiated as a test-run, the sauropods and herd beasts, and even the larger carnosaurs responded to Draco as if with the understanding of language, even across geographical ranges.

The critical moment, however, came just eight weeks ago, when he was finally paired with a *T. rex* – a specially-grown control group, bred specifically for that purpose.

Tyrannosaurs were indomitable – a quirk of evolution, inherent in history's greatest super-predator.

This proved true at the genetic level.

Presented with a full-grown male rogue and a sexually mature female, the male rex had promptly tried to kill him.

Draco, however, had met his rival in the middle.

Wasting no time with mental dominance, he had simply torn the rogue male's throat out with his own powerful tyrannosaur-jaws.

The female, he had taken as his mate, just like a normal rex.

This at least established dominance.

Promptly upon the conclusion of the experiment, the troop of Ottos attempted to establish control over their own creation.

It was that mental flex that produced that psychic stench, which Shanna recognized so well, activating chemical reactions in the brain, promoting specific actions or even pain in a primitive mind.

This time, however, it backfired.

Draco had turned upon his creators, his jaws still slathered red with the rogue male rex' blood, and his new queen bowed at his heel.

At the first touch of that mental static, that psychic scent of sulfur, Draco's eyes had narrowed.

As a group, the gathered troop of Ottos had felt the mental flex reflecting back at them.

The two closest had promptly dropped dead of embolisms.

As the two little lizards had toppled over, twitching, Draco had stepped forward and stomped them into the dirt.

Then he had turned to the others, his rumbling thunder of a voice barking out a single command.

"Stay!"

Like the sickle-claws under Otto's own influence, the remaining lizards had immediately dropped into a formal line, their gestalt minds utterly absent of individual thought or will.

As he spoke, Draco's scaly lips had drawn back over twelve-inch teeth in an obscene parody of a smile.

"I am taking over this operation."

And it was at that moment, two-thousand miles away, on the other side of the continent, that Shanna had suddenly snapped awake, stirred from her frightening dream, sitting up and blinking, wide-eyed in the dark.

In the aftermath of the dream, she tasted that psychic stench – that metal scent of sulfur – only now it was laced with dragon-fire and brimstone.

And the psychic echo of deep, rumbling laughter.

CHAPTER 15

There was one other that sensed the emergence of Draco.

Lily had been just eighteen when she had first come to the Mount. When KT-day had struck one year before, she had been an underage dancer, working in LA, at a club called Susie's Bar under a fake ID.

That was where she had first met her 'sisters' in the Coven. Ginger had been a mother figure, Michelle, a big sister.

Perhaps not coincidentally, Lily was also one of the Mount's first pregnancies. She had actually shared the maternity ward with General Rhodes' assistant Sally, whose daughter, Dawn, had been born just eight weeks before Lily's own daughter, Sabrina – the first two births in the Mount – probably among the very first in the entire new world.

At the Mount, they represented the beginning of Dr. Shriver's Arc Project.

These days, Lily played her part dutifully. She worked for the Mount's maid and house-cleaning services, she raised her daughter, and she was the wife of an officer, who believed he was the girl's father.

No one knew the truth, although Lily wondered sometimes if Sally didn't suspect Sabrina's real daddy wasn't who she said he was.

But not even Sally suspected the *whole* truth.

Lily knew a little of Sally's story – how the young man who had fathered her own child unknowingly left her behind, believing her dead and gone.

But Sally didn't know about the young man *Lily* had met along that same path – a man who she'd met in the woods and spent a single night with – a young man who she had then tried to lure into a dragon's jaws – all to please her Coven sisters.

That young man's name had been Mark, and like Sally, herself, he had left her with a child.

Half-sister of Sally's own daughter.

Lily had never told anyone – not Ginger – not even Sabrina, herself.

But it was right after Sabrina was born that Lily first began to have dreams about a place called the Valley.

Neither was she alone. Among those on the Mount – who happened to be exclusively women – that claimed to have dreams or visions of some semi-mystical, post-apocalyptic Eden in the west, nearly all of them had done so after conception. Dr. Shriver himself had noted that correlation.

They all also spoke of a woman – the beacon that gave the Valley its light.

According to Shriver, that woman was very real. Her name was Shanna.

Lily wondered what her Coven sisters would have made of her visions of Shanna and the Valley. Ginger had always spoken of the 'feminine divine' as the Coven's guiding force – the power of the Goddess.

But now most of her Coven sisters had gone. Except for Michelle, who had betrayed them all.

And of course, Ginger, who had stayed behind to help Lily raise her child.

Ginger was also always sure to remind Lily that the rest of her Coven sisters were not actually *gone* – they were just elsewhere. Like Shriver himself, Ginger used the word 'escaped'.

Sally's daughter was not the only child on the Mount who had grown up with stories of someplace better, but Sabrina's stories were not of the Valley.

Aunt Ginger told tales of a settlement where their sisters had found their own freedom – to worship as they chose, so to speak.

And if that meant the odd member of the patriarchal oppressors had to get fed to a dragon?

Well... Ginger did not over emphasize that aspect, except to say that the villains of every mythology tended to meet with well-deserved bad ends.

A small price to pay.

Suffice to say, Shangri-La had a different flavor in the tales Aunt Ginger told.

Lily still remembered Sabrina as a little girl, looking up at Ginger wide-eyed, asking, "Can I go there someday?"

Ginger had smiled, nodding knowingly to Lily.

"Perhaps someday. When you're older."

Lily, for her part, didn't know for sure whether such a place truly existed – although it had once. In the days after KT-day, the Coven had lived in just such harmony, embracing both the Apocalypse and the new world with enthusiasm – at least, until those same patriarchal oppressors had taken it all away.

It was certainly not beyond the realm of possibility that her lost sisters were still out there somewhere, living as unencumbered and free as they had once before. Ginger certainly believed it was so.

Of course, Ginger had also been very interested in Lily's dreams about the Valley.

In fact, she had often spoken of Shanna as the Goddess personified –

the feminine divine made flesh – the brightest mortal light on Earth.

Lily, herself, might once have been a bright natural light in her own right – but she was a corrupted luminescence. After all, like Eve had been attracted to the serpent, it had been Lily who first brought a little parrot-talking lizard to the attention of the Coven.

And like Eve, that seduction had preceded their fall.

But as Ginger had also said, the feminine divine and the feminine profane were two sides of the same coin – both were symbols of angelic power.

After all, wasn't Lucifer himself once an angel?

In recent days, Lily had begun to feel a new presence, this time emanating from the east.

A far cry from her dreams of Shanna and a tranquil Valley, this was a dark presence – violent and powerful.

These dreams had been frightening – overwhelming.

Yet, just like Eve and the snake, for Lily, there was also a perversely seductive attraction.

She had spoken of this presence to Ginger, who had nodded knowingly, and her judgment was straightforward and simple.

Her dreams were a calling.

And while Ginger may have long referred to Shanna as the Goddess personified, it now seemed that there was a power *above* the Goddess.

Now there was the Dragon.

CHAPTER 16

Shanna had been looking forward to her time in the mountains. In the past several weeks, since she had first sat bolt-upright up in bed, shaken and sweaty from her dream of the dragon, with that invasive presence peering into her mind, her anxiety had grown worse by steady degrees.

That numb spot remained in her mind, her awareness only punctuated by its absence, as if something knew she was trying to see it, and was deliberately hiding from her.

The form it created was like a shadow-puppet – exaggerated and distorted – and it made her afraid.

She did her best to hide it, as her moods had a tendency to affect those around her.

Not surprisingly, Cameron had been the first to sense her unease. She hadn't said anything, but it seemed he was the one person she couldn't hide from, even in her mind – perhaps because she never *had* to – and maybe that was one of her single greatest blessings.

"Something on your mind, babe?" he'd asked her mildly, as if disinterested, touching the issue gently, like he always did whenever he suspected she was having one of her 'hunches'.

She had smiled disarmingly, telling him everything was fine, because she didn't yet know quite *what* to think.

Cameron had subsided amiably enough, not fooled in the slightest. And without being asked, he and Maverick had arranged stepped-up patrols along the entire perimeter of the Valley.

He had also suggested she forgo her trip to the mountains this year.

But Shanna had been adamant. The truth was, she wanted to know what Caesar and his tribe were feeling.

Around the Valley, the tyrannosaur packs had been on edge.

And once in the mountains, she had found the great apes were as well.

Caesar reported dreams, as did all the members of his tribe.

He had also followed her much further along on her trip back this year, risking the wrath of the *T. rex* accompanying her all the way to her parked truck, seeing her through to the Valley.

Clearly, Caesar was troubled.

As Shanna made her way back along the mountain road, she sensed a tempest brewing behind the scenes.

For one thing, the Food of the Gods seemed to have sprouted-up once again. It had been years since Shanna had felt that telltale stirring.

So far, there had only been one significant bloom that had blossomed far to the east, and as yet, there had been no corresponding nuclear strike – possibly an infection that had not been detected by the military, or perhaps had burnt out on its own.

But in the Valley, life went on as normal, seemingly unaware.

As she made her way down the familiar mountain road, she saw her usual escort waiting.

This time it was Big Red. His head popped up as Shanna's truck appeared on the hill.

The big red rex seemed especially attuned to her, even among the tyrannosaurs. He had now grown into full maturity, easily topping ten tons, by far the largest rex in the territory.

Big Red rose to his feet as Shanna drove up and parked, stepping out of the truck and extending her hand.

The big tyrannosaur lowered his head, his voice a rumbling purr, as Shanna patted him on his gnarled snout. But she sensed an anxious note of anxiety as her hands ran over his rough skin.

Just like Caesar and the apes, Big Red was troubled.

"It's okay, big guy," Shanna said soothingly. "It's good to see you."

Big Red grunted, comforted, if not pacified. He stooped, allowing Shanna to climb aboard, taking her place across his thick neck, and the two of them began making their way back towards the main Valley.

Shanna shut her eyes, letting the warm breeze blow through her hair – which, even though she was entering into middle-age, still showed not even a trace of gray. Cameron, who was only six years older, was already displaying a salt-and-peppering of white, but Shanna didn't look a day older than she had in her twenties.

According to Rosa, Shanna seemed to have the metabolism of a woman half her age – possibly another benefit of the purification element. It was possible, Rosa suggested, that Shanna might be looking at a greatly expanded lifespan.

Rosa, who herself was seeing her first weathering of crow's feet, had expressed a bit of envy. She had also made the unfortunate remark that, these days, she was actually using Maverick as sort of a barometer to measure how well she was holding onto her looks.

"I'm almost scared," she said, "that one day, he might not hit on me."

"I don't think you need to worry," Shanna had replied, as Rosa had not seen Maverick come in through the back with Cameron, standing behind her, grinning broadly.

"You still look pretty good from the back," Maverick had said. "For a spinster-old maid."

Rosa had glared.

"*God*, you're a pig."

Shanna smiled at the memory, but the truth was, the possibility of her own extended lifespan actually left her with a touch of melancholy, and even a little bit of fear, because it occurred to her to wonder what it might be like to watch as Cameron grew older, and eventually left her alone.

Shanna let out a wistful sigh and, beneath her, Big Red grunted as he sensed her sallow mood. She patted his thick hide comfortingly as they trundled along.

The big *T. rex* pushed past the thick foliage and the lake came into view.

The population of the Valley was growing but it was still sparse enough that Shanna and her giant mount attracted no attention as they made their way up the beaten path towards the remote corner of the lake where she and Cameron had made their home.

By mid-day, some parts of the lake would be full of fishermen, but this corner was secluded and, for the most part, private.

So it was that they came upon Shanna's daughter unawares.

Tyrannosaurs were remarkably light-footed, as are most predators, and Big Red's passage was quiet enough for Shanna to hear splashing up ahead. She patted Big Red's head for him to stop.

Shanna peered through the trees at her daughter on the lake.

Leanne had just turned eighteen and had grown into every bit the beauty of her mother.

She was, however, a bit bolder and more willful by nature, and that had gotten her into trouble in the past.

Right now was a good example of how that kind of thing happened.

As Leanne stood up from the water, Shanna realized her daughter was skinny-dipping.

Shanna sighed in exasperation, contemplating the young woman she had raised.

Leanne was very much like Shanna herself, both in looks and mind. Leanne's IQ at least rivaled her mother's, and Shanna could also sense a powerful empathic ability growing within her. In fact, as Leanne had grown older, it seemed that Shanna's senses had magnified along with her, as if her daughter's light amplified her own.

Over the years, Shanna had learned to hide her empathic presence from her somewhat mischievous offspring, just to keep one step ahead of her. She had mostly succeeded, as all good mothers do, but she suspected that if Leanne's own senses followed the same cycle of development as Shanna's had, her daughter would one day exceed her.

But for now, Leanne was still young – still young but grown – and despite all the unarguable similarities, she, like every mother's child eventually must, was proving to be very much her own person.

Leanne could be prideful and headstrong, and as Shanna's daughter, she had always been considered special by the community at large.

It was not, however, like it might have been in the old world. Leanne had never been subject to the many pressures that a young woman of position and physical attraction had historically been purvey to. She was neither vain nor callous – she had never been touched by such things, much as Shanna herself had not.

The attention of boys had also been minimal. Despite Leanne's obvious beauty, there simply had not been that many her own age around.

Still, she had very much become a young woman – and perhaps at the moment, Shanna thought archly, one being a little bit too daring about showing it off.

That was maybe something Shanna would have to speak to her about. For even in this sparsely-populated new world, one was never as alone as one might think.

A soft grunt from Big Red alerted Shanna to the fact that someone was, even now, coming up the path towards the lake.

Shanna knew who it was before she could see him.

It was often like that now. Her senses sometimes seemed to reach into normal humans, not just the beasts who shared that small piece of her DNA. It was not all humans, and some she felt stronger than others – perhaps those that had a touch of shine in them as well. Just like the boy coming down the path.

'Man', Shanna thought, correcting herself – Lucas was a year older than Leanne.

Shanna had often felt things from him in the past, more than with any normal human besides Cameron himself.

She had never let Lucas in on the things she knew and felt about him, and that was a kindness – it would have shamed him, for that would have meant she would have known how much he was in love with her daughter.

Lucas was of average height – lithe, yet well-muscled like a gymnast – and as backwards and shy as any comparable nineteen-year-old from the old world might have been cocky and arrogant. And when he was around Leanne, Shanna could sometimes feel the painful ping of his aching heart as it wafted off him like a scent.

It was at these moments when she lamented the fact that such things should so often bring pain, and she regretted her own lack of experience in such matters.

Now, as Lucas unsuspectingly approached her skinny-dipping daughter, Shanna sat back out of sight to watch.

Lucas was walking, head down, a creel full of fish hanging from one hand, his bow and fishing rod across his shoulders. He might have been humming or whistling a tune, but Shanna was too far away to tell.

Then, with the air of a man with nothing more on his mind than a new fishing spot, he turned towards the lake and beheld Leanne in all her glory.

Leanne hadn't seen him yet, and Lucas stood for a moment, utterly transfixed.

Then, a moment later – and Shanna loved him a little for it – he turned and hid his eyes.

Shanna floated her mind out to him, grinning at his embarrassment, and at the same time, feeling the almost pathetic pang of longing, and the perceived distance between him and her daughter – the simple torment of love in vain.

She smiled sadly, unaware that other eyes watched as well – cold, merciless eyes to whom the tranquil half-comic beauty of the scene before them was meaningless.

A moment later, a pack of sickle-claws burst out from the bush.

CHAPTER 17

They came with no warning at all. That's how sickle-claws were.

Their raids were like guerrilla assaults. Like some of the more primitive theropods, they remained outside of Shanna's influence. They were not particularly brainy animals – even less than the *T. rex*. A rex' behavior, however, was governed much like a dog's – tyrannosaurs lived in a world of sensory perception, scents and emotion.

Sickle-claws were different altogether – they were all aggressive instinct. Where *T. rex* had developed pair-bonding, sickle-claws' mating habits were more like the gang-mobbing seen in some of the more vicious modern birds. And their methods of killing were brutal and reptilian, often eating victims as they stood there, disemboweled and still alive.

There were three of them, and they darted from the brush, down the muddy beach, right towards Shanna's unsuspecting daughter.

Shanna kicked her heels but Big Red had already started forward, an enraged bellow erupting from his massive jaws.

Leanne looked up, startled, but Lucas had already reacted. With the quickness of a fox, he dashed into the water, grabbing Leanne up over one shoulder, naked and objecting, and went charging for the opposite bank.

Shanna caught a bit of her daughter's outraged thoughts and would have been amused if not for the sickle-claws closing the distance between them – closing it rapidly.

Lucas was headed for the trees. Although sickle-claws were mighty jumpers, they were not agile climbers. Up among the slender branches would be safe.

Big Red bellowed again, launching into a full run. The big rex could turn in speeds approaching thirty miles per hour for short bursts, and had the wind not been against him, his sensitive nose would have already ferreted the clawed devils out.

The distance, however, was too great – the sickle-claws would reach the retreating duo before Shanna and Big Red could overtake them. Lucas wouldn't make the trees fast enough to climb to safety.

Once he reached the base of the first tree, however, Lucas threw Leanne quickly off his shoulder.

His curt command reached Shanna's ears: *"Climb!"*

Leanne, who by now had spotted the charging sickle-claws, complied without hesitation, darting up into the branches like a squirrel.

Unslinging his bow, Lucas turned to face his charging pursuers.

He was fast with his bow – he fitted an arrow and launched the shaft just as the first of his attackers leaped upon him.

The arrowhead caught the evil beast directly in the heart, and the animal was probably already dead even before it entered its leap. Momentum, however, carried it forward, landing with its full weight on top of Lucas, knocking the both of them to the ground.

In a heartbeat, the other two sickle-claws were upon him.

There was a moment's confusion as they were briefly torn between piling on Lucas, trapped and struggling beneath their unfortunate companion's twitching corpse, or pursuing Leanne as she scrambled into the higher branches.

The second's hesitation put Leanne out of their reach, and the two of them turned to Lucas.

Fate, however, was kind, for Big Red's jaws got there first.

The massive, six-foot jaws smashed together around the first sickle-claw's comparatively tiny fourteen-foot body. The foot-long teeth dismembered the smaller theropod as efficiently as a guillotine.

Bizarrely, instead of running, the third sickle-claw attacked – which suited the big tyrannosaur just fine. Big Red brought his foot down and smashed the taloned beast into the dirt.

Shanna climbed down from Big Red's back and helped Lucas pull the dead dromaeosaur off of him.

"That was very brave of you," she said earnestly. "You saved my daughter's life."

Shanna turned her head up to where Leanne sat, perched among the slender branches, still buck-naked and dripping wet.

"And you, young lady," Shanna said, an arch-tone in her voice, "perhaps you should put some clothes on."

Big Red raised his massive head to the top branches. Leanne climbed aboard, an embarrassed, yet indignant expression on her face, as the big rex lowered her to the ground.

CHAPTER 18

Sally stood outside Rhodes' office, listening. The General was in there with Shriver alone.

Major Tom was otherwise occupied, coordinating airstrikes. And Sally suspected the good doctor had specifically not wanted Tom's input on this particular day.

The war had officially begun all over again, and now the blooms had begun to sprout with it. As Shriver had repeatedly said, it was always only a matter of time. The lull – whatever glitch had paused that aberrant repeating program – only meant that the enemy was regrouping and gathering strength.

A fatal, pessimistic prophecy that was now coming true.

The first bloom had blossomed seven weeks ago in upstate Wisconsin. This outbreak had actually been fairly isolated, and Hicks had reported it in at its late stages. In a hopeful display of optimism, Rhodes had, for once, foregone Shriver's recommendation and refrained from sending in nukes, instead initiating a series of targeted napalm strikes to prevent the spread of the chemical's infection.

Major Tom had expressed hope that might be the end of it. They kept an eye on the area, watching for any possible evidence that the bloom might expand outside the quarantine zone.

The next outbreak, however, had been far afield, and this one had struck outside one of their outlying air bases in Texas. A third had hit their only surviving Navy base, operating out of Florida. Both sites had been trampled flat by rampaging infected giants, and either one was too far to have been directly connected to the Wisconsin site.

And the fact that both sites were two out of a bare-few military installations they had left was highly suggestive of targeted outbreaks.

Any doubt was summarily erased in the following days after several more bases were also hit – all of them Arc Project communities, including a number of food-grow operations, spread across seven different states, all east of the New Gulf.

Significantly, the Arc Project targets had not been hit by blooms. The attacking beasts were all normals – sickle-claws and carnosaurs acting in unison, which absolutely *never* happened naturally.

Random chance was conclusively eliminated in favor of enemy action.

As each subsequent attack lit off like a string of firecrackers, Sally had watched the General's face age by the day.

There had been one moment, when he'd authorized his first nuke strikes in more than eight years, that she thought the cracks in the stone facade might finally be about to break.

Then he had sealed himself off. Sally had actually *watched* him do it, like a physical action. And the first thing he had done was initiate the next tactical strikes as 'hand-delivered' air-missions.

"Why?" Sally had asked.

"To make them *do* it," Rhodes had replied. "Can't get soft."

Sally had not been sure if he'd been talking about his pilots or himself.

Today, the deliveries were to be made at the hands of Major Hicks, the recently-promoted *Lieutenant* Wedge, and two new recruits, Brady and Biggs, both eighteen, on their first hand-delivery training missions.

As Sally stood outside his office door, Rhodes' voice carried through the door as his volume rose with frustration and temper.

"It hasn't been like this since KT-day," Rhodes was saying. "It's happening everywhere!"

Shriver's voice was deliberately lower.

"And they're tactical strikes," he emphasized. "Hitting specific targets. These blooms are not designed to spread, so much as to draw us out. This is strategy at work, like a cagey fighter getting his opponent to swing. Testing limits and capabilities. Getting them to reveal and to exhaust themselves."

"The nuclear response has always been at your recommendation," Rhodes responded. "What do you suggest we do now?"

Sally could have answered that question before Shriver even spoke.

The doctor was adamant.

"General," he said, "we need Shanna. And it's time to stop pussyfooting around. We need to find her. Our resources are growing thin. An eruption of blooms on the scale of KT-day will overwhelm us. If there's a cure for the Food of the Gods, we need it now. This has to stop once and for all."

Rhodes was silent. Sally could almost see him posed at the window, staring out, hands folded behind him, his back straight, standing on his feet, as he always was during times of action.

"You've always resisted my efforts to locate the Valley," Shriver said. "But we can't afford to wait anymore."

"It's been almost twenty years," Rhodes replied, "that you've been advising me to commit resources to search for this semi-mythical 'Valley' in hopes of capturing a woman who may or may not even still be alive. And all you've ever been able to tell me is that it's 'somewhere west'. I might remind you, that's a terrain that is not easily searchable.

That's tyrannosaur territory. It's thick with them."

Rhodes cursed unintelligibly.

"And why west? Why not east? Why not north?"

"Because that's where everyone who believes in it *says* it is," Shriver replied.

"That same logic would have us looking for Santa Claus at the North Pole," Rhodes said.

"There are several constants," Shriver responded patiently. "The same stories are told by a variety of different people, with no close associations with each other. They are exclusively women. Usually after they become pregnant. Although not always. Some are just more sensitive."

"To what?"

"To *her*," Shriver said, his own voice rising briefly. And then, again deliberately calm, "Dawn is one."

Sally's ears perked at the mention of her daughter, and her own blood pressure ticked up a notch.

Dawn had become a sore spot between herself and the General – ever since her daughter had tried to flee the Mount.

Shriver was quite correct. Dawn *was* one who felt the Valley. She had been dreaming of it for years – ever since her first onset of puberty, in fact – something that Shriver suspected was a contributing factor.

Sally, herself, didn't know why, and neither did she care. For what it was worth, she fully sympathized with her daughter yearning for a better life. And she supposed she should have seen it coming long before Dawn and her boyfriend, Justin, now both eighteen and sweethearts since childhood, had finally made their run.

Justin, unfortunately, was by this time a soldier, and his flight from the Mount, let alone with a viable female of productive age, was considered not only desertion, but a direct violation of Shriver's Arc Project dictates.

By definition, it was theft of a valuable asset.

They had not made it far. It had been Justin's platoon commander who had discovered his absence, along with a purloined truck and supplies. He had sent a squad out to round him up.

When they caught up to them, Justin had resisted arrest. In doing so, he had been shot and killed.

Sally still remembered the look on Dawn's face when she had been brought back to the Mount. Her daughter had barely spoken to her since.

"I don't blame you, Mother," Dawn had said briefly, and then refused to talk about it further.

Her tone had not been one of accusation, but of disappointment.

Sally wasn't sure what would have been worse.

Justin's mother, Kathryn, on the other hand, who had always hated the military as a matter of philosophical policy long before the end of the world, was not shy about laying blame, and had told Sally so in no uncertain terms.

Up to that point, Kathryn had considered the two of them friends, but that perception had ended abruptly and definitively in a confrontation that had required Kathryn to be physically restrained by both Kristie and Major Tom.

Rhodes had sworn to Sally he hadn't sent the platoon after Justin and Dawn.

At the time, Sally couldn't see where it mattered.

But leave it to Dr. Shrinker to show her how it did.

"Dawn has already tried to run," Shriver was saying. "She is clearly being drawn by something. And she is unique among others like her that she is not encumbered by a child."

"What does that mean?" Rhodes asked.

"It means she has the freedom to run," Shriver said. "And I believe she will attempt to do so again.

"I suggest," he continued, "that we simply let her go. Put a tracker on her so we can follow, and let her lead us to the Valley."

Standing outside the door, Sally's jaw dropped.

"Are you suggesting," Rhodes replied slowly, "that we let a teenage girl wander on her own out into the wilderness?"

"With a tracker, we can keep tabs on her," Shriver said.

There was a muttered curse, and the door to Rhodes' office was abruptly thrown open with a slam.

The General's eyes were furrowed in anger but widened as he saw Sally standing there.

He saw the look in her eyes.

Rhodes' own eyes softened and, for a moment, those cracks in the stone reappeared.

Sally said nothing, just stared back at him.

Rhodes glanced back at Shriver. Then he turned to Sally and his hand started to reach out, as if to touch her.

But then he stopped, the stone facade dropping once again.

"You heard?" he said. And before Sally could answer, Rhodes shook his head.

"I promise you," he said. "I wouldn't let that happen."

Rhodes looked at her earnestly.

"I had a daughter of my own once," he said.

Sally nodded, noncommittally.

"General," Shriver said quietly from behind him, "we have a lot more to talk about."

Rhodes' eyes narrowed over his shoulder at the doctor, before he turned back to Sally.

"Go home for the day," he told her.

Without a word, Sally turned to leave.

Rhodes stood outside his office, watching her go.

"I promise you," he said.

CHAPTER 19

If Dawn had heard them, she could have told her mother that Shriver's plans and Rhodes' promises were both moot. She was already planning to take the entire issue out of their hands.

The main hangar was divided into two main bays, with the aircraft located in the larger east wing that accessed the open cliff. The west-end contained the land vehicles, and opened up out of a narrower tunnel, which emptied out onto the westward slope.

This was the route the Coven escapees had taken years before, when they had simply blasted through the main gates. At the time, the Mount's security had been shaky and compromised in the aftermath of the seismic upheaval that had destroyed much of the facility. These days, the entrance/exit-way was more fortified – it would have taken a tank to barrel through.

Dawn, however, had a way around that, and she was planning on leaving tonight.

The guard at the gate this evening had been part of the squad that had tracked her and Justin down that day. Corporal Conner had been Justin's friend. He had grown up on the Mount with both of them.

Dawn remembered what happened well enough. To be fair, it wasn't exactly deliberate on the part of the soldiers. Justin had brought his own gun up – he might even have fired first.

He had died in her arms.

Tonight, she had a truck loaded with supplies and a key in the ignition. Corporal Conner had helped her arrange for both. He had also given her his duty schedule and the timing of the shift change, along with the code to the front gate.

Dawn had hidden in the hangar as she waited for Conner to take his post, ducking behind her loaded truck as the outgoing guard passed by.

She held off another ten minutes to make sure he was gone and out of earshot before she made her move.

That was when a voice spoke up behind her.

"What are you doing?"

Dawn turned to find Sabrina standing there.

Sabrina's dark eyes narrowed at her in the dim light of the hangar.

Justin had always remarked how much she and Dawn looked alike – he had called Sabrina the 'evil twin'.

Now she looked at Dawn accusingly.

"You're trying to escape again, aren't you?"

Dawn said nothing, glancing around nervously as Sabrina's voice echoed in the hangar.

Sabrina nodded to the guard at the watch-tower.

"That's Conner, isn't it? He helped you set this up."

Dawn frowned.

"I want out of here," she said, finally. "That shouldn't bother *you*."

"The last time you tried this, it got Justin killed."

Dawn's lips pursed. Sabrina still considered herself part of a love-triangle, even though Justin had never done anything but push her away.

"What do you want?" Dawn asked.

Sabrina glanced over her shoulder, lest someone besides the two of them might hear.

"Take me with you," she said.

Dawn blinked.

"You're kidding?"

Sabrina shook her head.

"I hate it here," she said simply.

"I don't think that's a good idea," Dawn said. "You know, being that we don't like each other, and all."

Sabrina smiled thinly.

"Take me with you," she said. "Or I'll tell."

Her eyes flashed in the dark.

"I'll pull the alarm. You won't get fifty yards." She nodded to Conner's shadow at the gate. "And you'll get *him* court-marshaled."

Dawn's eyes narrowed, glancing back at the gate and the dark woods beyond. Sabrina made a move towards the fire alarm on the wall.

"Okay," Dawn said quickly, simply giving in, having no idea what trouble she might be inviting.

The two of them climbed into the loaded truck. Dawn started up the engine, and rolled forward out of the tunnel, their lights still off.

Up on the watch-tower, Conner waved as their truck passed.

Dawn tapped in the code at the gate and the bars slid open.

Beside her, Sabrina was smiling broadly as they drove through.

The night forest beyond beckoned – dark and mysterious.

Dawn moved them forward slowly, aware of every bump in the road as they left the Mount behind.

Neither of them spoke, their eyes and ears tuned for any sign of pursuit, as the lights of the facility faded in the distance.

Their passage along the rough terrain, however, masked the first hint of rumbling in the earth, like seismic vibrations that might proceed a quake.

Or the impact tremors from giant footsteps.

CHAPTER 20

Naomi had again woken up screaming.

Jonah reflexively reached for her in the dark, pulling her close. At this point, he wasn't even startled by the somnolent outburst rousing him from his sleep – her nightmares had been coming every night and growing worse.

Crying, Naomi clutched at him, her body shaking. Jonah whispered in her ear, not for the first time, that it was just a dream, and that everything was alright.

At this point, however, he was beginning to doubt the truth of both.

After a moment, Naomi abruptly rose from the bed and dashed into the bathroom. The light flicked on and Jonah could hear her throwing up convulsively.

Morning sickness. She *was* pregnant again.

Jonah lay in bed, waiting for her to finish.

She had also been talking a lot more about the Valley.

They had found out she was expecting three weeks ago via an old testing kit salvaged from one of the pharmacy shops in the little downtown shopping mall.

The area was remarkably well-preserved – no doubt a factor of the high-altitude. Stores were still fully stocked with groceries. It was almost like modern living.

But Naomi had been pressuring him to leave, nevertheless. It was time, she said, to go find the Valley.

"You said it yourself," she reminded him, "what kind of life would a child have growing up alone? She needs people. And the Valley is there. I *know* it."

Jonah could have repeated all the same things he'd told her many times before. He could have reminded her that these were only dreams – he could have asked how she even knew this place was *called* the 'Valley'.

Moreover, how did she know the child was a *she*? Naomi didn't even seem aware she was making the distinction.

She had also spoken of a woman – somehow central to the Valley and prominent in her dreams – a woman called Shanna, and Naomi spoke of her by name.

Jonah shut his eyes.

What could he say? That she was being irrational? That they had a good thing going here? Or perhaps remind her that she had miscarried before and might do so again? He could even fall back on that old fail-safe that she 'shouldn't-travel-in-her-condition'.

In the bathroom, Naomi groaned as she finished retching, coughing up the last bits of food and liquid in her stomach. After a few minutes, Jonah heard the sound of a flush and running water – all amenities he was reluctant to leave behind.

Finally, she shut off the light and reappeared at the bedroom door.

She looked in at him, her eyes blinking in the dark.

"I want to leave," she said.

Jonah sighed.

"Okay," he said. "You win. Let's go."

CHAPTER 21

Dawn was breaking on the coast. It was a typical morning in the life of a fisherman.

Mark's boat had laid claim to one of the more lucrative spots in the area and they were in the process of spreading out their net.

His first mate was a young guy named Pete, and he had been telling Mark about a woman in the bar the night before as they fed out the slack.

Mark had not really been listening – there was no need – he'd been right there in the same tavern, and the woman in question was a barfly who was there every single night. Mark, himself, had woken with a mild hangover and, although that was nothing unusual, he'd begun to wish he'd just stayed home.

He'd come out anyway – basically because he felt like staying home *every* morning.

His life had reached a point of stasis, of sameness, that was beginning to become a burden. The monotony and continued hard-labor had taken their toll on his spirit.

Was this all there was? Did it just go on and on, growing more and more tedious, more tiresome, joints cinching ever tighter, back growing stiffer, hands more arthritic, every day until it was all over? Was this how the story ended? Not with a bang but a whimper?

Mark looked back towards land. There was nowhere else to go, no other life in sight.

And the one person who might have made it all bearable was gone forever.

Pete had asked Mark many times why he didn't just take a wife from town. But at this point, Mark was a forty-something bachelor in a community with an extremely finite population, most of whom were already married or with a common-law equivalent – either that, or they were kids twenty years younger.

Mark's usual reply was that he had been a loner all his life and wasn't about to marry just to have somebody there.

The truer answer, however, was that there was still someone else in the way – a woman almost twenty years gone now.

Someone he could never quite let go.

Pete was still telling his story, and Mark was nodding and answering at all the right parts, even as he stared vacantly out over the sea, when suddenly the boat was struck from below.

The impact was like being hit by a rising submarine. The fishing trawler's entire hundred-foot frame was shaken and the stern was raised completely clear of the water.

Pete blurted a curse as he was knocked over the railing, landing with a splash. There were shouts of panic from the rest of the crew, as the entire rear end of the boat was smashed apart. Shrapnel came flying across the deck as if from an explosion.

Mark held onto the railing as the boat up-ended, quickly filling with water, and the crew-members slid down the deck into the ocean. From his momentary vantage, Mark was the only one that saw what had hit them.

He only got a glimpse through the geyser of water, but it was enough.

It was a shark. A Megalodon – and a Meg with a head the size of a two-story building.

It shook the hundred-foot vessel in its jaws the way a dog might shake a cat. Its tail broke water far beyond the length of the ship, and it thrashed and rolled, tearing the main structure of the boat apart.

Mark could clearly see that the Meg's normally-solid-black eyes glowed emerald green.

Then the railing broke away in Mark's hands and he dropped into the ocean with Pete and the rest of the crew.

The boat had been reduced to floating wreckage, leaving the twenty men treading in the icy Pacific water.

"What the hell was that?" Pete shouted.

Mark looked around. The Meg seemed to have disappeared.

They were rather like Great Whites that way – once they'd hit a target and realized it wasn't food, they usually left well enough alone.

Usually.

Mark looked in the direction of the coast. They were nearly ten miles from shore – not a swim he would have normally cared to attempt in this rough water. And while the Meg might have vanished, and a fish that size would probably not be interested in anything as small as a human, there were any number of other water predators that might be swimming along at any time, just waiting to pick them off.

There were two lifeboats still lashed to the wreckage.

"Cut them loose!" Mark shouted, even as he obeyed himself and began swimming towards the boats. Pete and the rest of the crew followed, and within a few minutes, they had managed to free both craft from their moorings, setting them upright in the choppy surf. The crew clambered aboard and were soon headed back towards shore.

Miraculously, no one had been injured. As he glanced back at the wreckage of the trawler, Pete looked wide-eyed at Mark.

"What the hell hit us?" he asked again.

No one answered. Mark said nothing but he suspected every man knew what it must have been and none of them wanted to say it out loud – at least not until they were safely back on shore.

That Meg had been infected, Mark thought. Apparently, they were about to have another outbreak. The giants were back again.

They were within half-a-mile of the beach, and Mark was just beginning to relax when the second boat suddenly exploded out of the water.

Jaws over seventy-feet wide smashed together, engulfing the entire lifeboat, along with the men aboard.

It took less than a second, and in that heartbeat, Mark and every man on their own boat were momentarily paralyzed at the sight.

Not that it would have mattered.

The Meg's strike carried it more than two-hundred feet straight up out of the water – barely past its wing-like pectoral fin. Mark had time to gasp at the size of the body.

Then it fell sideways back into the ocean.

Right onto the other lifeboat.

The shark hit their stern and suddenly Mark found himself flying through the air, twisting like a badly-thrown boomerang. He flew more than a hundred yards before he felt the stinging, splashing impact as he hit the water.

He plunged deep, and immediately began kicking for the surface. Around him, the remaining crew scrambled as they all started swimming the last half-mile towards shore.

They had lost ten men with the first boat, and another four when the Meg had come down on the second, leaving half-a-dozen survivors to stumble their way up onto the sandy beach.

As a group, they turned to look back on the ocean.

Mark glanced to Pete. Then to the others.

Besides Pete and himself, four men had made it.

Fourteen men lost.

Mark looked grimly in the direction of town. Their wives would have to be told.

That was the first thing.

Then he would be taking his old pickup and heading for the Valley.

Shanna would have to be informed that a bloom had sprouted off the coast.

Elsewhere, however, the giants were already making their presence known.

CHAPTER 22

Shanna sat up on the hill, just below the road that ran behind Lucas' house, looking down to the field below, watching as Lucas and Leanne cavorted with the Valley's tyrannosaur First Family.

Lucas had been taking Leanne on laps around the field on Big Red's back, obviously trying to teach her how to ride – so far with little success, as Leanne mostly clung self-consciously to Lucas' back.

Shanna had stopped to watch them, staying just out of sight, hidden by the brush. She cloaked her mind as she approached, not wanting to alert her presence to Leanne.

Hiding from her daughter, she thought with a sigh. She found herself doing that a lot these days. A mother's instinct dies hard.

Leanne never looked up, although Big Red's nostrils flared, and he glanced in Shanna's direction. You couldn't fool that *T. rex* nose.

Sue was pregnant once again. She and Big Red had several broods together in the years since they'd lost their first, and their offspring had formed their own family unit, with several juveniles currently lounging about in the field like a lazy pride of lions.

That was another change that had manifested in rex' behavior. Once, Trix would have objected strongly to another pack sharing her territory, but these days, they seemed more or less at peace.

More than that, Sue and Big Red seemed to be behaving as a monogamous couple year-round, rather than the traditional annual tyrannosaur spring-fling pair-bonding – evidence of actual social evolution in *T. rex,* separate from physical adaptation.

Sue had not yet laid this season, but she had cleared away her grove of trees at the field's edge in preparation for a whole new nest. Currently, the big female reclined as her big red mate rounded another lap with Lucas and Leanne on his back.

Shanna turned her attention back to her daughter and her would-be suitor, as Big Red paused at the grove, allowing the two riders to dismount.

Leanne was laughing, clearly enjoying herself. Shanna had noticed that since the incident with the sickle-claws, Leanne had been back in Lucas' company again. In fact, they were spending a lot of time together.

So far, however, Lucas had made no attempt to let his feelings for her be known.

And for a young woman possessed of extraordinary latent empathic talent, Leanne was apparently completely oblivious.

Perhaps to some extent, that was a factor of her preoccupation with the *T. rex*.

As she had grown older, Leanne had grown more and more anxious to prove herself a worthy successor to Shanna, and she was very conscious of her station in the Valley, both with its creatures and its human inhabitants, both of whom she had begun to think of as 'her people'.

For now, however, she remained just the princess, not the queen – and a princess, Shanna knew, who still remained afraid, deep down, that her own abilities would never develop as her mother's had.

Now was forever, as Shanna remembered very well from her own youth. But she didn't think Leanne needed to worry. Shanna felt a powerful light growing within her daughter. In fact, she suspected it was Leanne's own desire that blocked her way.

Even now, their voices drifted up the hill, Leanne bemoaning that she just couldn't make the tyrannosaurs do what she wanted like her mother could.

Lucas laughed.

"Neither can your mother," he told her. "No one can *make* a rex do anything. She *asks*."

Quite an astute young man, Shanna thought, nodding affirmatively.

She actually felt sorry for him that he'd set his camp for her daughter. The only reason Leanne hadn't broken more hearts was because there just weren't that many around.

So far, Leanne had shown no signs of those type of feelings for Lucas, and Shanna could look deeper than most. There was no sense of infatuation – unlike a brief period when Leanne had been fourteen where she'd developed a crush on Maverick. Shanna had been exceedingly glad when *that* stage had gone by the wayside – although Maverick had at least been sensitive about it... sort of... for Maverick.

Lucas, for his part, seemed to understand that his feelings were one-way.

Peasant and princess, Shanna thought, as ridiculous as that might seem in such a small community. But she knew that was probably how they were seen by most – probably even how they saw each other. Perhaps it was even true.

Still, Lucas couldn't resist being in her presence, and had apparently decided it was worth it just to sit at her knee.

Shanna smiled sadly, even as she could feel the heartache wafting off of him in waves.

The moment's brief emotion sent out a stray spark and Leanne suddenly jumped, turning suddenly in her direction.

Shanna ducked down guiltily, hiding her mind quickly. She felt a bit low in doing so, but a mother had to use every trick she could. The time would come soon enough when Leanne would truly be on her own.

When Shanna looked up again, Big Red was standing, staring in her direction. Sue as well. Neither of them had ever forgotten that first lost brood, and as Sue prepared for nesting, the two of them were feisty and cat-nervous.

The juvenile rex lounging about in the field popped their heads up alertly at Big Red's low growl.

As the sound drifted up the hill, Shanna frowned.

Big Red's hackles were up. Something was wrong.

The big tyrannosaur had caught a scent and now his growl grew into a rumble. A moment later, Sue and the juveniles were standing by his side.

Alarmed, Leanne and Lucas were on their feet as well, looking alertly at the surrounding hills.

Shanna felt a stab of unease – just as she had waking from that dream not so very long ago, with that dark alien presence looking into her mind.

It was there, and then it was gone again – someone hiding from her mind – much like she herself had been hiding from her daughter's.

From the clearing, Sue's low, rumbling growl joined Big Red's own.

Then Shanna suddenly became aware of another presence, this one much nearer... and *much* larger. She had been so absorbed in spying on her daughter that she hadn't even noticed its slow approach.

Beneath her feet, the ground shook.

An impact tremor – a massive weight, striking the earth.

Again.

And again.

Behind her, the sky abruptly grew dark, as if one of the mountains in the east had suddenly stepped in front of the sun.

Shanna turned and looked up... and up...

... and up.

For a moment, all thought vanished in a moment of all-consuming awe.

It had been years since Shanna had seen an infected giant up close, let alone a sauropod.

Over the hill, its bulk seemed to fill the entire sky.

Brachiosaurus was already one of the most massive animals to ever walk the Earth long before the Food of the Gods.

The creature Shanna saw before her today was a titan unmatched in history or mythology.

And it was heading right towards the Valley.

Shanna rose to her feet, starting to flex her mind. For half-a-second, she thought it might be possible to deter the lumbering behemoth – nothing more than an impulse, just to change its direction.

But then, as she did so, she realized what this beast really was.

It was a rather dramatic distraction.

There was an RV truck parked on the road just above. Standing outside was a woman dressed in black.

Surrounding her was a pack of dromaeosaurs.

As Shanna looked around, more of the sickle-clawed beasts materialized out of the brush around her.

She sucked a breath, ready to scream, even though she knew it was already too late.

The sickle-claws, however, did not attack, but instead just circled around her, cutting off her avenue of retreat.

The woman in black raised what looked like an air-pistol in one hand.

Shanna heard a loud *phut* and felt a sting in her chest. As she looked down, she saw a dart sticking out of her shirt, just below her collar. Immediately, her head began to spin.

The woman in black smiled.

"The Dragon Lord wishes to speak to you," she said.

With her last moments of consciousness, Shanna pulled the tranquilizer dart from her chest.

Then she staggered and fell.

The world faded and went black.

CHAPTER 23

Cameron was enjoying some quality time, sacked-out in a hammock in his backyard, when Leanne and Lucas came running around the side of the house. As he looked up and saw them, Leanne saw her father's eyes go wide with alarm.

"Dad!" Leanne yelled frantically. "Run! It's coming!"

That was all she got out, before the living mountain came into view over the roof of the house right above them, rearing over a thousand feet high, its eyes glowing emerald green.

Shanna and Cameron's house was a seven-room cabin – the foot that came down was rounded like an elephant's and nearly the circumference of the house itself – the cabin was smashed in a single step.

Cameron looked at the broken lumber beneath the giant's foot.

"My *house...*," he stammered, outraged. "*Whathefu...?*"

Leanne and Lucas came running past him.

"Run, Dad! Run!"

Having no better alternative, Cameron turned and ran with them, all three of them shouting out warnings to the houses ahead.

Heads started poking out of windows. One of them was Maverick, who lived two houses down. His eyes went wide and he let loose with a blurted, "Holy *shit*!" before he broke out his back door and started running as well.

Big Red and Sue were at the monster's heels, with the juveniles tearing along behind. And as the giant beast lumbered towards town, they were joined by Trix and her pack of females.

Leanne had seen the rex-pack do this before with normal-sized sauropods, usually at Shanna's urging, in order to keep the cumbersome long-necked beasts clear of the Valley. While herbivorous, these giants were ill-tempered, and because of their sheer size, they were a serious threat to both life and property.

But despite their size, or more accurately, *because* of it, sauropods were usually easily corralled by the *T. rex*. Within their own era, the different tyrannosaur species were actually responsible for rendering the largest sauropods extinct throughout entire geographic territories, and this was primarily due to the tyrannosaurs' powerful jaws.

Until the tyrant dinosaurs came along, the biggest sauropods were always able to repel predators like the big allosaurs with sheer size. But by the Late Cretaceous, it became necessary for prey species to employ evasion and agility against the one-shot-one-kill attack-strategy of the great-skulled tyrannosaur species. The big sauropods were simply too slow to apply their greater mass effectively against the tendon-severing, bone-shearing bites of a *T. rex*.

Today, however, was something different.

The rex chomping at the infected giant's ankles brought to mind a pack of small dogs biting at the heel of an elephant. Big Red and Sue ripped away chunks of flesh the size of small cars from the monster's legs, but that was insufficient to bring the beast down.

It clearly hurt, though – the giant's roar was like a foghorn, echoing for miles throughout the entire countryside. The angered titan reared like a horse and brought its piston-like feet down to the earth with the force of an asteroid.

The *T. rex* pack scrambled out of the way. Sue, however, was not quite fast enough. The massive blunt-clawed foot barely clipped her, but Sue was flipped and thrown nearly fifty yards like a rag doll. She landed bonelessly, and lay limp and unmoving.

Lucas cried out, but his voice was drowned out a moment later, as Big Red's roar of anguish sounded across the entire Valley. In blind fury, the big red rex charged the giant sauropod maniacally, biting and tearing, before an off-hand blow knocked him sprawling as well.

Big Red lay stunned, blinking, gasping for air.

Lucas shook off a restraining hand from Leanne and ran to the fallen tyrannosaur's side.

The giant sauropod thundered past them on its way through the village. The fleeing townsfolk broke to either side as the colossus overtook and passed them by as well.

Leanne came running up to where Lucas sat with Big Red, with Cameron and Maverick right behind.

The big rex was stunned but not injured.

Leanne, however, could see that Sue had not been so lucky. It only took one look at her twisted and broken frame.

The sauropod continued on, clearly bothered by its savaged and bleeding ankles, which were now showing scrapes of bone, as Trix and the rest of the rex pack continued to pester and harass the lumbering titan.

There was another shriek of pain as Trix was also struck and sent flying, rolling to a stop a short distance away, where she lay motionless, her neck broken.

But now the giant sauropod veered its course away from the center of town. The remaining rex kept at its heels, unrelenting, following the infected colossus as its path now took it out of the Valley.

Big Red began to stir. Lucas patted the massive, bony cheek. He glanced over his shoulder at the big tyrannosaur's fallen mate, and he grieved for his friend.

And to Leanne sitting beside him, Lucas' sorrow was palpable. For one clear moment, she could feel it coming off of him like body heat.

Leanne blinked, suddenly consciously aware of the connection – it was the first time she'd felt such sensations from a normal human. The intensity of his grief overwhelmed her and tears began to roll down her own cheeks.

Cameron, however, had suddenly stopped, turning to stare to the east in the direction the titan had come.

Leanne looked up at her father quizzically.

"What is it, Dad?"

But as soon as she asked, she felt it as well.

"Shanna," Cameron said.

CHAPTER 24

Lily knew what was coming.

One of the many things that Ginger had taught her early on was the inherent power in the role of the lowly maid.

A maid has keys to doors and access to private dwellings where no one else can go. Lily had already demonstrated the truth of this years ago when she had let Shriver's little talking lizard out of its cage.

She also had access to all the freshest gossip, and today the big item was that Sally's daughter, Dawn, had once again fled the Mount, just last night, and that her mother had gone absolutely ballistic in General Rhodes' office only a short while earlier that morning.

Ironically, this had been reported to her by Sally's former friend, Kathryn, when Lily had done her rounds in the med-unit that morning.

Ever since Kathryn's own son, Justin, had died at the hands of the Mount's power-structure, she had warmed considerably to both Lily and Ginger – Ginger who was always there with a piece of supportive wisdom and sage advice – with just an ever-so-slight twist of agenda.

Kathryn reported this latest news with bitter satisfaction.

Rhodes had apparently actually been on the defensive: "I didn't *let* anything happen."

But Sally hadn't been trying to hear it. Purportedly, she had laid right into him: "This was what Shrinker *wanted*!"

Rhodes' fallback had been, "This is what *Dawn* wanted. She didn't *ask* us."

Kathryn had smiled grimly.

"Karma's a bitch," she said.

Lily had not commented, just stoically performed her duties.

No one yet knew that Sabrina had gone as well. Lily had not reported her daughter missing.

Lily had received her visions and had consulted with Ginger, and she wanted Sabrina as far away from the Mount as possible when everything began to happen.

They had been setting things up for weeks now.

Lily wasn't allowed into the more sensitive areas without an escort, but she'd had the necessary keys and codes for a long time. That was one of the benefits of being married to an officer – all Lily needed was to engender trust – and Captain Stevens was secure in his marriage, his wife, and the daughter that wasn't his.

Pushing her cleaning cart nonchalantly out of the elevator, back to the maintenance level, she dallied through the shift-change until the area cleared out. Then she took her purloined keys and codes, letting herself down into the stairway that led to the lower levels – the restricted sections that led to the power-station.

As she made her way, she could already feel the thermal heat emanating from below, and the air was heavy with the ponderous beat of the generators that powered the entire Mount.

Just outside the main power room was a ventilation shaft. Bending a knee, Lily produced a wrench and began to work on the grating until the metal screen pulled loose.

There was skittering movement from inside, and three Ottos hopped out.

One of them ran up her arm and perched on her shoulder like a parrot.

Lily patted the little creature as it chittered and chirped.

Inside the ventilation shaft, there was additional movement. Lily didn't know how many more of the little lizards there were, but they always seemed to group-off in threes.

The creature on her shoulder chittered as the two others hopping about at her feet led her to the main control panel.

Lily was shaking in anticipation and she almost screamed aloud when a voice spoke up behind her.

"What do you think you're doing?"

Lily turned to find Michelle standing there.

Tall and strong, Michelle had always been the Coven's primary enforcer. At least, until she had sold them out to Rhodes – sold them out to *power*.

Michelle stepped forward. Physically, Lily knew she had no chance against her.

On her shoulder, the first Otto hissed, spreading its claws. The other two scurried to either side, their miniature sickle-claws tapping.

"I asked you what you think you're doing?" Michelle said again.

Now Lily stepped forward, patting down the little lizard posturing on her shoulder.

"Don't you *feel* it?" she said. "You were one of us, once."

Lily reached out and touched Michelle's hand.

Michelle blinked, gasping, and Lilly could *feel* the rush, like a shock of static – or like a sudden chilling wind.

All three Ottos chittered, and the one on Lily's shoulder spoke aloud, parroting her voice.

"Don't you *feel* it?"

Michelle stepped back, wobbling slightly.

As she did so, one of the other two Ottos scampered up to perch on her own shoulder.

Michelle glanced at the little lizard and then back at Lily.

She nodded to the control panel.

"Go," Michelle said. "Get up top. I'll handle this."

Lily smiled.

At the grating to the ventilation shaft, there was another skittering and several more Ottos poked their heads out, watching.

Lily turned back into the stairway as Michelle pulled open the control panel.

She had just reached the maintenance level when the lights in the Mount went out.

CHAPTER 25

Rhodes had been in a meeting with Major Hicks and Major Tom, as well as Dr. Shrinker, when Sally had burst into his office.

"My daughter is *gone*, you son of a *bitch*!"

Rhodes started to rise from his desk.

"Listen," he began, "it's not what you think. We just found out ourselves."

He was cut short, however, as Sally pitched her coffee cup at him. Rhodes ducked as it shattered on the wall, and he stared back at her, thunderstruck.

Sally turned her eyes venomously to Shriver and actually took a step in the doctor's direction before Tom intercepted her, shaking his head.

"Easy," Tom said. "We'll get her back."

Sally had burst into furious tears.

"Like the *last* time?"

She pushed away from Tom.

Rhodes had followed her out, but the conversation had not gone any better from there, with their voices now echoing across the entire chamber, and finally ended up with Hicks and Tom escorting her to the elevator.

"Take a breath," Tom advised her. "I'll send Kristie over to see you after her shift ends."

A breath, however, had not helped, and an hour later, she reappeared at Rhodes' door. The others had gone and the General was sitting in his office alone.

Now a bit more composed, Sally informed him she was resigning her post, and without another word, she turned and began cleaning out her desk.

Rhodes rose to his feet, as was his custom during times of stress, and stood watching her from his office door. When he finally spoke, his voice was deliberately calm and professional.

"If it's all the same," he said, "I'm going to choose not to accept your resignation at this time."

Sally didn't look up at him.

"I swear to you," Rhodes said, "I did not want this to happen."

Sally said nothing, but tears again started to stream down her face.

She had not yet thought beyond clearing out her desk, which for the most part consisted of a few office supplies and pictures of her daughter. Neither did she have any particular idea of what her actions might mean going forward.

Dawn was already out there somewhere, and this time, she had been gone for several hours before the alarm was even sent. The on-duty guard was being questioned – a friend of Justin's, from Sally's understanding, who she suspected was in on it.

What Sally actually had in mind was to go after her, the logistics of which having not yet even been a consideration. Truthfully, she knew that it was highly unlikely it would even be allowed to happen.

Rhodes stood over her desk, the granite pillar holding up the world.

Then he bent down next to her, his hand touching her arm.

"Sally," he said, and just for a moment, she thought she heard a break in his voice, a crack in the stone. "I am so, *so* sorry."

Sally squeezed her eyes shut, tears rolling down her cheeks.

Behind him, the emergency phone in his office rang.

Rhodes frowned, glancing over his shoulder, before he turned, stepping back to his desk and putting the phone on speaker.

It was Captain Stevens from the aircraft carrier stationed in the gulf below.

"Sir?" Stevens said, and Rhodes immediately straightened at the Captain's tone. "I think we've got problems. We've got incoming."

"What do you mean, 'incoming'?" Rhodes said.

And at that moment, the lights went out and the phone in his hand went dead.

"What the hell?" Rhodes said aloud. He turned and pulled the blinds on his window, letting the light in.

Sally blinked at the sudden glare. Tentatively, she got up to follow Rhodes into his office.

This was not the first blackout they'd experienced on the Mount, but preceded by Stevens' aborted call, it did not bode well.

In the sudden stillness, Sally was now aware of a rumbling, like a seismic disturbance.

Again, that was not exactly an unusual occurrence – according to Shriver, tectonic activity had increased all over the region by a factor of ten.

Rhodes was just reaching for the handheld radio he kept at his desk when it suddenly sparked alive, and Captain Stevens' voice barked through the static.

"General, sir! We've got..."

And then the message cut off.

"Stevens?" Rhodes began, but then his own voice died in his throat as one look out the window to the gulf below told him all he needed to know.

The aircraft carrier seemed to explode upward in a geyser – a hundred-thousand tons of steel knocked clean out of the water.

And through the deluge, they could clearly see the seven-hundred-foot vessel locked in the jaws of a giant Megalodon.

There was an explosion as the fuel lit up, even as the boat itself came apart in the mega-shark's jaws.

The Meg crested. A normal adult Megalodon might reach seventy feet or better – an infected giant could beat ten times that, and the monster shark's leap carried it more than its full body-length clear of the water.

Sally gasped. Rhodes cursed.

Never once had a Meg been seen this far up the gulf.

Rhodes' radio barked again. This time it was Hicks.

"Uh, sir? I think we've got problems."

Sally felt the force of impact even before she turned to look out at the surrounding mountains.

Their vantage was predominantly to the east, and their view to the north and south was narrow, but it was enough.

"My God," Rhodes whispered.

The mountains had come alive.

Sally remembered KT-day, and how the infected giants had suddenly appeared in the cities – beasts of all kinds – a helter-skelter assemblage – carnosaurs, ankylosaurs, ceratopsians.

This was something different than what they'd seen before.

It was a marching procession of giant sauropods – brachiosaurs, diplodocids, and titanosaurs, their eyes all glowing emerald green with the Food of the Gods.

Above their heads, the skies were filled with circling pterosaurs.

More than that, as the giant beasts advanced on the Mount, they were clearly moving in uniform formation.

Shriver had once estimated the weight of an infected titanosaur as in excess of a hundred thousand tons.

From the seismic tremors of their footsteps alone, the Mount itself began to tremble.

CHAPTER 26

The first wave of monsters struck the base of the mountain, and the impact was like the wrath of the gods. The massive long-necked giants reared, bringing their elephantine feet down in thundering blows that shook the very earth.

Within moments, avalanches of volcanic rock started tumbling down.

Inside the Mount, support tunnels began to collapse across the entire complex.

Sally and Rhodes were nearly knocked off their feet.

From the high cavern ceiling above, lights flickered as the back-up generators tried to switch on, but for some reason, they were not kicking in, as if the secondary circuit-breaker had been disconnected.

Rhodes' office lay at the eastern-most point of the administrative level. The stairs that accessed both the top deck and the hangar below were located out in the main cavern, on the south side, opposite the elevator on the north, and now the stairwell doors slammed open as Hicks and Major Tom burst out onto the floor, both carrying flashlights, shining their beams into the semi-darkness.

"General?" Hicks called out, his voice echoing in the open chamber. "Are you alright?"

"Right here, Major," Rhodes called back, coming out to meet them. "What the hell is happening?"

"We're sustaining serious damage all over the Mount, sir," Tom replied. "Structural integrity is compromised on all levels."

Even as he said it, there was another impact, shaking rocks loose from the ceiling above.

"I've scrambled all the ground troops to the hangar bay, and a prep crew up to the top-deck," Hicks reported. "I'm getting reports that several tunnels have already collapsed."

Hicks shook his head. "I don't know how many casualties."

"What about the Caverns?"

"Stable so far, sir."

"We've got to get the civilians clear," Rhodes said. "What kind of transport do we have available?"

"We've only got one transport chopper available in the hangar, sir," Tom said, his face sober. "That's not near enough to get everybody out."

Rhodes took a deep breath. He turned to Hicks.

"What about our fighter jets?"

"We've lost the aircraft carrier, sir," Hicks replied. "That took out the majority of our localized air force. Choppers. Jets. Everything. And after all the recent blooms, almost all of our F16s not stationed on the carrier have already been relocated to outlying bases. We might be able to scramble from one of these, but right now all our communications are down."

"What have we got on the platform up top?"

"Right now, we've got four combat choppers on the top-deck. All being prepped as we speak."

Rhodes nodded to Tom.

"You get down to the hangar. Load up that chopper with as many civilians as you can. Whoever you can't get out by air, pack the land rigs and take the rest out by ground."

"Out the west side of the Mount?" Tom shook his head doubtfully. "Sir, do you have any idea what's going on out there?"

"Send armed troops out first," Rhodes said. "Do your best to clear a path for the civilians." He nodded to Hicks. "We'll try and cover you by air."

"What about you, sir?" Hicks asked.

"I'm going with you," Rhodes replied. "We're going to need every available pilot. That means me too."

He turned to Tom.

"Get every ground-trooper to the hangar bay and start sending up the civilians."

"The intercom for the Caverns is down," Tom said. "I haven't been able to raise them."

"Damn it," Rhodes cursed. "That's not supposed to happen. Even with the power out."

Tom's eyes were grim.

"My wife's down there, sir," he said.

Rhodes nodded.

"Understood," he said. "Major, you get to the hangar. Get that chopper ready."

Then he turned to Sally.

"I guess it's up to you," Rhodes said. "Those people's lives are in your hands. I need you to get down to the Caverns and start bringing people up."

Wide-eyed, Sally nodded. She glanced at Tom and they both turned to go, but Rhodes caught Sally by her arm.

He met her eyes earnestly.

"I'm depending on you," he said.

And for just a moment, the cracks in the stone reappeared.

"I've told you before," he said, "I used to have a daughter. You remind me a lot of her."

Now those cement cracks seemed to shore together as they once again took the load.

"It's been a lot of years," he said. "And for what it's worth, you've made the end of the world a little easier for an old son-of-a-bitch like me."

Rhodes turned to Hicks.

"Let's get up top, Major," he said.

Rhodes nodded to Tom.

"Go get your wife," he said. "We'll be watching your back."

CHAPTER 27

Tom led Sally down the winding staircase, their flashlight beams chasing each other across the steps in front of them, even as the entire structure shook all around, sending rocks bouncing off the walls and stairs into the circular chasm below.

The hangar was seven-hundred feet beneath the administration-level and the Caverns another two levels below that.

Tom could see Sally was scared, and he kept a grip on her hand as they made their way in the dark.

Dust quickly began to cloud the air. Without the power, the ventilation systems had shut down and it was quickly growing stifling in the stairwell. Tom tried not to think about potential gases that might be leaking up from the bowels of the mountain.

The stairway rocked beneath their feet. Tom knew the interior architecture well enough, and was confident the stairs themselves were solid, but they were still mounted on the cavern walls. Enough shaking could potentially tear them loose.

Tom wiped the sweat from his eyes – he was beginning to scare himself. He glanced over at Sally, and squeezed her hand.

"You doing okay?" he asked, as much for her benefit as his own.

Sally nodded, wide-eyed, clearly fighting panic. She'd often complained about claustrophobia just riding in the elevator – the closed space of the stairwell in the dark must be overwhelming for her.

But Tom had known Sally for a long time, and she also suffered from an acute case of responsibility, and Tom knew how to activate her, just as Rhodes did.

"Hang in there," he said. "Those people down there are counting on us."

Sally shut her eyes, but nodded.

It had been nearly ten minutes since the lights had gone out and the first tremor had struck – ten minutes to make it down seven hundred feet of stairs in the dark. Now they were finally reaching the hangar-level.

The commons were still another two levels and eighty more feet below.

As they stopped at the landing that led into the main hangar, Tom turned to Sally.

"You can do this," he said.

And then, just to make it personal, he told her, "*Kristie's* down there.

I'm counting on you."

Sally shut her eyes, but nodded again.

"Just lead them up here. I'll be waiting."

Tom gave her hand another squeeze.

Sally squeezed back. Then she took a breath, setting her teeth, and continued on down.

Tom turned to the doorway to the hangar. With the power out, the code lock was inoperable. Fortunately, that was at least one contingency they had prepared for. He pulled open the lock and turned his key – privileged to an officer – and unlocked the door manually.

Inside, the hangar was dark. The main opening over the cliff let in a portion of daylight, but the overhead lights were still off, casting the open bay in a ghostly half-light.

Tom had expected the bustle of soldiers, prepping weapons and vehicles, as per-orders, but the open space was absolutely still.

He frowned. On *any* given day, there should be at least two dozen men working the main hangar. He peered into the semi-dark, shining his light, trying to see. He jumped as the breeze blowing through the cavern pushed the heavy door to the stairwell shut behind him.

Then, as his eyes began to adjust, he caught a hint of movement.

His ears detected a low hissing growl that morphed into a birdlike warble.

He turned his light in the direction of the sound.

As the beam illuminated the chamber, his blood ran cold.

"Oh my God," he whispered.

The hangar bay was the scene of a slaughter.

Bodies of soldiers lay strewn across the floor, torn and bloody, ripped utterly to pieces.

Standing over the remains, their eyes reflecting back his flashlight beam, was an entire *pack* of sickle-claws.

And skittering around at their feet, was a gaggle of those smaller lizards that Tom knew all too well.

"Oh you little *bastards*," he said aloud.

His own voice was mimicked back at him, echoing across the hangar in tandem stereo.

"Little *bastards*."

The first of the sickle-claws came at him in the half-darkness.

In an instant, Tom had his pistol out and fired, catching the onrushing dromaeosaur in mid-leap. Undaunted, with seemingly mindless aggression, a second and third immediately followed, but Tom dropped both of them in their tracks with two successive shots.

With his back to the stairwell door, Tom opened-up fire as the sickle-claws now attacked in a flock, and the hangar echoed with the sound of gunshots and screeching dromaeosaur death-cries.

Then the assault abruptly stopped.

Tom frowned. That was extremely uncharacteristic of sickle-claws.

He wasn't sure how many of them he had hit – it was difficult to see in the dim light – but for some reason, the attacking wave had paused.

He shined his light and he could see the remaining beasts just standing there, bobbing their heads, their eyes reflecting like headlights in his flashlight beam as they ogled him in that oddly birdlike fashion.

Tom began edging his way back towards the stairway.

He didn't see the movement behind him until Michelle stepped out of the shadows and clubbed him across the back of his head.

Tom dropped to his knees, his pistol falling from his hands.

Dazed, he turned to see Michelle smiling at him in the dim light. She was holding an M-16 automatic rifle.

An Otto perched on her shoulder like a parrot.

She raised her rifle and Tom heard a snap as she pulled back the bolt, glancing over her shoulder as she did so.

"I've got him," she said aloud. "Go ahead. Light it up."

Now Tom saw Ginger stepping out from the shadows. She had been hiding behind the transport chopper.

In her hands was a can of gasoline, and as Tom watched, she tossed a match towards the helicopter.

Tom could see her smile as the hangar suddenly lit up and the chopper burst into flame.

The path of fire followed a trail of gasoline spilled across the floor of the bay, streaking towards the lot of parked land-vehicles. In moments, the entire hangar was ablaze. The cavern opening sucked wind, feeding the fire.

Her eyes lit up like neon by the billowing flame, Michelle again turned back to Tom. Her smile was both beautiful and terrible.

"Sorry about this," she said, as she raised the rifle. "I always kind of liked you, Tom."

But at that moment, another tremor reverberated through the mountain, this one harder than all the rest.

An avalanche of rubble broke loose from the hangar's ceiling, and the ground shook hard enough to throw them all to the floor.

A large slab of rock dropped right on top of the burning chopper, igniting the fuel tanks, and now the whole thing exploded.

Standing right next to it, Ginger was nearly decapitated by a flying rotor blade. Tom heard a guttural – and wholly satisfying – grunt as she toppled over, her torn throat spurting blood.

Michelle regained her feet quickly, but Tom used the moment to make a dash for the stairwell. A volley of gunfire erupted behind him, ricocheting bullets off the walls, even as he crashed against the door, wrenching it open and diving through.

In seconds, Michelle was on his tail, but Tom had already turned, catching her unexpectedly with a hard punch just as she appeared at the doorway.

Surprisingly, she didn't go down, and Tom found himself grappling with her for possession of the rifle.

For a slender woman, she was surprisingly strong. Tom was forced to use his full weight to twist the gun from her grasp, following through with a back-swing, bringing the rifle butt against the side of her head, and Michelle finally dropped.

But now the sickle-claws were moving on him again, burbling like goblins as they came at him in the dark.

Tom opened up with the M-16 as they appeared at the doorway, the flash from the muzzle lighting up their flailing claws and the splatters of blood as he chopped them down.

He was backing up, and just turning to look for the top step, only to find Michelle was already back on her feet.

Tom let out a blurted curse, bringing the rifle around, but she had already let loose with a spinning kick that caught him flush, sinking deep in his gut, and knocking him down the stairway.

Gasping for wind, Tom twisted as he fell, reaching for the railing, but instead, his head struck the heavy metal steps.

The world went dark and he tumbled limply to the bottom of the landing.

Michelle stood, wiping blood from her brow, picking up the rifle, even as the sickle-claws funneled into the stairwell behind her.

One of the Ottos ran up her arm and perched on her shoulder.

Michelle smiled.

"Always liked you, Tom," she said.

CHAPTER 28

As Sally made her way down the stairs in the dark, the rumble in the Mount grew louder by the second. In the circular corridor, the echo was nearly deafening, as avalanches of concrete and rock broke away, bouncing off the metal staircase, sending pieces flying like shrapnel.

She had just reached the maintenance level above the main Caverns and was wondering why no one had yet tried the stairway, when suddenly something moved in front of her flashlight.

Sally shrieked involuntarily, and was answered by a responding scream as her light pinned a woman huddled on the steps. When she looked up, Sally recognized her face.

Lily stared up at her, wide-eyed and fearful.

"What are *you* doing here?" Sally demanded, pulling Lily to her feet. "Where is everyone?"

Lily blinked.

"I... uh... I was in maintenance when the quake hit. I couldn't get out. Everything went dark."

There was another answering rumble. Sally shined the light upwards as more rocks broke away from the walls.

"It wasn't a quake," she said.

She gave Lily a tug.

"Come on. We've got to get to the Caverns."

Lily shook her head.

"I tried. The doorway's blocked."

Sally shined her light down to the level below and she could see rubble piled up against the entrance. It looked like part of the stairway had broken away as well, causing her to worry about the steps beneath her own feet as the tremors continued to shake their moorings.

Even as she thought it, another monstrous impact shook the mountain, nearly knocking them both from their feet. Sally clung to the railing until the tremor passed.

Cautiously, she began to make her way down, looking back over her shoulder at Lily.

"Come on. Help me clear this away."

Lily hesitated, but after a moment, she followed.

Propping the flashlight on the steps, Sally began pushing aside the rocks, coughing as the dust gathered. The last wedge of concrete, however, was too heavy for her to move alone. She looked up irritably at Lily who was still just standing there.

"What are you waiting for? Help me!"

Obediently, Lily joined her and the two of them pushed the last obstruction aside.

The metal doors were bent on their hinges from the impact, and for a moment, Sally was afraid they might be stuck. But as she strained, there was a creak and the door swung open.

Sally grabbed up her flashlight, motioning to Lily, and pushed her way into the Caverns.

The overhead lights were out, just like the rest of the complex, but she could see gathered lanterns and lights clustered in the middle of the chamber. She heard a murmur of voices and struggled to see in the dim light.

A crowd was gathered – mothers and daycare workers huddled with their children in the center of the commons.

Sally spotted Kristie, standing at the perimeter like a guard. Sally stepped forward, waving.

"Kristie? What's going on? Why...?"

That was all she got out. She saw Kristie start to wave a warning before something struck her in the head from behind.

Pain exploded in her skull and Sally dropped to the floor. The blow had nearly knocked her unconscious. For a moment, she thought she'd been hit by a falling rock, but when she tried to rise, staggered and dazed, there was a sudden blast of machine-gun fire aimed at the ceiling, accompanied by screams and cries from the crowd.

Sally turned and saw Kathryn standing over her, an automatic rifle in her hands, and now she brought the muzzle down and leveled it at her head.

"Don't move, Sally," Kathryn said.

Behind her, Lily stood at the door, breath sucked in an aborted scream.

Kathryn glanced at Lily over her shoulder.

"Go on," she said, nodding to the huddled crowd. "Get over there."

Immediately, Lily complied.

"Kathryn," Sally stammered. "What in God's name are you *doing*? We've got to get these people out of here."

Kathryn's eyes narrowed.

"Your General shouldn't have killed my son," she replied.

There was another creak at the stairway door. Katheryn turned, raising her rifle.

But as the door pushed open, it was Michelle standing there, holding Major Tom at gunpoint. He seemed to be staggering, his scalp lacerated and bleeding.

Standing at her side like attack-dogs were half-a-dozen sickle-claws.

And sitting on her shoulder like a parrot was Otto.

"Go on," Michelle said, giving Tom a shove.

Tom stumbled. Kristie separated from the crowd, hugging him to her, wiping the blood from his brow.

Michelle caught Sally's eye and smiled.

Sally shook her head disbelievingly.

"Are you crazy?" she asked. "This whole mountain is coming down. We're *all* going to die."

Michelle shook her head slowly.

"No," she said. "We're not."

Her smile broadened.

"Not *all* of us."

And even as she spoke, the rumbling in the mountain abruptly ceased.

The sudden silence was deafening, and was only punctuated by the continuing clatter of falling rock.

Michelle looked down at Sally, eyes narrowed. The little Otto chittered on her shoulder.

"You know," Michelle said, "this is something I've wanted to do for a long time."

And with that, she brought the butt of her rifle hard across the side of Sally's head.

With a groan, Sally dropped limp and unconscious at Michelle's feet.

CHAPTER 29

The lights were still flickering in the stairwell as Rhodes and Hicks made their way to the top deck. Hicks had already radioed Wedge and Biggs to meet them up on the roof. He hoped to hell they were already prepped.

Then the lights went out completely – again, something that was never supposed to happen. The power to the top deck from the administration-level was supposed to be on its own relay.

"Dammit," Rhodes cursed. "Where the hell is Shriver? This back-up system was his baby."

As he spoke, it occurred to them for the first time to wonder about the Doctor.

"He was headed to his lab, last I saw," Hicks said.

Rhodes stopped, shining his light back down at the level below. Shriver's lab was on the administration-level, clear at the opposite end of the compound, and they had both seen the interior struts along the westward section had collapsed.

"You're not thinking of going back for him?" Hicks asked.

Personally, Hicks would have been happy to leave the old bastard to rot.

Rhodes looked torn.

"We can't just leave him," he said finally. "Besides, we might need him. You get up top. *I'll* go get him."

As if to contest the point, the mountain rumbled.

"I don't think that's a good idea, sir," Hicks said.

Rhodes smiled.

"I'm pushing seventy years old," he said. "According to Arc Project protocol, I'm one of the expendable ones." He slapped Hicks on the shoulder. "If I'm not up top in fifteen minutes, you get the hell in the air, and consider yourself promoted to General."

As he turned to go, however, the mountain itself decided to take the matter out of his hands.

The heaviest impact yet sent a cascade of rubble tumbling off the walls.

A chunk of rock struck the General in his head.

Rhodes dropped limp, blood gouting from his scalp, and he started to tumble down the shaking stairwell.

Clinging to the rail, Hicks lunged and caught the General's arm, arresting his fall.

The mountain, however, wasn't helping, threatening to shake the entire stairway loose. Riding out the tremor, Hicks pulled Rhodes up on one shoulder and began clambering back up the steps.

But then the rumbling suddenly stopped.

Gasping under the double weight, Hicks paused, listening.

Rubble continued to clatter from the walls, but it seemed that the steady pounding on the mountain itself had ceased

Had the titans broken off their attack?

But in the sudden silence, he could now hear gunfire from up above. "What the hell?"

Hicks kicked open the door to the top-deck, blinking, momentarily blind in the glare of the overhead sun.

Amid the sound of gunshots, there was the sound of screeching birdlike yodels.

Hicks looked around the platform and paled.

Wedge and Biggs had made the roof after all – they were the only ones still alive – and three of the four combat helicopters were ablaze.

Both pilots were currently pinned-down, backed-up against the last remaining chopper, and they were surrounded by an entire pack of sickle-claws.

And hopping about at the swarming dromaeosaurs' feet, amid the bloody, left-over carnage that had been the prep-crew, was a troop of those damned little talking lizards.

Hicks tossed Rhodes off his shoulder, and grabbed his sidearm. Dropping to one knee, he began to fire.

He dropped four of the attacking sickle-claws right away before the others realized the danger from behind and broke off to either side.

Hicks also took the opportunity to pick off a few of those skittering lizards at their feet as well.

He *hated* those little bastards.

"Wedge!" he hollered. "Get that chopper started!"

Hicks glanced skyward. Above them, the sky was a spiraling tempest of pterosaurs – all infected giants. And now he realized that circling among them were what looked like giant eagles – something new to the unnatural fauna.

He muttered a curse. They had been supposed to provide air cover, but Hicks could see they would be hard-put simply to escape at all.

The sickle-claws now turned their attention to him.

Hicks started to pick his shots more deliberately – if they mobbed him, it would be over in seconds.

With the momentary distraction, however, Wedge managed to get the helicopter started. Biggs jumped on board behind him as the chopper abruptly lurched from the tarmac into the air.

There was a blast of wind from the spinning rotor blades as the unwieldy aircraft careened recklessly in Hicks' direction. He ducked as Biggs blasted a covering volley of machine-gun fire and the dromaeosaur pack momentarily fell back.

Hiking Rhodes' limp body up over his shoulder, Hicks reached up as the chopper passed over, and Biggs caught his outstretched hand, hauling them both aboard, even as the wobbling aircraft launched into the air.

"Go!" Hicks shouted at Wedge, as he and Rhodes tumbled into the hold.

And here was where they were actually lucky that the circling pterosaurs were infected giants – the winged dragons were well-known to go after choppers, but the sheer size of these beasts made them less nimble, and Wedge took them up high and fast.

From the altitude, Hicks looked down upon the Mount.

The mountain was surrounded by an entire battalion of infected sauropods – gigantic two-thousand-foot, hundred-thousand ton monsters. Hicks had no doubt at all, the regiment of them was quite capable of bringing down the entire mountain.

Yet, for whatever reason, the titans seemed to have pulled back from their onslaught, and now simply stood in formation, like soldiers awaiting orders.

Hicks pulled his radio from his belt, hailing for Tom or anyone to answer, but all he got was static.

He looked back at the other two men grimly, then down at the unconscious General, as the chopper rose above the clouds and left the Mount behind.

CHAPTER 30

Dawn and Sabrina had been keeping to the highlands.

They had been driving for hours and as the morning sun broke over the mountains, Dawn pulled them over to an old abandoned service station, hoping to siphon gas.

"We shouldn't be stopping," Sabrina objected. "We've already got half-a-dozen cans in back."

Dawn, who was already regretting bringing her along, shook her head.

"The tank's running low," she said. "We have to stop and refill anyway. And you never know when we might find another station. Best to conserve our supplies and salvage wherever we can."

Up to this point, they had been traveling mostly in silence, but Dawn knew that was too good to last. They had been at odds most of their lives, and there was no reason to expect that to change now. But at least, so far, they had avoided bickering.

They were already several peaks over from the Mount and had covered more than two-hundred miles, even at the slow pace they'd been forced to crawl along at over the unmaintained roads in the dark.

But better that than running into any inhospitable prehistoric wildlife.

This had been foremost on Dawn's mind as she stepped out of the relative safety of the truck.

Consciously not looking at Sabrina, she also pulled the keys from the ignition as she got out.

Not that she'd considered the possibility that Sabrina might simply drive off and leave her if she allowed her the opportunity – perish the thought. But better safe than stranded. She stuck the keys in her pocket.

She also carried an M-16 rifle over one shoulder – a gift from Corporal Conner. It brought a modicum of comfort, although she'd never fired a weapon before in her life. She had actually spent several minutes just determining how to switch the safety off.

Once they had a little breathing room, she would pull over and fire a few practice shots, just to try it out. At the moment, it mostly functioned as a talisman.

"Will you hurry up?" Sabrina called impatiently, glancing back in the direction they'd come, as if soldiers might appear on their tail at any moment.

Dawn felt a small spark of irritation. Ignoring Sabrina, she hunted around the grounds until she found the station's storage tanks. Slipping in a siphon hose, she filled the truck's tank.

As she stood there, shivering in the chilly morning air, waiting for the tank to fill, the mountain wilderness around her was quiet and still.

That was when she first became aware of the tremors in the earth.

Dawn had felt quakes often enough growing up – they were common at the Mount. But earthquakes tended to be a few moments of sustained shaking, some more pronounced than others.

This was more like a steady drumbeat. Staccato and repeating.

Like footsteps.

They had been traveling mostly through thick forest, as well as in the dark, but the trees surrounding the immediate area around the service station had been cut away. Now the sun had risen, and for the first time, they had a good clear view of the surrounding peaks.

Dawn walked over to the drop-off at the edge of the clearing and looked down into the canyons that lay between.

It took a moment for her to register what she was seeing.

At first, she thought the mountains themselves were on the move.

"Oh my God," she whispered.

She turned and ran back to the truck, pulling out a pair of binoculars. She returned to the drop-off and focused in on the surrounding valleys.

"What are you *doing*?" Sabrina asked, getting out of the truck, and walking briskly up beside her.

Dawn turned, wide-eyed, and handed her the binoculars. Frowning, Sabrina put the scopes to her eyes and looked.

They had both lived in the Mount their entire lives and neither one of them had ever even seen a live sauropod except in video.

But the beasts they saw moving through the canyons below were infected giants, each of them like a walking mountain all by themselves. Their very footsteps shook the Earth.

And all of them were marching east.

"They're headed to the Mount," Dawn whispered, looking back the way they had come. "Oh my God. *Mother...*"

Sabrina lowered the glasses, and looked at her somberly.

"Get back in the truck," she said.

Dawn stood hesitant, but Sabrina grabbed her by the arm.

"There's nothing we can do," she said. "Let's get the hell out of here. *Now.*"

Dawn stood a moment longer, taking one last look at the marching procession of monsters advancing on what had been her home.

Hating herself, fighting tears, she finally turned away.

She climbed in the cab, starting up the truck, and pulled back out onto the mountain road.

"Don't think about it," Sabrina said. "Just drive."
Helpless, Dawn simply nodded.
Sabrina did not look back.

CHAPTER 31

The Mount was not the only human habitation to be hit that day.

In no less than a dozen attacks, battalions of monolithic giants rampaged in coordinated mayhem over nearly every single military establishment east of the New Gulf.

Nor were they all sauropods – in these secondary attacks, the giant long-necks were joined by horned ceratopsians and tank-like ankylosaurs, and even a variety of carnosaurs, including the biggest carcharodonts, all operating in tandem.

Distress calls from these facilities went unanswered, from the farming communities, to the outlying air bases and weapons depots. Each and every operation that was hit was smashed and razed to the ground, completely and utterly destroyed.

With the exception of one, and that was the Maelstrom nuclear base.

Here, the giants held back, surrounding the site at the perimeter, even as the on-site military launched everything in their entire arsenal, short of the nukes themselves, at the gathered behemoths.

Conventional weaponry had long-since proved useless against infected giants, let alone in numbers, but the giant beasts' seeming reluctance to pursue their rampage across the base itself apparently instilled the mistaken belief in the site's defenders that their bullets and munitions were holding the monsters at bay.

Alas, such was not the case.

With a deliberate, strategic acumen that had not been seen before, particularly in regards to mass incidents involving infected giants, the true intent was revealed once the ammo began to run low.

At that point, the base was flooded with sickle-claws, who went in and slaughtered the on-site troops hand-to-hand.

It was a tactic that preserved the infrastructure of the base, and more importantly, the operational network for the nuclear silos and the warheads within.

Once the human population was cleared away, the new wardens took over.

Troops of Ottos followed the sickle-claws into the complex, taking up positions at the consoles and desks.

The infected giants remained immobile along the base perimeter, now an immovable guard surrounding the site.

And so the reigns of nuclear power changed hands.

CHAPTER 32

The new King had arrived to take his rightful place on the mountain.

Draco stood on the top deck of the Mount – what the subjects of its former lord had called the Dark Tower.

Draco liked the name. He had a flare for the dramatic – another distinction that separated him from his lizard-like genetic sires.

In preparation for his arrival, Otto and his dromaeosaur troops had cleared away the bodies of the slaughtered soldiers from the top deck platform – devouring the remains and tossing the bones over the side – and now the regiments of sickle-claws stood in formation at Draco's feet.

Troops of Ottos were scattered among them, some perched on the dromaeosaurs' backs, others skittering at their heels. But all of them bowed in deference to their master, awaiting orders, hanging on his every move, in abject obedient servitude.

All was as it should be.

Almost.

There was still the matter of the Food of the Gods.

Draco looked out around the mountain, surveying the brigade of living monoliths that were now his personal guard, as well as the circling pterosaurs above – which were also accompanied by flocks of giant eagles, Draco's own contribution to the mostly Mesozoic wildlife – stronger and more agile than pterosaurs, they were also close relatives of sickle-claws, and therefore easier to control.

All these giant beasts were still in the early stages of infection, before the madness set in. For right now, he owned them – the great beasts stood at attention, mindlessly waiting for their instinctual buttons to be pushed, operating with a complete absence of will.

But soon enough, even the simple cognition of a sauropod would ultimately fail and they would become uncontrollable.

He had a finite window to deal with it before that happened.

But even now, the first steps were being taken.

There was a rustling among the sickle-claws and a chittering among the Ottos as two human figures appeared at the stairwell leading to the lower floors.

The first was one of the group of females who called themselves his 'followers'.

That amused Draco to no end. Humans were such base creatures, unique among living animals that they would forfeit allegiance to their own kin – their own *kind* – to their very species' survival.

And for what? Personal vindication? Abstract ideological belief? Personal power?

How had such a contemptible species dominated the Earth?

Draco supposed the answer was simple enough – it was the absence of competition.

Until now, that is.

And perhaps fittingly, the human race had sowed the seeds of their own destruction.

This female – his *follower* – was a prime example. In order to overthrow the dominance of Adam, this Eve and her Coven of deceivers had let a very large serpent into their Garden.

As of now, they suited his needs and he would deign to accept their worship.

This particular woman was currently acting as liaison with the remaining human population sequestered below, which for the moment, he was generously allowing to live. He had even restored the power, allowing ventilation to the lower levels so they wouldn't suffocate.

Draco turned to regard his human lackey, who called herself Michelle – a rather prosaic name, Draco thought. If he chose to keep her alive, perhaps he would give her a new name that suited him better – one that marked her proper role as a pet.

Michelle stood with an entourage of sickle-claws and an Otto perched on her shoulder.

At her side was an old man, looking bloodied and the worse for wear.

"Yes?" Draco said, speaking down to his creature, his voice a rumbling thunder, enjoying the visible tremor in the tiny mammals that stood before him. "What have you brought for me?"

Michelle looked up at her new god.

"This is the man you asked for," she said. She shoved the old man out in front of her. He stumbled and fell at Draco's feet.

"This guy's the big brain," Michelle said. "I had to dig him out of a pile of rubble, but I think he'll live."

Draco nodded slowly.

"That remains to be seen."

He loomed over the old man, who adjusted his glasses, looking up with wide eyes.

"Speak your name, human," Draco said. "And what value you present to me."

Trembling, the old man rose to his feet.

"My name is Dr. Victor Shriver," he said, his voice a shaking tremor.

Draco nodded.

"And I understand you are the resident *expert* on the work of a certain Professor Nolan Hinkle."

Shriver swallowed nervously.

"I once operated as liaison to Professor Hinkle and the United States government." He cleared his throat. "I have been studying his work for more than thirty years."

Draco nodded again.

"I know your name," he replied. "It is scrawled all over the literature. Rather like a dog that marks a tree. As if that makes it his."

Draco leaned close, his broad nostrils sniffing Shriver's fear.

"But," he said, "a preacher who simply repeats verse without understanding is no more a Holy man to his congregation than a parrot."

Now Draco reared up to his full height and turned, gesturing grandly out to the giant guardian behemoths that stood their posts in the canyons west of the Mount.

"Look out upon *my* congregation. They are truly empowered such as gods. Yet, that very divinity is killing them. They are dying."

Draco turned back to Shriver.

"You have been brought to me as purported authority. And so I ask, is it within your power to save them?"

"I have been looking for a cure for the Food of the Gods," Shriver said, "for almost twenty years."

"I see," Draco replied. "The very definition of an academic. One who can recite written text by rote memorization, minus the virtue of practical application or critical thought. Are you telling me that, in all that time, you couldn't come up with a solution?"

"I believe it can be done," Shriver said. And now he spoke with more confidence. "Professor Hinkle had a daughter. For a short time, she continued his work. She claimed she was close to a cure."

Draco's leathery lips pulled back over twelve-inch spiked-teeth in a parody of a smile.

"Yes," he said. "I know of Shanna. The living blood of the Creator."

Dr. Shriver nodded eagerly, volunteering the rote phrase that he had presented to General Rhodes a thousand times over the course of the last two decades.

"We need Shanna," he said.

Draco sighed.

"I had surmised as much myself," he said. "And our audience has satisfied me that I clearly don't need *you*."

And with that, Draco stepped forward, bringing his massive foot down on top of Shriver, squashing him into pulp.

There was a brief, involuntary cry from Michelle as blood splattered her face.

Draco wiped his foot disgustedly on the tarmac, as if he'd stepped on a slug. He turned to Michelle.

"It would be to your benefit," he said, "not to waste my time with such relics again."

Michelle nodded, the very picture of obedience.

"Understood," she said.

Several of the Ottos hopped off their sickle-clawed mounts and began picking at the pieces of Shriver smeared across the tarmac.

Draco turned, looking to the west.

He had not expected much from Shriver and had gotten exactly that. He knew well enough who and what he needed.

Shanna waited, somewhere beyond the mountains.

But soon, she too would be his.

CHAPTER 33

Mark saw the results of the giant sauropod's rampage when he and Pete arrived in the Valley. It seemed his warning was coming a bit late, and by the looks of things, probably would have been mostly useless anyway.

The tracks left by the infected beast had left entire houses smashed inside of a single giant footprint. A two-block-wide swath had been mowed right through the center of the community. From the hillside, as they had first arrived into town, it looked like a path left by a giant rototiller.

"*Jesus,*" Pete whistled through his teeth.

Mark took quiet note that it was just a solitary set of tracks. A single beast had done this – one infected giant – not yet even entered into the rage-phase – simply strolling through town.

But that wasn't what brought the vacant look of fear to the townsfolk's eyes as he passed through the Valley.

Shanna, apparently, was gone.

And clearly, she was already sorely missed.

As Mark and Pete parked his pickup and began walking the streets, they caught snippets of conversation, and Mark could almost *feel* the escalating levels of anxiety and fear – a near-constant buzz of low-grade hysteria.

And frankly, looking at it from the bigger picture, Mark couldn't blame them.

If Shanna really was gone, how different might life in the Valley suddenly become for the rest of them?

First and foremost, Shanna's influence had been a mellowing effect on the beasts.

And while that was congenial enough in regards to *all* the prehistoric fauna, most problematic were the *T. rex*.

Being just a touch tyrannosaur-phobic himself, Mark couldn't help but think of Junior, who was now a full-grown, nine-ton male – never the most trustworthy of creatures to begin with, but at least in Shanna's presence, he was less inclined to relentlessly hunt him down.

The Valley's tyrannosaur population also went a long way in suppressing the presence of other predators – sickle-claws in particular. How long before *that* changed too?

And amid the wild speculation buzzing out of the mouths around him,

Mark himself privately wondered what might happen among the people themselves.

The Valley's community had been living for nearly two-decades basically ungoverned. To Mark's knowledge, that was unique in human history. Surely, that had to have been Shanna's influence as well.

What happened when human nature took over?

Of course, there *was* Leanne. Mark heard her name bandied about. And it was said she might one day be an even brighter light than her mother. Shanna herself had said that.

But she was young. So young.

As once were we all, Mark thought, as he and Pete approached the remains of Shanna and Cameron's cabin.

A crowd had gathered on the site as the townsfolk came together to help with the clean-up, and by the time Mark and Pete arrived, most of the loose debris had been cleared away.

Cameron had taken the opportunity to conduct an informal town meeting, and was currently fielding questions from the crowd, standing in front of the footprint that had once been his home, with his burly pilot-friend, Maverick, acting as sort of a half-assed moderator.

Mark had known Cameron for a long time – they had arrived in the Valley together – and Mark thought him an unlikely administrator, as the man clearly thought himself. Nevertheless, Cameron conducted the meeting with a poise born less from community spirit than from the simple and honest fear for the woman that he loved – and also in recognition of the reverence in which she was held by the Valley's people as well.

As it turned out, they had some idea who had taken her.

When Cameron had said the name, it had left the crowd subdued.

It wasn't spoken about much, but most survivors in the new world had at least a nodding acquaintance with a certain parrot-talking little lizard – a ghoul that most of them had first seen dining on human corpses in the aftermath of KT-day – a ghoul that had turned out to be something much more.

Otto was known to the people of the Valley.

And every one of them *hated* those little bastards.

Cameron also had some idea where Shanna had been taken.

The townsfolk were also familiar with the Mount, via the handful of military-men who had first come into the Valley with Shanna. Mark recognized Wilkes and Garner, standing at the forefront of the crowd.

"Our... intelligence," Cameron said, "suggests that the Mount... has fallen."

Mark glanced at Pete. Cameron did not elaborate on the specifics of

119

their 'intelligence', but Mark suspected he knew where it was coming from.

He also suspected Cameron already had a course of action in mind. The gathered military men were evidence of that.

With more political savvy than Mark would have given him credit for, Cameron allowed a rolling suggestion to murmur its way through the crowd – that they try to arrange some sort of armed response – to raise an army – perhaps even take on the Mount itself.

Cameron waited for the option to be given voice before he deftly batted it aside.

"We're clearly dealing with infected giants," he said. "Did you all *see* that thing?" He indicated the twelve-foot deep footprint where his house used to be. "That was just *one*. And from what we've gathered, we are likely looking at a full-on bloom." He paused for effect. "Perhaps one of the largest ever."

Cameron shook his head.

"We literally have less than half-a-dozen military-men in the Valley, and they all agree that in such a scenario, infiltration is our only option." He shrugged. "If we want her back, we're going to have to sneak her out."

He waited just long enough for every person in the crowd to start volunteering before he quieted them down.

"We've got a plan," he said.

CHAPTER 34

After the crowd dispersed, Mark followed Cameron back to Maverick's house, one of the cabins on the lake that had escaped untouched by the giant sauropod's rampage. Mark instructed Pete to wait for him at the local bar – an order his first-mate was only too happy to obey – before knocking on Maverick's door.

Cameron himself had answered. Nodding at Mark – who, besides being a member of the Valley's original settlers, was looked upon as sort of the defacto leader of the Fishing Community – Cameron opened the door and allowed him in.

Gathered inside, along with Maverick and Cameron, were all the Valley's representative military – Johnson, Wilkes, Garner, Cooper, and pilot Bradbury. Mark took note that Allison's son, Lucas, had joined them as well.

And sitting in the middle of the room was Leanne.

Shanna's daughter looked strained, her eyes red and sunken. Rosa sat attentively beside her, dabbing her brow with a wet cloth.

"I'm sorry," Leanne was saying, "I just can't see anymore."

"She's been describing visions," Cameron explained to Mark.

Garner nodded.

"What she's been describing is the Mount," he said. And then, with a shake of his head, "None of it sounds good."

Mark frowned. He'd had his own experience with General Rhodes. As far as he was concerned, nothing that started there sounded good.

"Otto's taken over the Mount?" Mark asked.

Cameron shrugged.

"We think so." He nodded at his daughter. "She's only getting bits and pieces. But she's pretty sure that's where they've taken Shanna."

"What's your plan?"

"Well," Cameron replied, "just like I said outside. We're going after her."

"The Colorado Rockies? How are you going to get there?"

"By air," Maverick volunteered. "My old man's got an old cargo plane he's been restoring."

"We've also still got our old military chopper," Bradbury added. "We've kept up the maintenance. It should be fine to fly."

"Who's all going?"

"Just who you see here." Cameron turned to the room. "Maverick's father has been collecting weapons and surplus from leftover military and National Guard bases in the surrounding areas for years, so we're going in armed. Maverick's flying the plane. Bradbury's got the chopper."

"And I'm going too," Lucas said quietly, standing unobtrusively in the back.

Mark glanced at Cameron. "He's a kid."

Cameron sighed, raising an eyebrow to Mark.

"Yeah," he said. "We've already had that conversation."

"Big Red was gone this morning," Lucas said. "Sue's dead. And now Shanna's gone. Big Red can feel her just like Leanne does, and he's going to follow."

Lucas eyed them all defiantly.

"Big Red is my friend. Shanna is... well, she's Shanna."

He shrugged his shoulders – nineteen years old and as implacable as a mountain.

"I'm going," he said.

"And you're taking your daughter too?" Mark asked mildly.

"Barring locking her up, leaving her behind wasn't going to be an option," Cameron replied. "Besides, like it or not, she's the closest thing we've got to a crystal ball. The military boys can lead us to the Mount, but we're going to need Leanne to lead us to Shanna."

Leanne and Lucas both stared back resolutely. Cameron recognized the fearless determination of youth. He even remembered it in himself.

Although, it had been a long time.

For a moment, he considered volunteering to go along, but he reminded himself the last woman who'd counted on him, he had let down.

Besides, he had his own responsibilities these days.

"So what should I tell my people back home?" Mark asked.

And now Mark saw the determination in Cameron's own eyes – again, something Mark remembered from a long time ago.

Cameron nodded affirmatively.

"Tell them we're going to get her back," he said.

CHAPTER 35

They took off early the next morning. Cameron had been hoping to avoid a crowd, but he supposed there was no avoiding it, and it seemed that nearly the entire Valley had shown up to see them off, crowding the lot in front of Maverick's father's old barn.

Garner, Johnson, Cooper, and Wilkes loaded up into the chopper. The rest of them boarded the old cargo plane with Maverick.

Mr. Wilson had spent most of the night doing last minute checks and repairs on both of the old aircraft. And as Cameron's group arrived with the sun, he had handed the keys to the chopper to Bradbury.

Then, with a resigned air, he gave the cargo plane keys to Maverick, eyeing his son earnestly.

"Not one scratch," he said.

Maverick had grinned broadly as he fired-up the old engines. And as he turned the big plane onto the dirt road they were employing for a runway, there was a loud *thump* as the plane's wing struck something, possibly a tree.

Cameron heard a muffled curse from Maverick's father outside – "Watch where you're going, you dumb shit!" – and then he felt the forward momentum pull him back in his seat.

The gathered crowd could hear Maverick's yodel as he leaned on the throttle, gaining speed and, with one final lurch, he launched the ancient aircraft up into the air, banking sharply as he veered east into the rising sun.

Cameron's stomach lurched right along with it. It had been a long time since he'd flown with Maverick, and three out of the last four times they had crashed.

In more reserved fashion, Bradbury lifted the chopper up out of the old air-park, and they left the Valley behind.

After his initial exuberance, Maverick settled down and smoothed-out their ride, dipping or breaking one way or another only when he feared his passengers might be lulled to inattention by the steady drone of the engines.

Bradbury brought the chopper up beside them, keeping pace at air-speed, and before long, they had left the Cascades in their mirror and the first of the Rocky Mountains came into view on the eastern horizon.

Rosa napped. Lucas, who had never flown before – at least, not since his infancy – stared fascinated down at the distant earth below, while Leanne detailed the geography of what he was seeing.

Cameron, meanwhile, shut his eyes and allowed his thoughts to turn to Shanna.

He had been in almost constant motion for the last two days. But now there was nothing to do but wait. And speculate.

Shanna was alive – of that much he was certain. He could *feel* it. As for what she might be going through, he had no clue. He wasn't like Leanne – he got no *imagery* – no visions – but he knew she was out there somewhere.

And he knew she was waiting for him to come find her.

Just like he always had before.

Cameron closed his eyes and tried to relax. He had barely slept since getting rousted from his hammock by a giant sauropod the day before and he let the drone of the engines lull him. His eyelids fluttered and he began to dream.

Sometimes our subconscious is where our awareness magnifies. In his dream, Cameron felt Shanna's presence strongly – hers and one other.

For weeks now, he had been hearing Shanna moan in her sleep, but she had been reluctant to talk about it, simply tossing it off as bad dreams.

But now, he understood.

In his dream, *knowing* it was a dream, he had the sense of a dark and terrible presence – a massive dark shape that spoke in a rumbling chuckle, with vile good humor – and in the middle of that indistinct shadowy form, he saw spike-like, ivory-white teeth and glowing eyes.

From Shanna, he felt fear, and so fear touched his own heart. The great black shape raised a giant clawed hand that seemed to grow even as it reached out for him, stretching over the mountains from the east.

In the awareness of his dream, Cameron struggled to wake.

That was solved a moment later when the plane suddenly lurched violently to one side.

The aircraft was briefly upended, throwing the passengers roughly from their seats.

Rosa started awake, tumbling out onto the floor. Leanne shrieked as she was thrown bodily into Lucas' lap.

Cameron thumped his head smartly on the arm of the seat next to him, bringing him fully back to consciousness.

"Jesus, Maverick!" he yelled up to the cockpit. "Take it easy, will you?"

"That wasn't me," Maverick called back. "Something *hit* us!"

Maverick's voice carried none of its usual self-assurance, and Cameron felt the clinging chill of fear left over from his dream return like a gust of cold wind.

"*Something?*" Rosa demanded. "What do you mean *something?*"

"Oh my God," Leanne said, pointing out the window. "Look!"

Part of their starboard wing had been completely torn away, as if bitten off by a passing shark. The plane wobbled as Maverick held them level with difficulty.

In the sky beyond, banking towards them like a dreadnought, was an eagle – an eagle with a wingspan of better than four-hundred feet.

As it bore down upon them, they could see its eyes glowed green.

"We're crippled on that wing," Maverick called out. "If that thing hits us again, we're going down."

The giant raptor drew closer, arching to bring its taloned feet forward, as if reaching out to snatch a fish out of a river.

Then suddenly it jerked to one side, and veered away.

Behind them, Bradbury had brought the chopper up to intercept. Their side-panel was open. Garner and Wilkes were both poised at the opening, machine guns blasting.

Their heroic gesture, unfortunately, was also their last.

The giant bird turned in mid-air and its talons lashed out, catching the chopper in one massive claw. The gigantic beak came down an instant later and the chopper came apart. Then it exploded into flame.

"Jesus," Rosa whispered.

Leanne covered her eyes.

Now the raptor turned its attention back to them, even as the plane struggled like a wounded sparrow with its half-wing.

"We're losing altitude," Maverick said, shaking his head fatalistically. "We've got to take her down."

The terrain below, however, was dead center of the Rocky Mountains – as bad a potential landing strip as you could possibly find on the entire North American continent.

Maverick arched them into a dive as the giant bird closed the distance rapidly behind them. The claws stretched out once again.

The talons latched onto the rear of the plane, catching the fuselage mid-center, tearing through the metal like paper. The claws flexed and the entire rear half of the aircraft was torn away.

Within the cabin, a sudden windstorm ripped at the passengers. Rosa was yanked from her seat and went sailing past Cameron, falling towards the gaping opening. With a desperate lunge, Cameron reached out and snagged her shirt. There was a loud rip of fabric and Cameron thought he was going to lose her anyway before she turned and grabbed onto his hand. With a grunt, he pulled her into the seat beside him.

Leanne lost her own grip and started to fall – only to be stopped by Lucas, who caught her by the hair. She yelped in pain, but he held on until she managed to latch on to one of the remaining seats.

Behind them, the giant eagle had discovered the tail portion of the cargo plane to be nothing but an unappetizing shell and tossed it aside, banking after them once again.

But now the ground was rushing up at them at terrifying speed. Maverick wrestled frantically with the controls.

"*Do* something!" Rosa screamed.

"*Do* something?" Maverick countered fiercely. "Oh shit! I never thought of that. I should *do* something!" He glared over his shoulder. "Just shut the hell up and hang on!"

They were in near free-fall. The mountains below looked like hungry jaws. The peaks were covered with snow, like sharp white teeth.

Maverick heaved mightily at the wheel, jerking them upright as they came in fast.

The plane hit the uppermost peak, blasting the powdery surface into an avalanche, throwing the passengers to the floor once again. The angle was steep, and without missing a beat, the plane began to slide.

Snow-covered trees snapped like twigs, sheering away the remainder of their damaged wing, sending them into a spin. The passengers inside were tossed like dice, the centrifugal force pinning them back against the walls.

They bounced like a pinball over rocks and trees until, with a final shuddering lurch, the aircraft finally slid to a stop.

For a long moment, everyone lay too stunned to move.

Then Leanne sat up, turned, and threw-up directly into Lucas' lap. Lucas was too shaken even to object.

"My God," Rosa said hoarsely. "We lost the chopper."

"We almost lost *us*," Maverick said, unlatching from his seat. "You're welcome, by the way."

Cameron tried to stand, and found his legs rubbery. He turned to the others. Rosa likewise clambered shakily to her feet. Leanne was again noisily sick – this time, Lucas moved aside, letting her bend over the seat.

Their load of supplies had been upended and whatever hadn't been secured had been sucked out. Looking through the torn opening, Cameron saw a swath mowed behind them through the trees.

He climbed out, sinking two feet into the late spring snow. Rosa climbed out beside him as Maverick took stock of their remaining provisions.

"Hey," Maverick called to Lucas, as he began tossing packs out the back. "Give me a hand here."

Leaving Leanne still hunched over her seat, Lucas turned to help, and soon they had a pile spread out along the snow.

They had just started going over what they had left when the sky above them suddenly darkened.

As they looked up, the giant eagle had recovered its target and descended down upon them like a storm.

They stared up helplessly, with nowhere to run. Cursing, Maverick turned, grabbing for the pack with the rifles.

But in the breath of a moment, it was all already over-and-done. The giant raptor's talons latched onto the ravaged hull of the cargo plane, snatching it like a clam shell off the beach.

With a hurricane flap of its wings, it launched back up into the sky with its prize.

Cameron blinked as he realized Leanne was still inside.

Lucas, however, was already moving.

As the massive wings hoisted the battered aircraft off the ground, Lucas caught one of the loose cables dangling from the wreckage.

Lucas was yanked into the air with a jerk and dragged along behind as the giant bird lofted itself once again into the sky.

Cameron stared helplessly as bird and prey became quickly smaller with distance. The mangled plane looked like a child's toy in its claws as the giant raptor bore it away, with Lucas dangling from the cable and Leanne trapped somewhere inside.

Maverick shook his head.

"I'll tell you this – that kid's crazier than I am."

Cameron said nothing, just watched the departing bird and its stolen bounty until it disappeared on the horizon.

CHAPTER 36

Lucas could feel the cable starting to give. Inside its metal casing, it really wasn't much more than a few wires twisted together. It was certainly no tow-rope and definitely would not support his weight much longer.

He spared a look at the jagged mountain peaks, so far below.

The bird wasn't helping. Each flap of its giant wings was like being yanked into the momentum of a speeding roller coaster. Lucas struggled against the wind, pulling himself inexorably, headfirst into the freezing blast. Unable to gain a purchase on the flailing cable with his feet, he was forced to climb hand-over-hand.

Leanne was hidden somewhere within the cabin. Lucas' greatest worry – aside from the weakening cable – was that she might fall from the ragged opening.

Lucas was also concerned the giant bird might decide to drop the tattered aircraft as he had seen normal-sized birds do to oyster shells, shattering them on the rocks to get at the tasty innards.

After a while, this last fear began to fade. The giant raptor had reached cruising altitude and stretched its wings into a glide, flapping now only intermittently. The bird clearly had a destination in mind. It had its metal prize clutched tightly in its claws and was probably headed for its lair.

That meant they had a little time.

The less frequent pumping of the massive wings also enabled Lucas to climb more easily against the wind. He was in partial free-fall now and so, thankfully, his arms weren't forced to bear his full weight.

But he was still close to exhaustion. His shoulders and back burned, and the muscles in his hands and arms were near the limit of their endurance. It seemed as if it had been forever since they left the ground, and when he finally put a hand on the torn metal of the cabin, still dangling from his dubiously straining cable, he barely retained the strength to pull himself aboard.

He gasped for breath, even as the blast of icy wind tried to keep it from him. Blinking wind-blasted tears from his eyes, he peered into the darkened compartment.

"Leanne?" he called hoarsely, straining to see in the dark.

There was a low moan from the front of the cabin.

Leanne had made her way up to the cockpit and she clung to one of the pilot's seats. As the plane lurched and tossed, she hung her head over the armrest, and was repeatedly and noisily sick.

"Leanne!" Lucas shouted over the wind.

"Lucas?" she groaned, looking up from the seat. "Oh God, can you please go shoot that thing or something?"

Lucas looked around. He had personally tossed the pack with the rifles out of the cabin.

Not that shooting it would help, anyway. A bird that size wouldn't be injured by a bullet, although it might irritate it enough to drop them.

Lucas climbed his way up to the cockpit and hunkered down next to her as she remained prostrate over the seat.

Leanne looked at him earnestly.

"Please tell me you have a plan."

Lucas didn't answer. He looked around the cabin quickly. The curved beak would make short work of their protective metal shell once the bird finally touched down.

His bow and quiver were still strapped to the side paneling but an arrow would be less than a splinter to the giant raptor. The hunting knife at his side was equally useless.

Then he spied a large green duffle bag he had not spotted before, strapped securely beneath what had been Cameron's seat.

Maverick's father had outfitted them with a variety of war-surplus. A quick glance inside brightened Lucas' spirits considerably.

The giant bird now seemed to be angling towards one single peak, banking and dipping sharply as it veered in close.

Leanne groaned again at the sudden drop, dry-heaving once again.

"What's happening?" she managed between convulsions.

"He's bringing us in. Hang on."

There was a sudden drop and a violent crash as the cargo plane landed hard among the rocks. The giant bird had dropped them nearly fifty feet into its nest and the impact left them both momentarily stunned.

The creature wasted little time – the hooked beak peeled back the roof of the cabin like a sardine can. Lucas imagined it would likely be disappointed by the relative lack of meat within the bulky metal shell.

But the beak came down anyway and Lucas moved quickly, grabbing up the green duffle.

The grenades inside were probably twenty years old and he would be lucky if the first one didn't go off in his hand the moment he pulled the pin.

Above him, the digging beak was easily the width of the entire cabin, but it prodded through the metal cylinder with surprising dexterity, searching for the tiny human prey.

As it felt its way toward the cockpit, Lucas hooked the bag around the tip of the beak and tugged slightly, the way he did when he fed the *T. rex* raw meat. The giant bird felt the resistance and pulled back.

Lucas yanked the pin on the grenade and popped it back inside the duffle with the rest. A moment later, the bag was pulled from his hands.

Through the opening torn in the cabin roof, Lucas could see the giant raptor snap its head back, tossing the duffle down its massive gullet.

There was a wet, muffled, bursting sound, like a belch, from deep within the giant creature's throat, and the lightly-colored breast feathers suddenly stained bright red.

The giant raptor shrieked – or rather, it attempted to – the exploding grenade had ruptured its voice-box, and what came out was a hoarse, shrill whistling.

Then there was a louder explosion as the rest of the grenades went off a split-second later, and the entire neck of the giant raptor suddenly blew out, splattering them in a torrent of blood.

The giant bird staggered, spreading its wings, and stumbled to the edge of the peak.

It actually managed to launch itself into the air. Its flight, however, was short-lived, dropping into an almost immediate glide, as it soared out over the dizzying depths below.

Then the glide fell limp and the giant bird began to tumble, rolling, falling from the sky.

Clambering from the broken plane, Lucas and Leanne cautiously made their way to the edge of the precipice, and watched the creature's spiraling tumble into the canyons below.

"Was that," Leanne asked breathlessly, "what you had planned?"

"Uh..., yeah," Lucas replied agreeably. "That or something like it."

"Well," Leanne said, "I guess that wasn't *too* bad then."

Then she wiped disgustedly at the blood that had drenched her clothes.

"I just wish we could have gotten out of the way first."

Lucas didn't answer. He held his hand up over his eyes, shielding the sun as he looked back in the direction they had come. Then he sighed deeply, shaking his head.

"What?" Leanne asked.

"I'm trying to figure out where we are. And how far back we left your father."

"How far do you think?"

Lucas turned away, walking back to the plane.

"At least fifty miles," he said. "Maybe more."

He began rummaging around in the ruined cabin.

Leanne stared at him, dumbfounded.

"What do you mean, 'fifty miles'?" she demanded. "How are we supposed to find them?"

"Well, actually," Lucas said, "I don't think we can."

He turned and looked at her, his face serious.

"We're on our own."

Leanne struggled with this briefly.

"So what are we supposed to do?" she asked.

Lucas continued with his rummaging.

"Well," he said, "first I'm going to salvage what we can out of this plane. Then we make camp for the night to rest up. Then start out in the morning."

He shrugged, gesturing at the precipice drop behind her.

"I want a good night's sleep before I try climbing *that*."

Leanne turned and looked down to the canyon floor, which was impossibly distant – you really almost couldn't even *see* it. She staggered with a wave of vertigo.

She stepped back from the edge.

"No," she said. "No way. I can't do it."

Lucas looked back at her sympathetically, and suddenly Leanne wanted to hit him – slap him, do anything to shut him up before he could speak – before he said what she knew he was going to say.

He said it anyway.

"We've got no choice, Leanne."

She shut her eyes. Lucas waited patiently. He could actually see the panic and frustration bubbling beneath her surface.

Then she let out a deep and desperately unhappy sigh.

"Okay," she said simply. "What do I do?"

They began preparing camp for the night.

CHAPTER 37

Fifty miles west of the Valley, a giant was dying.

The infected brachiosaur that trundled through the Valley the day before had been heading west – mostly aimlessly, for it was as close to mindless as was possible for a living vertebrate animal of its size to be.

It had not questioned the impulse that had guided its trajectory through the Valley, nor was it truly aware of the outside presence that influenced its tiny mind in that direction. But now that its simple purpose was accomplished, that subtle mental pressure had been abandoned and the hapless giant was left to its own devices.

But it was not the chemical that coursed through its veins that was killing it – not yet, for an infected beast might endure for weeks or months – the lumbering giant was being delivered a death by a thousand cuts.

The tyrannosaur pack had pursued the beast doggedly from the Valley, displaying that trademarked *T. rex* stubbornness.

Trix' surviving pack of adult females had been joined both by Sue and Big Red's juvenile offspring, as well as Rudy and Junior and the rest of the rogue pack of males that patrolled the outskirts of the Valley. For nearly two days straight, they had pestered and harassed the giant beast, their great jaws digging at its ankles, tearing out great chunks of flesh, until finally digging deep enough to damage tendon and bone.

The giant sauropod was dimly aware of the pain, and had attempted on several occasions to stomp and chase its tormentors away, but they remained undeterred.

Not only was the great beast beginning to bleed out, the steady, piranha-like assault was clearing the flesh from its feet, and the giant brachiosaur was starting to stumble.

And when it finally staggered forward, no longer able to support its titanic weight, the impact of its fall could be felt all the way to the coast.

The giant beast lay stretched-out, nearly two-thousand feet from nose to tail. Its limbs had been broken in the fall, and now a low guttural moan escaped it – a base, miserable foghorn of a wail, for it was still alive, and might remain so for a while.

But the surrounding pack of tyrannosaurs saw no need to wait – their quarry was down, its shattered limbs pinned under its own weight, and now they moved in and began to eat the helpless beast alive.

And so the chemical that infected it was passed on.

As the pack of *T. rex* swarmed over the dying giant, ripping away ever greater chunks of meat, the Food of the Gods was now ingested into their own systems.

Before long, their eyes began to glow emerald green.

CHAPTER 38

Big Red had been on the move for nearly two days straight, and as the sun began to drop over the mountains, the big tyrannosaur finally settled down to rest, curling up under a grove of trees.

He had already left the peaks of the Cascades behind him, and looming before him were the first pinnacles of the mighty Rockies.

Around him, the beasts were on the move – creatures of all kinds – herd beasts that included both ceratopsians and sauropods. And as he made his way further east, he saw the first signs of carnosaurs, traveling along with the plant-eaters, in a mass migration – all moving eastward into the mountains.

So far, he had ignored them, focusing on his own goal. The other creatures had likewise given him a wide and respectful berth, and he had not yet been stirred by the pangs of hunger to attack.

In truth, there would likely be no need, for that was one of the inherent effects of the Food of the Gods – the chemical itself *was* food – an infected beast attacked out of aggression, not hunger.

In his repeated assaults on the infected sauropod, Big Red had torn away and ingested several large mouthfuls of meat, and the chemical was now coursing its way through his veins.

Already, the telltale green glow lit up his eyes in the dark.

And while he was not truly aware of it, he had already grown in stature. He had left the Valley as the biggest rex in the territory, at well over ten tons. In the two short days since, he weighed-in at more than half-again.

But while he was so far unaware of these changes in himself, as the chemical took hold, the beacon that drew him grew correspondingly brighter, its draw growing ever stronger.

Shanna was somewhere beyond those mountains. She was in distress and danger. Big Red could feel her fear.

There was also the burgeoning awareness of another – the same dark presence that had set his teeth on edge for weeks now. As his senses continued to expand, that presence came into sharper focus, and he recognized it for what it was.

A rival and a threat.

Either one was unacceptable.

Big Red lay awake in the dark, his eyes glowing emerald green, and a low growl rumbled from his chest.

When he finally slept, he dreamed of Shanna, and of a dark

forbidding presence – and of the battle that waited for him somewhere in the days ahead.

CHAPTER 39

As Mark and Pete headed back to the coast, Pete suddenly sat up in his seat, pointing out his window.

"Wait, what's that?"

They were just reaching the first burgeoning slope of the modest Coastal Mountains that bordered the west side of the Valley. Mark looked in the direction Pete was pointing, and first noticed birds and pterosaurs circling above, like vultures over a carcass.

Then he saw what had attracted the flying scavengers' attention on the plains below.

"Oh *no,*" Mark said.

He pulled the pickup over to the side of the road and the two of them got out. Mark grabbed a pair of binoculars.

A miniature mountain seemed to have grown at the base of the slope.

It was the infected brachiosaur that had meandered its way through the Valley.

As unlikely as it seemed, the rex pack had apparently managed to bring the giant beast down.

Mark shook his head, amazed. He was certainly never one to doubt the stick-to-it stubborn determination of a *T. rex.*

And currently, it appeared that every tyrannosaur in the Valley was piled on top of the mammoth carcass, gorging their fill.

All that infected meat.

Looking through the scopes, Mark could see their eyes, already glowing green.

"*Ohhhh* boy," Mark breathed.

Without Shanna's influence, the *T. rex* were poised to become dangerous again anyway, let alone infected with the Food of the Gods.

As he adjusted the binoculars, Mark saw Junior among them, popping his head in their direction.

That big SOB couldn't possibly be scenting him all the way from here.

Could he? Not *already.*

Mark shook his head. It didn't matter – today or tomorrow – the stubborn beast would come for him soon enough. Only now, it would be as an injected giant.

Here or at the coast, the Valley had just become an inhospitable place.

Mark knew what he had to do. He lowered his binoculars and turned to Pete.

"Come on," he said. "Back in the truck."

"Where are we going?" Pete asked as he clambered in beside him.

Mark backed up and turned around.

"We're heading back to town," he said. "We've got to warn them they've got a bloom about to sprout up right here in the Valley."

Mark pulled the truck into gear.

"Then," he said, "I'm sending you to the coast to warn everybody there."

"What about you?" Pete asked.

Mark shrugged.

"We need Shanna back," he said. "And I'm going after her."

CHAPTER 40

Cameron, Rosa and Maverick worked their way down the eastward slope of the mountain. They had salvaged what they could from the wrecked plane, loaded up as much as the three of them could carry, and then they had been on their way.

Maverick had taken a moment to bemoan the demolished aircraft. This would not be the first time he'd been forced to hand his father the keys to a totaled wreck.

"*Ohhhh* boy," he groaned. "Dad's gonna kill me for this"

At the moment, however, that was a secondary concern – they had crashed right near the top of one of the highest peaks, and were looking at a minimum of two days hard travel before they even got down out of the snow pack.

Their rescue mission had now instead become one of survival, with dubious prospects, at best.

Hopefully, once they got down out of the worst of the mountains, they would be able to find a salvageable vehicle, something Maverick might be able to get up and running. They kept their eyes open for any old houses or work sheds, or possibly an old logging site.

They at least had weapons, rifles and ammo, along with several days' worth of food. They had a tent and the means of starting fire.

Cameron supposed it could be worse.

Maverick and Rosa passed the time with idle barbs back and forth – Neanderthal-pig – prude, spinster-old-maid. Rosa asked him if he'd ever flown a plane that hadn't crashed. Maverick said he didn't think so.

Cameron was mostly silent, lost in his own thoughts, oblivious to Rosa and Maverick's rather halfhearted bickering.

He believed Leanne was alive. Just like Shanna, his daughter had taken a subtle empathic place in his mind. Cameron was sure he would have felt *something* if Leanne had died.

On the other hand, none of their prospects looked good. Not for the three of them, not for his daughter, or for Shanna herself.

They didn't even precisely know where they were.

And as the sun dropped over the peak of the mountain, the temperature immediately began to drop, forcing them to set up camp for the night.

Cameron glanced back the way they had come. Six hours on foot – they had put in maybe twenty-miles and seen absolutely nothing but mountains, snow, trees and forest.

The area had been remote *before* the world had ended. It could be days before they even found a road, let alone a working vehicle.

But there was nothing to do but trudge onward. They had to survive first.

They began gathering wood for a fire.

CHAPTER 41

Lucas and Leanne spent their first day making their way down the eastern front of the mountain.

Leanne had been an adventurous child, and had done her share of climbing, all over the trees, hilltops, or any of the relatively modest terrain in her home Valley. This, on the other hand, was something entirely different. The view from the precipice alone was enough to freeze her in her tracks, threatening another bout of vertigo and vomiting.

Once they started down, however, it grew quickly worse. The cliff-side was nearly a sheer drop.

Lucas prodded and coaxed her along. Faced with this impossible climb, he tied their waists together with a length of rope – hugging close to the minuscule fissures in the rock, he tugged at her like a dog on a leash whenever Leanne was reluctant to follow.

And reluctant was not the word – at one point, she had simply frozen-up completely, unable to move. Accompanied by Lucas' softly-murmured instructions, she had been navigating a particularly egregious section of cliff-side that actually seemed to push outward, leaning her *back* over the abyss, and she made the mistake of looking down over her shoulder.

For a moment, the world swirled in a sheer spin, and vertigo struck her with such force that, for a moment, she thought she had already started to fall.

She clung to the rock like a barnacle against the surf. There were a few seconds where she might have actually blacked-out. The next thing she was aware of was Lucas urging her on.

"Leanne," he said, finally, after ten minutes when she still wouldn't move, "I'm going to keep going. If I have to pull you, you'll fall. If you fall, *I'll* fall. You can't go back up. You have no choice."

She stood paralyzed until she actually felt the tug of rope at her waist. Cursing, fighting tears of anger, she began to move again, her mind now focused on hating Lucas instead of the dizzying drop below. She clung doggedly to that hate until they finally reached the base of the mountain.

They hiked another couple of miles until they found a small clearing by the river.

Leanne was exhausted, scratched-up and sore. And it didn't help to see Lucas, apparently fresh as a daisy, bustling about, gathering wood, calling out instructions as he prepared camp.

Lucas was not exactly barking orders. In fact, he actually seemed to be taking pains to be gracious, but nevertheless, Leanne felt her blood pressure begin to rise.

Although she wasn't quite willing to admit it, she was unaccustomed to being *told* to do anything, no matter how tactfully.

Lucas' response, however, when she finally called him on the matter, had not been helpful.

He simply looked at her with a confused, and rather pained expression and said, "But you don't *know* anything, do you?"

It was all she could do to keep from pitching a piece of rock at him – the river that bordered the clearing had smoothed-out any number of stones that would be perfect for throwing.

Instead, she turned away, fists clenched, walking off her own steam.

"Leanne..." Lucas began.

She ignored him, stooping by the water's edge to wash off the dirt and volcanic dust that had embedded into her skin.

"*Leanne!*" Lucas suddenly shouted.

A split-second later, the deceptively calm river seemed to explode.

There was a massive, dark shape behind the splashing water and Leanne had the impression of jagged, eight-inch teeth.

The crocodile's head was easily six-feet long, and it had been lurking invisibly only inches beneath the rippling surface.

Momentarily paralyzed, Leanne stared numbly as the massive jaws lunged towards her.

A moment later, it fell limp, almost at her feet. Protruding from its left eye was one of Lucas' arrows.

Her heart pounding, Leanne turned, gaping, to where Lucas stood, his bow drawn, and another arrow already notched in the string.

"Step away from it, Leanne," he said, and put a second arrow in the creature's other eye.

Then, as Leanne stood there, still frozen, Lucas bent and quickly began to cut away meat from the scaly hide, keeping a wary eye on the surrounding water for any of the croc's sure-to-be-arriving companions. He glanced up at Leanne as he piled the reptilian steaks at her feet.

"Dinner," he said.

Leanne paled.

They decided, at Lucas' carefully-neutral suggestion, that the river might not be the best spot to make camp.

Fortunately, an hour's hiking through the thick woods brought them to an old, abandoned cabin. The place was sparse with supplies and there was definitely no vehicle, but it was equipped with a fireplace and a barbecue. Lucas grilled the croc steaks he had cut.

Leanne sat still and quiet with embarrassment.

As Lucas worked the fire, she finally spoke, her voice uncharacteristically subdued.

"You must think I'm an idiot," she said.

He turned and looked at her, his face a shadow in the fire, but she could see the earnest reflection of his eyes.

"No," he said. "I don't think that at all."

Then he had looked hurriedly away, as if embarrassed himself.

Leanne fell silent as Lucas began setting up a bedroll on the floor, allowing her the single bed.

Outside, the sun had set behind the mountain as the moon approached from the east, rising above the trees.

Leanne thought of what might be prowling about in the woods around them. It was so different from the security of her Valley.

She wondered what lay in store in the days ahead. She wondered about her father and mother, and if she would ever see either of them again.

She tried not to be afraid.

On the floor in front of the fire, Lucas started to snore.

Smiling a little, Leanne rolled over in the rustic little bed and tried to sleep.

CHAPTER 42

The next day's travel was easier than the first, but Lucas and Leanne still had to fight their way through heavy vegetation. The Mesozoic flora had heavily overgrown, and the moisture created by the new plant-life added a degree of humidity that was new to the region – the new fauna was lush and healthy.

Now that they were working their way along the basin floor, there were also signs of predators, including a few big ones. One track they came across had to have come from a large allosaur, maybe even a carcharodont.

There was no rex spoor though. For whatever reason, probably Shanna's influence, most of the tyrannosaur species seemed to have migrated west.

Sickle-claw signs, on the other hand, were quite well represented, and already a few small species had harassed them from a distance – frightened off after Lucas had skewered two of their number with arrows.

Still, Lucas demonstrated an easy familiarity with the forest, and his confidence was catching. Leanne started to relax, and stopped taking his instruction personally.

Lucas, for his part, saw no point in telling her they had slim chances of surviving this little misstep in their rescue mission, and neither did her father and his party. They were faced with several hundred miles of hard travel across a predator-filled terrain.

Thus uninhibited by troubling reality, Leanne began to study Lucas himself.

She'd known him at least peripherally all her life, and knew that from the time he was eleven years old, he had mostly raised himself.

That night, as they camped out by their fire, in the crook of a large tree, she finally asked him about it.

"What was it like," she asked, "after your parents died?"

He glanced up at her over the fire.

"I was a kid," he said. "I guess I was scared. I cried a lot at first. But the next day, I just got up and went to work out on the field like usual."

His face reflected thoughtfully in the firelight.

"That was how they raised me," he said. "They were old for being parents. My father never used to talk about it – not really. But my mother always told me that they wouldn't be around forever. And my dad? Well, he just worked on preparing me for it."

Lucas shrugged.

"I guess he did his job. I'm alive."

"Do you miss them?" Leanne asked.

Lucas nodded.

"Every day," he said.

Leanne settled down next to him. The night was chilled and they huddled together. Lucas tensed a little as Leanne leaned close.

"I'm sorry I stopped coming around after your parents died," she said. "I know you were alone. We were friends. I should have been there. But I just disappeared from your life." She looked apologetic. "I guess I was scared too."

"We were both kids," Lucas replied.

"I think I can understand now what it must have been like," Leanne said. "Being alone. I'm afraid I'm never going to see my parents again either." She looked up at Lucas. "I've been being prepared too. I'm going to have to fill my own mother's shoes someday. And I'm scared that I can't do it."

"Why?" Lucas asked

Leanne thought for a moment.

"Maybe it's the responsibility. My mother... I see how much she means to the people in the Valley. And I just can't *do* the things that she can."

She sighed in frustration.

"I can't even do the things *you* can."

She shook her head.

"But it's all already mapped-out. I'm supposed to carry on when she's gone. And she may already *be* gone. That means that even if we somehow make it back home, I'm supposed to carry the weight of the whole Valley. And apparently pass it on to my own daughter someday. And I'm nowhere near ready for it."

They sat silent a moment, watching the cracking fire. Then Lucas asked quietly, "Pass it on to your daughter? Do you have a father picked out?"

Leanne smiled a little.

"No," she said. "Nothing like that." She shrugged. "The pickings are a little slim in the Valley."

Lucas cleared his throat. "Ah."

He lay back into the crook of the tree.

Leanne fell silent, settling in next to him. Soon her breath deepened and she slipped into sleep.

Lucas sat awake a while longer. He was very much aware of the warmth of her body. Her words, however, struck a bitter chord in his heart.

He looked down at her and was struck again, as if for the first time, by her sheer beauty. But at the same moment, he realized the distance between them, and the truth of her words – more than that, the truth *behind* her words.

If they failed in their mission, if Shanna truly *was* gone, it *would* fall to Leanne to carry on.

And, Lucas thought resolutely, if that was *her* responsibility, then it was *his* to bring her home safe.

Right at that moment, he made a silent vow, a promise to himself and to her that he would protect her.

Not for himself, or for any hopeless hopes he might entertain, but for *her* – and for the future. He would watch after her for that reason, and that alone.

Lucas told himself this.

He told himself he was a liar.

And it was with this ache in his heart, like the embers of their slowly dying fire, that he finally nodded off to fitful sleep.

But in his dreams, the embers burned on.

CHAPTER 43

Shanna had never been to the Mount, but she recognized it from her dreams.

And as the chopper circled the top-deck platform, she recognized as well the dark presence that waited within.

When she had awoken, they had already been in the air. The first thing she had been aware of was the drone of rotor blades, and she had looked up expecting to see the woman in black who had taken her.

Instead, she found herself surrounded by a troop of sickle-claws, sitting there in the chopper cabin beside her. Their beady eyes stared, blinking back at her, their voices wavering between a low, snakelike hiss and their characteristic birdlike warble.

Shanna looked to the cockpit, and for a moment, she had the impression that the chopper was flying itself. Then she saw the little lizards, standing on the seats and over the dash, hopping about like jabbering gremlins, pulling on the controls one way and then the other.

"Where are you taking me?" she had asked.

All three of the little lizards bobbed, staring back at her. As one, they spoke in the voice of the woman in black.

"The Dragon Lord wishes to see you now."

Now the chopper circled in for a landing.

Waiting for her on the tarmac was another woman, standing there with another troop of sickle-claws.

Yet another Otto sat perched upon her shoulder.

As the chopper landed, the woman stepped forward and slid open the door to the cabin.

The sickle-claws flocked outside to stand in disciplined formation beside her. The woman leaned into the cabin, eyeing Shanna with interest.

"So," she said, "*you're* Shanna. I've been hearing about you for a long time."

The woman extended her hand, motioning Shanna out of the chopper.

"My name is Michelle," she said. "And you'll need to come with me."

Beside her, the sickle-claws cackled in light, trilling caws. The Otto on her shoulder chittered.

Shanna took Michelle's hand, climbing out of the cabin, and as she did so, she felt a small spark of her shine.

It was different with different people, but it was always a window.

From Michelle, what she felt was an utter and total lack of empathy. Some people, like General Rhodes, were shut off, letting nothing out at all. Then there was the woman in black, from whom Shanna had felt a deep, overriding hatred and smoldering anger.

Michelle was different – she was an absence of human morality – utterly amoral and self-serving – unabashed.

Rather like the lizard perched upon her shoulder.

Michelle led Shanna down the stairwell into the caverns below.

And while it was her first time at the site, she could see that there had been some obvious renovation to accommodate the Mount's new lord.

For one, the human-sized doorways to the stairs and upper levels, along with the entire walls around them, had been torn away.

And on the cavernous administrative-level, what had once been General Nathan Rhodes' office was also gone, the interior architecture completely removed, leaving an opening that looked out over the cliff onto the New Gulf below. What was left more resembled the bastion of a medieval castle.

The new master of the house stood with his back to her as Shanna was led into his presence.

A regiment of sickle-claws stood at attendance. And curled like a cat at his knee, was a female rex.

Draco turned to regard Shanna as Michelle brought her to stand before him.

The rex female perked at Shanna's presence.

Draco looked down at his mate, his leathery lips pulling over saber-teeth in a dragon's imitation of a smile.

"She knows you," he said, his voice a low, thundering rumble. "As do we all." Draco bowed graciously. *"Mother."*

He reached out a taloned claw, stroking his queen's scaled head.

"For aren't you mother to us all?" Draco said. "Your DNA exists at the very base of my genetic code. And that of all our kind."

He made a sweeping gesture to his Queen, and then to Otto and the sickle-claws.

"I look into your mind," he said, "and I recognize that part of you in myself."

Shanna stared back, and tried to feel any kind of a shine from him, but he was completely sealed-off. He had been hiding from her for a long time – much like Otto had. Rather like the way Shanna had learned to hide from Leanne.

"Why have you brought me here?" Shanna asked.

Draco eyed her, his oddly expressive stone-face seemingly amused.

"Don't you know?"

Shanna said nothing.

Draco nodded to Michelle.

"Leave us," he said.

Michelle nodded and obediently retreated from the chamber, taking Otto and her entourage of sickle-claws with her.

Draco turned to Shanna.

"Come with me," he said, stepping past her, towards the westward wing of the administrative-level.

He led her clear to the opposite end of the compound, where the cave's ceiling had partially collapsed. But Shanna could clearly see this had once been a scientific lab. And she could guess who it had belonged to.

"This," Draco said, "was once the proprietary of one Dr. Victor Shriver."

Draco again showed his teeth in that parody of a smile.

"I believe you knew the late doctor?"

Shanna nodded, noting the descriptive reference to the 'late' doctor – as she was no doubt meant to.

"Then," Draco continued, "perhaps you are aware of his obsession. And his frustration."

Pushing back the rubble, Draco uncovered a sealed compartment mounted in one corner, that took up an entire wall of the chamber. With a flick of his claw, he pried open the latch, revealing the contents within.

Sealed inside were dozens of vials of glowing green.

The Food of the Gods.

Shanna had expected something like this. The brachiosaur in the Valley had been a very obvious tell.

The Food of the Gods had destroyed the world once. Seemingly, it would not be put to rest until the job was done. Madness and death had always followed wherever it had blossomed.

"Dr. Shriver," Draco said, "spent many years searching for a cure. Or perhaps 'cure' is not the right word. He sought to *perfect* the chemical – to eliminate the adverse side-effects. Ultimately, he failed. I have spent some time perusing his records."

Draco leaned down close, looking Shanna eye-to-eye.

"The missing ingredient," he said, "according to Dr. Shriver, is *you*."

The leathery lips pulled back again.

"It turns out," Draco continued, "that he has records of your own work from many years ago."

Shanna shut her eyes. She remembered it well. Back in New York – a coerced effort on her part. And it had all ended on KT-day.

"You were once charged with completing the task started by your father," Draco said. "I charge you once again."

Shanna looked up at him.

"Why?" she asked simply.

Draco's answer was equally simple.

"Because," he said, "it is my intention to use the power of the Food of the Gods to wipe away the scourge of humanity from off this Earth once and for all."

Shanna stared up at the face of her captor, searching for his thoughts.

"What is it about us that you hate so much?" she asked him.

"Oh, it's not just you," Draco replied. "Not just humans. It's mammals in general."

His teeth flashed again, this time in an exaggerated grimace of distaste.

"They are... *soft*," he said. "Like slugs and worms and rats and other disgusting things you squash beneath your feet. I would see every last one of them gone."

"So why would I possibly help you?"

Draco eyed her meaningfully.

"In acquiring this stronghold," he said, "I have seized its assets, including its nuclear arsenal. You will do as I ask or your Valley will be a dust-cloud."

"So why not just do it then? If you want all of us dead?"

"Because the Valley is not the only enclave of humans left on Earth," Draco replied. "Yours is a difficult species to irradiate, and nuclear fallout causes widespread ecological destruction. It is not my intention to destroy the natural world. Just *you*."

Shanna nodded.

"You've obviously been experimenting on your own. You have Shriver's records, including all my preliminary work. You've got access to large stores of the chemical as it exists, and have the capacity to create more. What do you need me for?"

Now Draco frowned.

He turned from her, head down, musing. For a long time, he didn't answer.

But when he did finally speak, Shanna detected the first sign of agitation in his voice.

"Because I can't *do* it," he said. He turned a dangerous, challenging eye upon her. "I have already spent... years."

He shook his head.

"I have distilled it, refined it, and have succeeded only in purifying it. My own version of the recipe does not correct the side-effects. In point of fact, it exacerbates them, as the more potent octane works even faster."

Draco turned to face her again.

"You see beyond it," he said. "You see past the mechanics of DNA and understand the poetry of it. You comprehend the spiritual. Perhaps it is a mammalian trait – the product of a race that suckles on a mother's breasts rather than be born into the world ready to kill. Perhaps..."

Draco paused, turning a speculative eye upon her.

"Perhaps," he said, "it's just *you*."

He eyed her a moment longer.

"Do you read poetry?" he asked. "I studied it for a while. And I could recite every line I ever read. But I could never write it."

Now Draco's eyes grew distant.

"Its mystery," he said, "is beyond me."

Shanna regarded Draco and suddenly understood him a little better.

Perhaps he wasn't so different from Otto after all.

It was not her mammalian '*softness*' that he hated. Draco only hated what he feared, and he did not fear '*softness*' – that was just something to fixate on.

What he really feared was what he lacked in himself – and perhaps this was what he truly inherited from Otto – the absence of the creative spark. All the knowledge in the world wasn't much help if you couldn't have a simple idea.

Draco had the Maelstrom base and all its nuclear weapons under his control. He had the Food of the Gods at his disposal. In his hands, was the power of total destruction.

But he needed *her* for the act of Creation.

At that moment, Shanna knew what she had to do.

And in that moment, she began to hide from him in her mind.

"Okay," she said. "I'll do it."

CHAPTER 44

Mark kept to the high ground as he made his way east, which provided him a vantage of the surrounding canyons.

All around him, the beasts were on the move.

It was clear that the Valley wasn't the only place blooming. The infection of the Food of the Gods seemed to have spread far and wide, in almost every animal he could see.

The beasts were all in the same early stages of advanced growth, already approaching full size, but not yet showing signs of impending madness – as if they had all been infected at once.

Which, Mark thought, suggested that this outbreak was anything but random.

He wondered if the Valley's tyrannosaur pack would be joining this mass exodus of beasts.

It seemed highly likely. And that meant Junior, who would now be infected himself. Mark shuddered at the thought. Junior had been a handful as a two-foot hatchling.

Mark glanced self-consciously over his shoulder, as if the big rex might appear on his tail at that very moment. At least he'd managed to get some lead time. The roads had mostly been clear. He had passed into Idaho early that morning and was just now reaching the first of the western Rockies.

His final destination was still the better part of three-hundred miles as the crow flies, but he knew the way well enough. He had taken a brief detour to the Mount once, almost twenty years before. But he'd certainly never expected to be going back one day, let alone of his own volition.

He also started running into his first road obstructions once he'd gotten into the higher mountains. The thicker foliage meant more on the highway, and he was periodically having to pull over and clear the path.

The further east he went, however, he began to discover that a lot of the clearing had apparently already been done. A number of the roads seemed to have been in use.

Mark was ambivalent at the implications. He could attest personally that signs of human habitation were not necessarily a good thing.

He kept his rifle handy any time he left the relative safety of his pickup.

His current route, however, seemed to have finally run into its first significant obstacle with a large tree that had fallen across the road.

Mark pulled over and got out.

It was a large tree and it effectively blocked both lanes. Neither was there any way around it, with thick brush on one side and a drop-off on the other. He had brought a chainsaw for the express purpose of cutting his way through potential dead-falls, but the trunk was more than four-feet across.

Mark sighed. That was the thing about these mountain roads – there weren't a lot of alternate routes once you got out in the boondocks. The last turn-off was twenty-miles back.

He was debating whether to pull out his chainsaw and give it a try when he heard the rustling in the brush.

Mark turned, grabbing up his rifle.

Whatever it was, it sounded *big*.

Then there was a heavy thump as a large shape suddenly emerged where it had been hiding almost invisibly among the trees.

Mark found himself staring into the face of a giant gorilla.

The creature reared up behind the fallen log, standing over twenty-feet high.

Then there was an abrupt rush of movement in the surrounding brush, and two more giant hairy beasts stepped out onto the road behind him.

Mark already had his rifle out and aimed...

... but now he slung it back over his shoulder.

The first of the big apes vaulted over the fallen tree, raising its massive hands.

It signed a greeting.

Then it grunted, pointing to a pair of patches of empty fur on his shoulder and forearm – bullet wounds that Mark remembered putting there himself almost two decades before.

Caesar growled, struggling with vocal chords not yet evolved for the task.

"*Shahh-nahhh*," he said.

Mark nodded.

"Yeah, right. *Shahh-nahhh*. You know, I'm actually happy to see you guys."

Caesar grunted in return. Behind him, Cornelius and Dr. Zaius hooted.

Mark nodded to the fallen tree across the road.

"A little help?" he asked.

Caesar turned, gesturing to the two others, and they set to moving the massive log out of the road.

Mark climbed back into his pickup and started the engine. As he drove past the dead-fall, Caesar fell into lumbering step beside him, with the other two following along behind.

Mark leaned out the window.

"You know, for what it's worth," he said, "I'm sorry I shot you."

Caesar growled, holding up two fingers.

Mark nodded.

"Yeah, I know," he said. "Twice."

Caesar grunted begrudgingly as they made their way down the road.

CHAPTER 45

Leanne was learning her way around the woods.

It was something of a relief not having to ask Lucas about every little thing – how to start a fire, find food or fresh water – and she was getting rather casual about her bathroom breaks as well, thank you.

So far, they had also been lucky about close encounters with large theropods, although they'd had a few more run-ins with dromaeosaurs. Fortunately, given enough time to spot the nasty, sickle-clawed devils, Lucas' proficiency with his bow rendered them largely immune – he could drop them at a hundred yards or better.

Of course, arrows would do them little good against a large carcharodont. Just last night, after they'd taken refuge in an old abandoned motor home, a large carcharodont-carnosaur, probably a Giganotosaurus, had passed through their camp.

The big carnosaur appeared to be tracking a scent. Lucas thought it had probably been stalking them for some time, drawn to their unusual human smell, and it had followed their trail right up to the motor home's front door.

Inside, Lucas and Leanne had sat breathless – motionless as mice with a cat outside their hole.

The carcharodont, however, perhaps confused by the odor of rust and unappetizing metal, only nudged the motor home a couple of times, rocking it easily back and forth, before finally giving up and going on its way.

As Leanne began to learn the ropes of wilderness survival, she also began to develop an appreciation for Lucas' skills. Most particularly, she was increasingly grateful for his skill with his bow – they had certainly not gone hungry, and by this point, Leanne was willing to forgive him for the incident with the songbird when they were kids.

Lucas was also quite an adept fisherman. And not only that, he was able to balance their diet by picking out natural plant-growths – greens and roots that were edible, along with the odd natural fruits and berries, separating them from the ones that might poison them.

As she adjusted to life outdoors, Leanne realized she felt quite secure in Lucas' company, and considered how different things might have been if he wasn't there.

She had begun to admire him, and not only that, to depend on him as well.

And perhaps naturally, in this primordial environment, one day, her feelings towards him began to change.

It was early morning and she had awakened from their night's camp to find his bedroll empty. Momentarily alarmed, she had relaxed when she saw him hunched over the small stream by which they'd camped.

He had his shirt off and was both washing it in the clear water and using it as a washcloth on himself. Leanne found herself watching him, admiring the toned muscles in his back as they rippled under his skin.

For the first time, her gaze turned speculative. And when he'd turned around suddenly to catch her eyeing him, she started and flushed furiously.

Recovering quickly, she had made a sarcastic comment about him needing a bath and had turned away.

Nevertheless, a small seed had been planted in her mind, and it was one she didn't quite know how to deal with.

She recognized the *nature* of her feelings readily enough. In her adolescence, she had developed an infatuation with Maverick – one that her mother had disapproved of strenuously.

Overall, however, that sort of thing had occupied a rather minor portion of her thoughts, which was really not so surprising, considering the circumstances of her upbringing.

In the old world, things would have been different – there would have been peer-pressure, and she would have been actively pursued. But for better-or-worse, the world had changed. Growing up, there had been few peers – something that had left her rather ignorant of her own beauty.

Despite her bold and headstrong manner, Leanne had a few confidence-issues, which was perhaps most evident in her frustration at being unable to duplicate her mother's empathic abilities, despite Shanna's assurance that Leanne's potential far exceeded her own.

It didn't even help when Shanna had pointed out that her own abilities did not truly manifest until she was older, and then only after her pregnancy. In the manner of youth, Leanne did not want to simply follow in her mother's footsteps, but step beyond them.

So, perhaps it was not surprising that as these unexpected feelings for Lucas began to emerge, she found herself awkward and embarrassed.

And that night, after yet another day of hard travel, when they had bedded down for the night, this time in the hollow of a massive dead tree, she had tucked herself far off to one side, as far from Lucas as the small space would allow.

And Lucas? He had seen the look in her eyes that morning and had finally stopped lying to himself. He loved her. For better-or-worse. For rejection or not.

As the fire crackled, he moved over next to her and sat down.

Leanne stiffened. Although they'd slept in close proximity for weeks now, she suddenly felt a surge of discomfort and impropriety.

Then she caught his eye, and this time she didn't look away.

Lucas, as helpless before that gaze as if hypnotized, felt himself leaning forward.

Then Leanne suddenly jerked back, her eyes wide – she opened her mouth and began to scream.

Lucas started, blinking and confused, pulling away as if burned.

Then he turned in the small space and found himself staring into a mouth full of massive, ivory-white teeth pressed against the narrow opening to their shelter, and inhaled drooling, carrion breath.

Adrenaline shot through him and he fumbled frantically for his bow, knowing it was useless, and already too late.

Then there came a familiar grunt.

The jagged-toothed maw pulled out of the opening and Lucas stared disbelievingly out into the clearing.

"Big Red?!"

There was an answering grunt. The massive body reclined in front of their shelter and Lucas scrambled out, shouting joyfully.

But as Leanne followed him, their joy was short-lived.

Big Red was massively grown. And as he reached his massive head down to sniff at them, they could see the green glow in his eyes.

"The Food of the Gods," Leanne said. "He's infected."

Lucas patted the scaly hide soothingly, but when he turned to Leanne, his eyes were drawn and somber. He knew the pattern of infection well enough.

"It's going to kill him, isn't it?" he said.

Leanne looked back sympathetically, helplessly. She nodded.

Lucas shut his eyes.

"How long?"

Leanne reached up and touched the massive snout. Big Red sniffed at her affectionately, ignorant of the chemical coursing through his blood that was killing him.

"He'll grow," Leanne said. "Like the sauropod in the Valley. Probably almost three times the size he is now. And once his growth tops out, then... well, it begins to eat away at his brain."

She shut her eyes, not wanting to finish.

"And then it kills him," she said. "Just like rabies."

Lucas stared up at his giant friend and Leanne could see he was fighting tears.

"I'm sorry," she said, touching the *T. rex'* broad snout again – and even as she did so, she felt a small tingle emanating from the big tyrannosaur – a small spark of the empathic sense that Shanna had always assured her would one day come.

Big Red was still friendly for the moment, but Leanne could feel the pressure building from within, and when there was no more outlet, it would manifest into rage.

One day, not long from now, it would burst its way free.

And at that moment, she felt another spark, this one even stronger – only this wasn't from Big Red – or even from Lucas.

It came from the east – a sense of something dark and powerful, yet still far away.

A creature not of madness, but of similar rage.

It left a sense of burning sulfur in her mind – mental fire and brimstone.

Leanne shuddered involuntarily as she turned to the east, breaking into goose-flesh as if with an icy, winter chill.

She had spent most of her life pining for the day when the gift of empathy would finally come to her.

Now, for the first time, she felt fear that someday, it just might.

And someday soon.

CHAPTER 46

Dawn and Sabrina were on foot. They had left their truck almost five miles back.

It was ironic – they had enough gas to make it clear across the country, food for weeks, spare tires – Corporal Conner had even changed the oil.

But after encountering a dead-fall blocking a narrow mountain road, Dawn had attempted to turn them around and gotten the truck stuck in the ditch.

They had spent the next three hours trying to get the damn thing free.

Now they found themselves hoofing it on a road that probably hadn't seen five vehicles a year *before* the end of the world.

They had taken what food they could carry. Dawn carried her automatic rifle, which she still had never even fired once.

Excepting the last several nights curled up in the back of the RV, neither one of them had ever spent a single night outside in their lives.

"You know," Sabrina suggested, "it might be better to just head back to the truck while we still have daylight."

Dawn glanced at her tiredly. They had been hoping to find an old service station – something that might have tow-equipment. At this point, they hadn't yet given up hope on circling back to try and free the truck, but the area was remote. And as the sun started to tip into early afternoon, their prospects were looking dim.

Sabrina stopped.

"I'm serious," she said. "We have no idea where we are. We could be walking for miles before we find anything."

"No one asked you to come along," Dawn replied shortly. "If you want to go back, then go."

Dawn turned her back and kept walking.

Sabrina eyed her coldly.

The truth was, she had never intended to complete this trip in Dawn's company, and the Valley had never been her intended destination.

Dawn may have been having dreams about Shangri-La, but Sabrina had been having dreams of her own.

Before she'd left the Mount, she had confided these dreams to her mother, and Lily had told her it was time for her to leave.

Their Coven sisters were still out there, her mother said, and it was time for Sabrina to go and seek them out.

Sabrina hadn't wanted to leave her mother behind, but Lily told her she had her own role to play back at the Mount.

She'd been visited, she said, by the Dragon.

So Sabrina had hitched a ride with Dawn, initiating a journey she'd fantasized about ever since she was a kid.

And ever since they'd entered the Idaho Rockies, she knew they were drawing near.

She could feel it. Perhaps the Dragon was guiding her as well.

Dawn wanted to continue on and seek out the Valley.

Sabrina was tempted to let her.

But Dawn should not have turned her back on her like that.

It was a moment of arrogant conceit that Sabrina was not prepared to tolerate.

It called up too many instances of privilege while growing up on the Mount – all those scuffles on the playground for which Sabrina was punished. Dawn was the Mount's first birth, the General's goddaughter – the pampered princess.

Then there was what had happened to Justin.

Part of Sabrina longed to tell Dawn about those nights together she knew Justin never had – just to rub it in her spoiled face.

Instead, she stepped up silently behind her.

Because now they were out here all alone.

Dawn had her rifle, but no idea how to use it.

Sabrina quietly reached for the knife in her pack, eyeing Dawn's unprotected back intently.

So intent, she didn't notice the rustling in the bushes until the shadow blocked out the sun.

Then she looked up and screamed.

Looming above, staring down at them from over the trees, was the fierce, scowling face of a giant hairy ape.

Dawn started at Sabrina's scream, almost in her ear, first looking back, and then up as the giant beast stepped openly into the path. Dawn gasped, stumbling back, grabbing clumsily for the rifle over her shoulder.

Sabrina screamed again, as another giant ape stepped out onto the path behind them.

And then a third – they were surrounded.

Dawn fumbled with the rifle, her arms tangled in the shoulder strap. But before her fingers found the safety, a great hairy hand reached out and snatched the weapon away.

Dawn staggered back and fell.

The big ape stared down at her with a low admonishing growl.

Sabrina crouched beside her, holding up her knife.

Then there came the sound of a honking horn.

The big ape standing over them glanced over his shoulder and stepped aside as an old pickup truck appeared on the road behind him,

Dawn and Sabrina stared wide-eyed as the pickup rolled to a stop and a man got out, stepping up beside the giant ape.

"Are you two ladies lost?" he asked, smiling.

Dawn and Sabrina sat mute, too paralyzed to speak.

"Sorry if my friends scared you," the man said.

He turned to the twenty-foot gorilla standing next to him.

"This here is Caesar," he said. "Those two are Zaius and Cornelius. Caesar here was up scouting on the hill when he saw your truck stuck a few miles back. He backtracked you to here. We figured you could use a hand."

The man tipped his hat.

"My name's Mark," he said.

CHAPTER 47

Jonah had been flying for three straight hours, and the steady drone of the Cessna's engine was beginning to lull him to drowsiness.

Lounging in the cockpit beside him, Naomi had been alternately napping, and staring vacantly out the window, but there wasn't much view as Jonah had kept them above the cloud cover.

It was ironic, Jonah thought. He had offered to let her drive – he always did, and she always declined. It didn't matter how many cracks she made about how lousy a pilot *he* was, or how adept and confident she herself had become behind the controls, she always preferred to be chauffeured.

But now they were beginning to run low on fuel and Jonah was looking for a place to gas-up. They were passing through southern Idaho and their map showed an air base shortly ahead.

It was also getting dark. Jonah had originally been headed for a commercial air-terminal further north, but sometime in the twenty years since the map had been drawn, the place had been smashed flat.

Still, it was best to count their blessings. Beyond this little detour, their trip had so far been remarkably free of hazards – no increment weather, and more importantly, no pterosaurs – which was why they stayed at high-altitude. The danger-spot was when you got low to the ground.

But now they dropped below the clouds in the direction the map indicated the air base lay and, right on cue, Naomi sat up abruptly in her seat.

"Oh *no*," she said, as she looked out the window.

With a spark of alarm, Jonah's eyes turned quickly in the direction she was pointing – he was expecting pterosaurs, or possibly one of those giant eagles that had more recently inserted themselves into the new ecology.

But Naomi was pointing at the ground.

Jonah banked for a better view, hoping the air force base hadn't been trashed as well.

But the base was still there. Unfortunately, the facility appeared to be active – and busy.

"Uh oh," Jonah said.

He glanced at Naomi, who shook her head. The last thing they wanted was contact with the military.

Jonah was torn – they had to land somewhere soon. He was tempted to turn back towards the smashed air-terminal up north. Perhaps they could still salvage some fuel. There were also a few smaller private air-parks dotting the area.

Then Naomi tapped his shoulder, nodding behind them.

An F-16 fighter jet had appeared on their tail.

Their radio barked alive.

"Attention, unidentified aircraft. You are trespassing in restricted airspace. You are instructed to land immediately."

A second fighter appeared, pulling up beside them.

Naomi waved cheerfully through the window. She turned to Jonah with a shrug.

"You better land," she said.

Jonah sighed, allowing the two fighters to escort him down to the runway.

As they touched down and coasted to a stop, they were immediately surrounded by a platoon of armed guards.

Jonah groaned. They'd been through this routine before.

"You know," he muttered, "we're in a damned Cessna. We can't be that intimidating."

Naomi nodded agreeably.

"Funny," she said, "how the end of the world seems to make people paranoid about every little thing."

As they climbed out, the two fighter pilots joined the platoon of guards. The leader stepped forward, removing his helmet, and introducing himself formerly.

"My name is Major Dwayne Hicks," he said, "and on the authority of the United States Military, I'm placing you under arrest."

Naomi smiled broadly.

"*Major* Hicks now, is it?" she said. "Good to see you again, Major. It's been a long time."

CHAPTER 48

Cameron, Maverick and Rosa had been hiking their way out of the mountains for five days. It had taken them almost forty-eight hours just to make it below the snow-pack, but even then, the terrain remained hard and difficult travel.

It was nearing sundown on the fifth day when they finally stumbled onto an old logging road.

For the first time, they had started to see evidence of human habitation – there were signs of campfires, although most of it seemed very temporary, with little left behind.

The old logging road, however, showed signs of recent regular use, and a lot of the overgrowth had been cleared away. There were also tire tracks that looked like they came from an RV.

More importantly, they now at least had a trail to follow, and one that, according to their compass, continued east. It was also a welcome change from picking their way through the dense forest.

But they were still at high elevation, and while they had made it down below the snow-level, that did not stop the temperature from dropping rapidly with the setting sun. As it grew dark, they started gathering wood for a fire, and began to set up camp for the evening.

The three of them huddled close as the darkness settled in on the mountain. Maverick produced a can of pork and beans, prying it open with his knife and passing it around.

"Apologies in advance if this has me repeatin' later," Maverick said, smiling.

Rosa eyed him archly.

"Maybe I'll sleep outside the tent," she said.

At that moment, there was the snap of a broken branch that sounded as loud as a rifle shot, echoing from somewhere in the not-too-distant woods.

The three of them froze.

"Maybe not," Rosa amended, edging a little closer to the two men.

Maverick grabbed up his rifle.

They sat, listening intently, like a troop of deer at a brook. So far, the forest had been seemingly empty, but they knew that was too good to last.

Cameron pulled a flashlight from his pack and shined it into the trees.

The thick foliage revealed nothing.

"Just a falling branch?" Rosa ventured hopefully.

Then something moved in the shadows, and they heard a distinctive birdlike warble.

"That," Maverick said, bringing his rifle up to his shoulder, "sounds like a sickle-claw."

"What's a sickle-claw doing in the mountains?" Rosa objected.

Then there came another crack of a breaking branch, and this time it was followed by a much deeper rumble – a heavy growl that might have echoed out of a prehistoric bear cave.

"That was no sickle-claw," Cameron said, standing up.

There was a heavy, thudding impact as a nearby tree was pushed over, and now a massive shadow reared up above the surrounding brush.

A moment later, a second shape appeared behind it.

The firelight illuminated a great, shark-toothed head, more than six-feet long, looking down at them from over the trees.

"*Ohhhh* shit," Maverick breathed.

It was a carcharodont – a big one – big enough that a shot from Maverick's rifle wasn't about to do anything but piss it off.

And there were two of them.

Maverick raised his rifle anyway, aiming for the eye.

Then suddenly a light shined from the creature's back – the glare of a flashlight beam – and they realized that someone was sitting astride the beast's shoulders like a horse.

There was a crunch of heavy footsteps as the giant theropod stepped into the clearing. The second beast followed a moment later, also with a mounted rider.

The shadowy shape on the lead carnosaur's back let out a loud and piercing whistle, and suddenly there was a rush of motion in the trees.

There was an answering birdlike screech and half-a-dozen sickle-claws broke from the brush like a flock of flushed pheasants

The pack of dromaeosaurs formed a tight semi-circle around the campfire, their eyes reflecting back like jack-o-lanterns in the firelight.

Maverick glanced sideways at Cameron and Rosa.

"Okay," he muttered, "*now* we're screwed."

But then the bushes rustled again and another shadow materialized, stepping fully into the firelight.

It was a woman – dressed in black, adorned with bones and handmade braids. She was holding a rifle of her own – it looked like an M-16.

She reached up and patted one of the sickle-claws on its neck. The clawed beast cooed like a pigeon.

A moment later, several other figures emerged from the trees – all women, all dressed in black.

All holding guns.

The woman perched astride the lead carcharodont tapped the beast's massive head and the carnosaur kneeled, allowing her to dismount.

As she turned to regard them, they could now see the little lizard clinging to her shoulder like a parrot.

A little creature they knew all too well.

The woman was smiling as she approached. She raised her automatic rifle, regarding Maverick's *30.06* with amusement.

Behind her, the rest of the Amazon troop all raised their own rifles, and there was the sound of several bolts being snapped into place. The sickle-claws stood at attention like trained attack-dogs. Above their heads, the two carcharodonts began to growl.

The woman in the lead nodded to Maverick meaningfully.

"You might as well put your gun down," she said.

On her shoulder, the little lizard tittered.

Maverick looked over to Cameron and Rosa, who both shrugged. Maverick sighed, lowering his rifle.

The woman in black stepped forward.

Maverick offered her his most charming smile.

"So," he said, "what's your name, honey?"

The woman offered a charming smile right back.

"You can call me Christine," she said.

Then she stepped forward and struck Maverick across the temple with the butt of her M-16. He dropped unconscious at her feet.

Still smiling, Christine turned to Cameron and Rosa.

"And you," she said, "will be coming with us."

CHAPTER 49

It was nearly dawn by the time they reached the settlement. It looked like it had once been an old logging camp, but to Rosa, it seemed more like a pagan survivalist fantasy.

The encampment was apparently all women, and all of them heavily-armed, with military-style weapons. Rosa could only guess from where.

They also rode carcharodonts like horses and the sickle-claws responded to them like trained dogs.

Even Shanna couldn't do that.

But Rosa suspected the little lizard perched on the shoulder of the leader – the one who had introduced herself as Christine – had something to do with that.

They had bound both Cameron and Maverick as they escorted them through the forest, but for Rosa, they had left her hands free. She wasn't yet sure if that was favoritism or lack of concern. She had made a brief effort to doctor the gash Christine's rifle butt had left on Maverick's forehead, but had been admonished by their captors.

Maverick, still a bit dazed, had simply shrugged.

"I'm fine," he said, with blood still running down his cheek.

The two big carcharodonts trundled through the brush, clearing a path as they went. The rest of the troop followed on foot, with the pack of sickle-claws at their heels.

Once they reached the main entrance, Christine let out another piercing whistle and the front gate began to roll open.

A guard looked down from the tower as they passed, armed with an automatic rifle like the rest of them.

It was a large facility, surrounded by a high steel fence. The grounds were wide and spread out, once to accommodate logging trucks, but now allowing for the free movement of fifty-foot theropods.

There was a stable near the entrance, likely a former maintenance garage, where four more of the massive carcharodonts lounged. A smaller, adjoining barracks housed the troops of sickle-claws.

As she led the group of them across the grounds, Christine tapped the carcharodont's head and the big carnosaur bowed, allowing her to dismount. She motioned to the other rider, who led both mounts to the stable.

On Christine's shoulder, the little lizard hooted and jabbered, and in immediate response, the troop of sickle-claws flocked as a group into their own shelters, like birds lining up across a telephone wire.

Rosa's eyes cut over to Cameron and Maverick, who both frowned.

The three prisoners were now attracting attention from the rest of the Amazon tribe.

Maverick shrugged, regarding the exclusively female entourage as they gathered around.

"It could be worse, I guess," he said. "I've actually had some pretty good weekends that started out like this."

Rosa glanced at him sideways.

"You're already bleeding, Maverick. Why don't you try shutting the hell up?"

Christine smiled, nodding as she was rejoined by the second rider, who held her rifle aimed and ready, eyeing Maverick meaningfully.

"Good advice," Christine said.

As she spoke, another woman separated from the crowd.

Like the others, she was dressed in black, but she was also adorned with an assortment of colorful beads braided into her hair and clothing.

Witch-doctor priestess regalia, Rosa thought.

"These people aren't military," the woman said. "Where did you find them?"

"They were coming down out of the mountain," Christine replied. "I think they were in that plane that went down."

The second woman nodded.

"You think they came from the Valley?"

Christine nodded.

"I do."

The second woman turned to Rosa.

"You know Shanna then?" she said.

Rosa's eyes widened, but she didn't answer, again glancing nervously at Cameron and Maverick.

"It's okay," the woman said. "You can talk to me. My name is Luna. We welcome sisters here. And we've been aware of Shanna and your Valley for a long time."

Rosa remained silent, taking pertinent note of the stable full of sickle-claws as well as the little lizard perched on Christine's shoulder.

"You might say," Luna continued, smiling gently, "that we have worshiped Shanna from afar. The goddess made flesh."

Rosa nodded slowly, even as she found herself thinking of all those sickle-claw raids over the years.

And as she regarded several large RV-style trucks parked along the perimeter – which, like their weapons, looked as if they had once been military – Rosa also now recalled Shanna's mention of tire tracks up on the hill the day that Lucas' parents had been killed – tread from a mysterious vehicle that could not be accounted for.

Allison had always been a bit of a witchy-woman, hadn't she? With something of a haunted past that she never talked about?

"Yes," Luna said, "we have long been aware of your friend, Shanna."

But now, her smile grew long-suffering.

"Alas," she continued, "It seems that her time has passed."

Luna reached out, tracing her fingers down Rosa's cheek. Rosa felt an odd crackle at her touch.

"Even a goddess," she said, "must know when to bow."

Luna nodded slowly, her eyes alight with the glow of a zealot.

"The Dragon Lord," she said, "has come into power."

There was a spark of static at the tip of Luna's fingers and Rosa jumped, startled, pulling away.

"What in the hell," Maverick said behind her, "is a *Dragon Lord?*"

Luna turned to regard Maverick and Cameron, and now there was a predatory lilt in her eye.

"You will learn that soon enough," she said. She nodded to Christine and the woman standing by her side.

"Teresa, will you please take these three to the pen?"

Luna looked at Maverick, studying him speculatively up and down. Then she turned and pointed to Cameron.

"That one first," she said. "Get him ready."

CHAPTER 50

"These women are nuts!" Maverick said.

He had tactfully waited until their armed escort had gone before speaking.

The three of them had been led to a makeshift stockade that looked like it might once have been a locker room, equipped with showers and plumbing. In place of bars, steel-wire fencing had been mounted to create a number of separate cells.

In a cell by himself, a man in military garb, lying on a cot, looked up as they were brought in.

Their escort, the one Luna had called Teresa, nodded to the soldier as they entered.

"New recruits, Donny," Teresa said. "Looks like you've been moved down the line again."

The soldier said nothing, but he didn't look happy.

Teresa beckoned both Rosa and Maverick to enter the first cell, but held Cameron aside.

"You're coming with me," Teresa said.

Cameron glanced nervously at Maverick and Rosa.

"Where am *I* going?"

"You're going to meet your mate."

Cameron blinked.

"My *mate*?"

Teresa slammed the cell door behind Maverick and Rosa, who stared back speechless as she led Cameron at gunpoint out of the chamber.

"Absolutely, certifiably *nuts*!" Maverick repeated.

Two cells over, the lone soldier shook his head.

"You don't know the half of it," he said.

He rose from his cot.

"Private Donny Cates," he said, introducing himself. "I've been here for a month." He shook his head. "There were three of us when I was captured."

"Where are they taking Cameron?" Rosa asked.

"Your friend," Cates replied, "is being groomed for the conception ritual."

Maverick and Rosa exchanged looks.

"The *what*?" Maverick said.

"Well," Cates said, "from what's been explained to me, it's sort of a black-widow spider-thing. They pick out a mate, and they have their 'rituals' until they get knocked-up. Then they feed the guy to one of those big lizards out there."

Maverick and Rosa blinked.

Cates nodded.

"What can I say?" he said. "They're nuts. They've gotten spacey living in these mountains. They think getting pregnant gives them visions."

Rosa and Maverick exchanged another look.

"Visions of what, exactly?" Rosa asked.

"Of dragons, I guess." Cates shook his head. "It's apparently been going on for a long time. We've got an air base about ten miles north of here and we've been having troops go missing for years now. But we never knew why."

"I guess that explains where they got all the military-grade weapons and those RVs outside," Maverick said. He regarded Cates. "And you've been here a month? How is it that *you've* lasted so long?"

The Private shrugged.

"The other two guys were just better-looking, I guess. I wasn't popular in high school either. Thank Heaven for small favors."

Maverick and Rosa absorbed this silently.

"Your friend," Cates said, "apparently drew the lottery ticket."

"You know," Maverick said, "I *almost* feel rejected."

"Well," Rosa volunteered, "if it's about procreation, maybe they're worried about missing chromosomes."

Maverick frowned, casting Rosa a dire eye. For a moment, his lips pursed, no doubt with one of his standard old-maid/spinster remarks, but instead he waved it off, turning back to Cates.

"So what about *her*?" he asked, indicating Rosa.

Cates shook his head.

"I don't rightly know. It hasn't come up since I've been here. Maybe they'll let her join up."

Maverick glanced back at Rosa.

"Well," he said, "in that case, she might just fit right in."

And with that, he turned away, lying down on one of the cell's two cots and fell silent – rather uncharacteristically, Rosa thought.

She wondered if, after all this time, she'd finally managed to hurt his feelings.

Maybe it was the circumstances, but she actually felt the impulse to apologize.

She noticed he was still bleeding from his scalp.

"Here," she said, sitting down next to him, "let me take a look at that."

"I'm fine," he said gruffly.

"Don't be stubborn," she said, and began to dab at the running blood with the sleeve of her shirt.

With a disgruntled sigh, he sat up, allowing her to dress the wound, something she'd done on an almost-weekly basis ever since they'd first met.

"I didn't mean the chromosome-thing," she ventured.

He looked up at her.

"Yeah you did."

Rosa nodded.

"Yeah," she admitted. "I did."

"So," he asked, "how do you feel about converting to dragon worship?"

"Well," Rosa said, falling into her standard bedside-manner, "I might get to feed *you* to a dragon."

"Does that mean we get to procreate first?" Maverick returned. "For an old-maid-spinster, you're still pretty hot."

Rosa nodded. That was more like it.

"And for a Neanderthal," she replied, "you're still a pig."

Maverick smiled and Rosa actually felt a little bit better.

Two cells over, Cates shook his head, rolling his eyes, and lay back down.

Rosa wondered what was happening with Cameron at that moment.

Or Leanne and Lucas for that matter.

If Shanna was waiting for help, so far, they were seriously letting her down.

Everything to this point had gone dramatically wrong, and there was no improvement in sight.

She sighed. For the moment, there was nothing to do but wait.

CHAPTER 51

Cameron was flying – whatever they'd injected him with was some pretty potent stuff.

The 'ritual chamber' was once a corner office on the top floor of the logging site's operations building. It had been tarted up like a honeymoon suite, and Cameron was currently laid-out across a king-size bed, doped-up on some kind of Spanish-fly aphrodisiac-from-Hell.

Christine and Luna had just brought in a young girl. Cameron guessed her to be no more than nineteen, introduced as 'Abbi', who was apparently his bride-to-be, black-widow-style.

In whatever distant part of his mind that was still capable of making such objective observations, he had to at least give them credit – they didn't bother with the pretense of dressing her up in white.

He actually tried to speak as they brought her in – something to the effect of, 'Sorry, I'm taken,' but all that came out was low, mumbling babble.

Christine and Luna had smiled.

Cameron hoped Shanna would forgive him.

Although, he supposed it was going to be a moot point – he would be eaten by a carcharodont once the act was done.

It seemed, however, that he was going to get a stay-of-execution, so-to-speak.

The 'ritual' was interrupted before it even started when Teresa suddenly appeared at the door, looking disheveled.

Through the hazy filter of the drugs, Teresa sounded like she was talking underwater – garbled whale-speak – and Cameron focused that same distant part of his mind attempting to decipher her words.

"The *General* is at the air base," she was saying. "They're setting the place up as the new headquarters."

Christine and Luna seemed to take this news with great interest.

Cameron nodded affirmatively, rather proud of himself for following along.

"The Dragon Lord," Teresa continued, "says it's time."

"Okay," Christine said, "get the mounts ready and let's go."

Luna nodded to Cameron.

"What about him?"

Christine shrugged.

"He can wait," she said. "Let him sleep it off." She smiled down at Cameron. "Looks like you caught a break, big boy."

Cameron grinned back apathetically.

"What about the carcharodonts?" Teresa asked. "They still need to be fed."

Christine smiled.

"Give them the soldier," she said.

CHAPTER 52

"We have to leave him," Leanne said. "He's losing it."

Lucas looked back at her helplessly. Big Red had stopped for a rare rest, breaking his inexorable eastward path for the demands exhaustion placed on him.

The big tyrannosaur's growth cycle was nearing its peak. And perched along his broad back like a pair of hummingbirds, too light to be noticed, Lucas and Leanne had begun to wonder, as the chemical slowly corrupted Big Red's mind, whether he even remembered his passengers were there.

Big Red's pace through the mountains had been relentless, and they had eaten up the miles with startling rapidity.

But now, they were nearing their destination. Leanne could feel it.

There were also a lot of other animals on the move, herd animals and predators alike – carnosaurs plodded side-by-side with ceratopsians and stegosaurs.

Lucas had never seen such behavior before. Droughts or other such ecological malfunctions could sometimes push entire populations along this way, but this forest seemed quite healthy.

And they were all infected giants, as far as they could see, silhouetted across the horizon.

All headed east.

None of the other creatures, however, pursued their goal with the obsession of Big Red.

As they progressed on, Leanne began to feel the pull as well. The sensation both excited and frightened her.

For his part, Lucas was glad, because it gave them something to talk about.

Things had grown rather stiff and uncomfortable between them. They didn't speak much, and there had been no repeat of their brief moment by the fire.

At first, Lucas thought Leanne might have been embarrassed. But as they grew closer to their destination, he began to perceive the more significant truth.

As they neared the Mount, Leanne had grown increasingly spacey – almost aloof. She described a dark presence – something terrible – close to the presence of her mother.

Combined and magnified by the life-forces of the wildlife itself, all of it together was stimulating unused senses in her for nearly the first time.

Lucas recognized what was happening well enough – Leanne was coming of age. The power within her had begun to emerge. Her focus on the world around her was shifting and her perspective was shifting along with it.

Now she would belong to the world.

Lucas stole a glance at her serene beautiful face and doubled his resolve that he would see her through to the end.

Leanne noticed him watching her.

"What?" she asked.

"Nothing," he said, turning away.

Ahead of them, the Mount now loomed on the horizon.

Within sight of their destination, however, Big Red had abruptly settled down to rest. That was how the Food of the Gods worked, Leanne explained. It was like a sugar-high – once full-growth was achieved, the excess energy resulted in sudden crashes, like a kid that will run all day long and then suddenly drop and fall sound asleep for hours.

Big Red sat down so abruptly his passengers were nearly thrown. His massive head dropped and his eyes squeezed almost immediately shut into sleep.

But through the cracks in his lids, you could still see the greenish emerald glow.

It was then that Leanne told Lucas it was time to leave him behind and go on their own.

They were in easy traveling distance now and Leanne could feel the madness starting to build within their giant mount. Soon he would become a danger to them.

Lucas shut his eyes. Big Red had been his friend – he couldn't bring himself to think of the big rex as a pet. For most of his life, in his solitary, often lonely existence, this simple animal had been there for him more than any human.

Then there was the dream that had been Leanne herself – an unapproachable impossibility, forever out of reach. But until now, the *dream* had always been there – the motivating illusion of hope.

It was time, Lucas realized, to let both of them go.

With them, it felt as if he was jettisoning part of his soul.

Leaving Big Red slumbering in the clearing, Lucas led Leanne into the forest, down the last leg of their journey.

And behind them, unnoticed by either, Big Red's head popped up. His green-glowing eyes blinked, focusing on Leanne and Lucas as he watched them go.

In his own dim way, he understood they were leaving him, and he also understood why.

He was a rogue now.

And the rogue walks alone.

CHAPTER 53

Cameron had fallen asleep. The last thing he remembered were the soldier's screams as they had dragged him out to the carcharodont stables.

The window above the bed was open, letting in the cool evening breeze – although the frame was, of course, barred. Cameron suspected that, drugs or no drugs, the would-be victim of the odd ritual sacrifice had tried to make a break for it.

The soldier below was apparently making just such an effort.

Cameron had lain there apathetically as the voices below drifted up.

The soldier had started off making a brave front, but that had not lasted long.

"Finally my turn to procreate?" he asked.

"No, Donny," Christine had replied, "just feeding time."

There had immediately followed the sounds of a struggle, accompanied by 'Donny's' voice, now a high-falsetto – "*No-no-no-no!!!*"

Lying there, Cameron felt a brief impulse to get up and look out the window, but he couldn't quite summon the will. Instead, he just listened.

The man's shrieks deteriorated into begging as they threw him into the stables, and then escalated once again into full-on screams, only to finally be cut off, abruptly and definitively, a few seconds later.

Cameron heard Teresa laughing.

"Now *that* guy was a screamer."

After that, Cameron drifted off again, and when he next awoke, it was full dark. Shaking off the cobwebs, this time he managed to roll over and get out of bed.

Still a bit fuzzy, he made a perfunctory attempt at the door, finding it predictably locked. Then he went to the window and looked out onto the grounds.

Down below, lit by torch-light, the tribe was putting on their war-paint, donning the same black garb as in the mountains the night before, and armed to the teeth with purloined automatic rifles.

The carcharodont stables were emptied out and all six of the giant carnosaurs were dressed and mounted, ready for war.

Christine was in the lead, with an Otto perched upon her shoulder. Teresa, apparently her primary lieutenant, also had one of the little lizards riding with her, and several more were mounted like jockeys across the backs of the battalion of sickle-claws at the carcharodonts' feet.

Luna saw them off at the gate, and Abbi, Cameron's bride-to-be, was mounted at the guard-tower as the procession moved out.

They were headed to the air base up north, Cameron recalled, blinking as his senses cleared and his faculties returned to him. They had gotten word 'the General' was there. That *had* to mean Rhodes.

Whatever had hit the Mount had driven the forces of the military to ground, and the air base was obviously where they had gone to regroup. This cult of dragon-worshiping Amazons clearly intended to pounce while they were still vulnerable.

Cameron tugged at the bars on his window in frustration. He looked around his gilded cage for anything he might use to lever them apart.

The bedposts, however, were made of wood and would be no match for the steel bars. Beyond that, the room was completely bare of furnishings. He also tested the locked door with a few experimental kicks and discovered that, besides the heavy dead-bolt, it was made of metal, not wood. No doubt a soldier or two had tried that as well.

Cameron had only just sat down again, racking his brains, when the ruckus started outside.

It began with a sudden bellowing roar, followed immediately by the sound of machine-gun fire and a woman's scream.

Jumping back to his feet and running to the window, Cameron looked out just in time to see something large hit the main gate like a speeding truck, directly below the main guard tower.

Perched in the guard-post above, Abbi was sent flying into the compound as if launched by a catapult. She landed heavily and was knocked unconscious on impact.

A great hairy, black shape burst through the wall, letting loose with a challenging roar. Two others joined it a moment later, and Abbi's tower was smashed to the ground.

Cameron recognized them well-enough. Shanna referred to them as her 'extended-family'. He had met Caesar himself. The other two would be Cornelius and Dr. Zaius.

There was the sound of more gunfire as the three other guard-towers were also smashed to the ground, accompanied by squalls and screeching caws as the reserve troops of dromaeosaurs came running to their defense, claws spread, only to be promptly crushed beneath giant hairy paws.

Cameron also saw troops of Ottos scurrying, scattering like rats, breaking for the fences, but the three big apes seemed to make a particular effort to smash each and every one of the scaly little bastards before they reached the safety of the bushes beyond.

It took less than two minutes.

When it was all done, an old pickup rolled through the demolished front gate, and Cameron laughed out loud, recognizing the beat-up truck even before Mark stepped out.

Cameron put his fingers to his lips and let out a loud whistle. Mark turned, spotting Cameron in the window, and he smiled and waved. He nodded to Caesar, and a moment later, a huge hairy paw appeared at Cameron's window, yanking the bars away, along with part of the wall.

Presently, they had Maverick and Rosa rounded up out of their cell, and the group of them gathered to where Luna and Abbi, along with the remaining guards, sat sequestered in the middle grounds, surrounded by the snarling twenty-foot apes.

Mark was also accompanied by two teenage girls Cameron had never seen before, and who now pulled up behind his pick-up in what looked like another military-issue RV. The two of them stared wide-eyed and blinking out the windows, apparently reluctant to join the gathered assemblage.

"Gotta tell ya'," Maverick said, slapping Mark's shoulder, looking up at Caesar, "I never thought I'd be so glad to see an eight-ton gorilla."

"How did you know where to find us?" Rosa asked.

"We found the tail of your wrecked plane a few miles back," Mark replied. "Caesar says he's been by this encampment before. We've been tracking you for the last twenty-four hours."

"Our group got separated," Cameron said, briefly describing the incident with the giant eagle.

"Once we got down out of the mountain," he continued, nodding to where Luna and Abbi now sat huddled with their Coven sisters, "that's when we ran into *this* troop of nutcases."

Mark glanced down at Luna, who sat, silent and sullen.

"We saw them feed that guy to the carcharodonts," he said, shaking his head, sparing Luna an arched eye. "You bitches are crazier than ever."

"You know her?" Maverick asked.

Mark nodded as Luna glowered back at him.

"We go way back," he said.

"So who are your friends?" Rosa asked, indicating the two girls still hunkered down in their front seat.

Mark waved to the two teens, beckoning them over. Looking apprehensive, they climbed out of the RV to stand hovering close to Mark.

"This is Sabrina and Dawn," Mark said. "They're both refugees from the Mount. They saw what happened there." He nodded meaningfully to Cameron. "It seems like your 'intelligence' was right on the money."

Cameron nodded.

"Which brings us to our next little problem," he said. "Guess where their little war-party is headed *now*."

Caesar had the answer to that one. He pointed north.

"*Huuu-mahhns*," he said.

Maverick nodded.

"That soldier said they had an air base a few miles north."

"They also," Cameron added, "said 'the General' was on-site. That's gotta be General Rhodes."

"General Rhodes," Mark mused. "No kidding."

He sighed, glancing up at Caesar, who grunted in return.

"They've got a lead on us," Mark said. "We better get moving."

CHAPTER 54

Leanne and Lucas had a stroke of luck shortly after leaving Big Red behind when they discovered a big 4x4 truck locked up tight in an old barn, less than three miles down the road.

Lucas, whose father had taught him rudimentary engine maintenance on their old farm vehicles, was able to get it started by jumping the battery from a gas-powered generator right there handy in the garage.

The old barn was completely unlooted and also yielded a treasure trove of other provisions – everything from canned goods, to stores of gasoline and tools, to medical supplies. It seemed remarkable that everything was entirely undisturbed, but a moment's thought suggested why.

There were no people here. Beyond the Mount itself, humanity was completely absent.

After they'd cleared the truck free of a few rather large spiders, they loaded-up and pulled out onto the main road.

In spite of the absence of humanity, the roadways themselves actually seemed well-used. The local wildlife had apparently been utilizing mankind's old trails rather than carving out their own. While overgrown with brush at the edges, the roads were clear, and their going was easy enough.

The truck itself, besides being big and powerful, was in excellent condition. Even the old CD player was in working order and they discovered a case of discs under the seat. Even the air conditioner worked. It was almost like an outing.

At least, that is, until Lucas nearly drove them off the edge of a cliff that had no rights being there – a new canyon that looked down into a brand new gulf.

It had been getting dark and, up to this point in their journey, they had not risked traveling by night. But with the added security of the heavily-constructed vehicle around them, they decided to press onward, the old truck's high-beams illuminating the path in front of them.

Fortunately, Lucas had been taking it slow. Despite the bright headlights, there were no roadside reflectors or streetlights, as there would have been in the old days, so Lucas had actually been creeping along at a pace not much greater than a fast walk.

That was still almost fast enough to drive them over the edge. The road was nothing but blackness ahead – and perhaps that should have been the tip-off, because there had been no illumination of trees.

The front wheel of the truck had already dropped over the edge before Lucas reflexively stomped the brakes, and the two of them were thrown roughly forward into the windshield.

For one dizzying moment, the truck seemed to teeter, and they stared down into the blackness of the drop-off. Lucas reversed the gas, spinning wheels. The truck's forward motion was checked, but the front tires were stuck over the lip of the ravine.

Lucas cautiously opened his door and stepped out, shining a flashlight underneath the front wheel-axle.

"Well," he said, "we aren't going anywhere tonight. Maybe we can get it out tomorrow."

Leanne didn't answer. Lucas turned to find her staring in the direction of the Mount.

"Leanne?" Lucas ventured. "What's wrong?"

Leanne turned to him slowly, her eyes wide and suddenly frightened.

"It knows I'm here," she said, her voice barely a whisper.

"What are you talking about?"

"Whatever it is that I'm feeling out here," she said, "it feels me too. It knows we're coming."

Leanne visibly shivered.

"I can *feel* it," she said. "It knows right where I am."

"You don't know that," Lucas said.

But at that moment, a pack of sickle-claws stepped out into the road behind them.

These were big ones too, one of the larger dromaeosaur breeds – they were lion or tiger-sized, probably weighing more than four-hundred pounds each, and they spread out in an arrow-shaped formation, like a flock of birds, as they advanced.

Lucas froze for half-a-heartbeat. His bow was in the truck.

There was something deliberate in these creatures' movements – something *directed*, that he'd never seen before.

"Get in the truck!" Leanne shouted.

His paralysis broken, Lucas instantly complied, leaping into the cab, slamming the door shut behind him, and gunning the engine to life. He stomped the gas, squirreling all four tires, trying to pull the front wheels free.

And then incredibly – absurdly – Leanne's passenger-side door opened.

She had never locked the door.

Grasping claws reached in and snatched her out of the cab, and she was gone, just like that.

Lucas made a leap for her door just as it was slammed shut in his face.

Then he felt a heavy jolt as the truck was shoved from behind.

There was a stomach-dropping shift in momentum as the truck rolled over the edge.

Lucas heard Leanne scream.

Then his head connected with something hard and the world went black.

CHAPTER 55

Something bad must have happened at the Mount, Jonah thought.

It appeared that the air base was being set up as a new headquarters, and in a scramble, at that. That couldn't possibly be good.

As he and Naomi were led across the tarmac from the runway, Jonah also took quiet note of the rather modest assets on display. Besides a bare minimum of ground vehicles, with no tanks, he counted only a dozen jet fighters, including the two that had escorted them in, along with maybe a half-dozen combat helicopters, and three or four more cargo choppers bringing in shipments.

And while the base was clearly mobilized and busy, with soldiers scurrying about everywhere – most currently occupied with receiving incoming cargo – Jonah estimated there were not much more than a couple hundred troops, all-told. If that.

He had known that the human race was an endangered species, but he hadn't known it was *this* bad. These were extinction-level numbers.

Then there were the ashen expressions on the faces of Hicks' armed two-man escort – Hudson and Brady, according to their badges, who looked barely old enough to shave.

Something bad had happened alright.

So far, Major Hicks hadn't exactly been forthcoming.

"Why are we being arrested?" Naomi asked, as they were marched along.

Hicks was stiff and formal.

"You were in restricted air space."

Naomi smirked.

"That's kind of arbitrary these days, don't you think?"

Hicks spared her an arched eye.

"*No*, actually," he replied emphatically. "Right now, it's anything but arbitrary."

Naomi frowned, glancing at Jonah.

"As long as we're on the subject," Jonah said, "why exactly are all of *you* here?"

"Because," a voice said, "things have gotten bad again."

They turned to the lone figure walking towards them and, although it had been nearly twenty years, they both recognized the stoic, chiseled face of General Nathan Rhodes.

Hicks snapped the two-man squad to a stop. Brady and Hudson both saluted formally as the General approached.

Rhodes seemed not to have aged so much as hardened like a rock wall. His head was bandaged, and Jonah could see the tissue around the white gauze was swollen and purple.

Definitely something bad had happened at the Mount.

Rhodes regarded Jonah.

"I remember you, son," he said. "You helped us out once. I thought you had potential. But you turned out to be a deserter."

Naomi laughed out loud.

"It's hard to call a man a deserter when he never even joined up," she replied. "Especially after he saved your asses."

She hooked a possessive arm around Jonah's elbow.

"And to be fair," she said, "he *didn't* desert. I *took* him."

Naomi squared her shoulders, eyeing Rhodes challengingly.

"The military already *got* one man of mine," she said. "You can't have *this* one. And if you don't mind, we were just passing through, and we'd be happy to be on our way."

Rhodes smiled thinly.

"Unfortunately," he said, "this time, there might not be anywhere for you to go." He shook his head. "Our enemy... has evolved."

He touched the bandage on his head.

"You asked why we are here," he said. "It's because we've gotten our asses handed to us. We've lost every surviving base besides this one. Most importantly, we lost the Mount, and all the assets that went with it." He leaned forward. "That Includes nuclear."

Rhodes allowed a moment for this information to sink in.

Then he turned and indicated the mobilized base.

"We're going to try and take it all back," he said, "but what you see here is all that we've got left."

The General turned to Jonah.

"We need pilots," he said. "You helped us out once, son. I'd be willing to forgive and forget an awful lot if you could do it again."

"And if we say no?" Naomi asked. "What then? You keep us as prisoners?"

Rhodes glanced at the two armed guards behind them. Then, with a nod, he waved them off. Brady and Hudson stepped instantly aside, clearing the way back to the runway.

"No," Rhodes said, "you're free to go."

Naomi looked back suspiciously.

"Just like that?"

"Just like that," Rhodes agreed. "But just remember, this time, there might not be much of a world left."

He stepped up close, looking Naomi in the eye.

"Not even the Valley."

Naomi blinked. She glanced at Jonah, and for the first time, she looked doubtful.

"We're in it for the species now, boys and girls," Rhodes said. He held up his fingers half-an-inch apart. "We're this close to going out forever."

He nodded towards the runway, where their Cessna sat waiting.

"There's your out," Rhodes said. "Make your choice. But you better be ready to live with it, because there aren't going to be any second chances this time."

Naomi's hand unconsciously stole to her belly. She hadn't even started to show yet. She turned to Jonah.

But before she could speak, a gunshot rang out.

Jonah actually felt the bullet whizz by his ear.

The shot struck Rhodes in the shoulder and he dropped to one knee with a guttural curse.

Hicks and the other two soldiers immediately pushed the General aside, their guns drawn, even as Jonah grabbed Naomi and pulled her to the ground, throwing himself in front of her.

There was a bellowing roar from the edge of the forest, and a crash as the perimeter fence was knocked down.

A massive carcharodont separated from the trees.

Astride its shoulders was a woman dressed in black and wielding an automatic machine gun.

At the monster-theropod's feet was a troop of sickle-claws. And among them were human handlers – armed Amazons with M-16s.

The woman on the giant carnosaur's back let loose a loud and piercing whistle and suddenly the brush broke apart, revealing half-a-dozen full-grown carcharodonts, all with machine gun-toting mounted riders.

There was an eruption of gunfire.

The lead carcharodont roared again.

Like horses breaking from the gate, they charged.

CHAPTER 56

Under a hail of gunfire and with the carnosaurs' roars echoing in their ears, Jonah grabbed Naomi's hand and they started running for cover. Hicks pulled the bleeding General along behind them, and they all ducked behind a nearby truck, as Brady and Hudson returned a layer of cover fire.

"Are you alright, General?" Hicks asked.

"I'm fine," Rhodes replied, chagrined. "I swear, I've bled more in the last couple of weeks than since the whole damned world ended."

He looked down at the blood running through his fingers as he covered the wound on the shoulder. Then he nodded to Hicks earnestly.

"Major, would you please go and shoot something."

"Aye, sir," Hicks responded, slapping a magazine into his rifle. He jumped up to rejoin the fight, even as several platoons of soldiers came running in their direction. The clatter of their gunfire joined the reverberating bellows of the big carcharodonts and the birdlike caterwauling of the sickle-claws.

Jonah snuck a peek over the hood of the truck.

Now as he looked closer, he could also see the familiar little lizards perched on the carnosaur-riders' shoulders.

"Oh *no*," he muttered.

Beside him, Naomi groaned.

"Oh, I *hate* those little bastards."

Rhodes popped up next to them.

"I told you things had gone bad again," he said.

Jonah glanced down at Naomi, and was tempted to remind her of the nice, cozy domicile they had left behind in Montana. Naomi saw the look on his face and shook her head.

"Don't even say it."

The initial battle was already not going well – the small-arms fire wasn't enough to take down a big carnosaur, and the carcharodonts simply charged unimpeded through the base. Jonah heard Hicks shouting for bigger guns, and several troops broke away from the fight, running for the armory.

But half-a-dozen sickle-claws split off as well, and the troops didn't make it thirty paces before the dromaeosaurs ran them down.

Mounted on the lead carcharodont, Christine grinned at the soldiers' screams.

She waved to Teresa on her own mount beside her, and pointed to the unguarded squadron of jet-fighters.

"Take them out," she said.

Teresa let out a loud whistle and the lizard on her shoulder squawked.

Two of the other big carcharodonts reared like horses, nearly throwing their riders, as they turned and charged directly into the first of the docked jets, knocking it off its wheels and igniting the grounded aircraft into flame.

There was a responding barrage of gunfire that went completely ignored by both big carnosaurs as they turned and barreled into a second jet-fighter. The grounds lit up in another explosion, sending shrapnel flying everywhere.

Then Jonah heard a screeching caw almost in his ear. He turned to find a trio of sickle-claws had discovered their hiding place behind the truck, and were already on top of them.

But before either Jonah or Rhodes could make a move, Naomi was on her feet, her pistol in hand, opening fire. She emptied her clip, dropping all three of the deadly clawed beasts, and kept firing until their sickle-taloned feet stopped kicking.

Rhodes looked up at her, his eyes wide.

"What?" she said. "No one frisked me."

A moment later, however, a larger shadow loomed as Teresa spotted them from the back of her carcharodont. She kicked her heels and the giant theropod started moving in their direction.

Naomi looked down at her empty pistol, glancing at Jonah and Rhodes.

"We'd better run," she said.

But then a single gunshot rang out, echoing from the perimeter of the compound.

Teresa jumped as the little lizard was capped off her shoulder like a tin can and went spinning onto the tarmac.

As if in response, her carcharodont-mount immediately started bucking, and Teresa now struggled to control the big carnosaur.

"Where did *that* come from?" Rhodes said, looking towards the fence.

The question was immediately answered as the surrounding brush suddenly erupted once again.

Hicks' voice rose above the others: "Holy *shit!*"

There was a mighty roar as a giant gorilla burst from the trees, beating its chest, even as it broke into a lumbering charge.

A moment later, there was a second crash, accompanied by twin, hooting bellows, as the enormous ape was followed by two more.

And at their feet, an old pickup squirreled between the giant hairy trio skidding out onto the tarmac – one man leaned out the passenger window, picking single shots with an M-16 while standing in the back, a brawny lunatic, unloading his own automatic rifle, firing widely, with explosive bursts in all directions.

Christine turned just as Caesar hit her carcharodont-mount broadside, knocking the big carnosaur completely off its feet, and she was thrown from its back. Christine hit the pavement hard, bouncing, rolling to a stop, and then lay still.

Caesar knew his way around carcharodonts – the saw-toothed jaws were dangerous weapons, capable of delivering a hemorrhaging wound that could take down a hundred-ton sauropod, but they lacked the bulldog jaw and neck strength of a tyrannosaur.

The big ape pounced on the downed theropod, grabbing its jaws in both powerful arms and *twisted* until he heard the sound of snapping vertebrae.

The little lizard that had been perched on Christine's shoulder squawked and bolted for the woods.

From the back of the pickup, Maverick drew a bead and blasted the little creature in one shot, sending it spinning in a splatter of blood.

He glanced down at Mark and Cameron in the cab of the truck.

"I *hate* those little bastards," he said.

Then he rose up and hollered to the military troops who watched wide-eyed, briefly stunned into inaction.

"It's those goddamned lizards controlling the others!" he shouted. "Shoot them first!"

Hicks nodded, turning to his troops.

"Do it!" he ordered.

Suddenly the barrage of return fire was aimed at the attacking riders instead of their giant mounts – which unfortunately for the riders left a very narrow margin for error, and two of them were hit almost immediately as the shots missed the lizards completely.

Once the scaly little rats were on the ground, however, Hicks' troops were able to pick them off like shooting gallery ducks.

And as the presence of the Ottos dwindled, the carcharodonts quickly began to lose focus.

Not the most intelligent of beasts to begin with, one of the big carnosaurs turned its head and snapped its own rider off its back like a sardine.

The sickle-claws, likewise, were suddenly less picky about their targets, turning on their handlers, and their hooting caws were now joined by the screams of the Coven.

Christine was just picking herself off the ground, only to discover herself confronted by four of the clawed beasts advancing on her.

Hicks, however, put a bullet through the first of them, just as it prepared to leap. With three consecutive shots, he took down the others in quick succession.

Christine promptly turned on him and opened fire with her M-16.

"*Jesus!*" Hicks blurted as he ducked aside and rolled.

Christine followed him in her sights, just as he turned and fired back. His shot caught her in the leg, and she fell to the pavement with a scream, clutching her thigh, dropping her rifle.

Cursing, she started to reach for her lost weapon, but Hicks was on her in an instant, hovering, with his own rifle up and aimed at her head.

"Seriously, lady," he said. "Don't move or I'll put the next one right through you."

Christine glared. Then she put her fingers to her lips and let out another piercing whistle.

It was an order to retreat.

The remaining Coven turned and broke for the fences. But now the sickle-claws were aggressively moving on them as well – simply being closer, they had become the easiest targets, and the Coven's screams mixed with the dromaeosaurs' birdlike yodels as they were torn apart.

Still struggling with her mount, Teresa finally managed to get the big carcharodont turned and moving for the trees, but now she was intercepted by Cornelius and Zaius, who tackled the giant carnosaur together.

Teresa was thrown clear. She rolled as she hit the concrete, and as the two giant apes pummeled her downed mount, she came up running and made a break for the woods.

Rosa, however, met her before she got there.

Parked just out of sight in Sabrina and Dawn's RV, just beyond the fence, with the two teens huddled behind her in the cab, Rosa was waiting with a purloined M-16 of her own. Stepping out of the rig, she caught Teresa with the butt-stock as she ran past, knocking her to the ground. Rosa pulled back the bolt, aiming the rifle at her face.

"Don't move," she said.

A second later, however, Rosa herself was struck from behind. Startled, she realized that Sabrina had tackled her, and was now struggling for her gun.

Lying on the ground, Teresa looked up, wide-eyed. Then she rose and bolted for the trees, disappearing into the brush.

Rosa had been taken by surprise and Sabrina was starting to gain the upper-hand when Dawn joined the fray.

"What are you doing?" Dawn demanded as she wrestled Sabrina away and the rifle went flying from both their hands.

Reaching into her pocket, Sabrina now produced a knife. With a wild yell, she stabbed out, slashing Dawn across the stomach with the tip of the blade.

Dawn screamed, pulling away. Sabrina stabbed forward again, but behind her, Rosa grabbed up a loose stick and brought it down hard on Sabrina's knife hand, sending the blade spinning. The teenager shrieked and Rosa pulled the stick back for a second swing.

Sabrina stared back at her venomously. Then she turned and ran, disappearing in the same direction as Teresa.

Rosa was tempted to follow her. Instead, she turned to tend to Dawn, who was crying, holding her bleeding stomach.

Within the compound, the three giant apes were finishing off the last of the carcharodonts and the battle was now turning into a route.

Once the big carnosaurs were all dead, the remaining sickle-claws turned and fled for the trees.

The last straggling members of the Coven also fled – they had taken more casualties from the carcharodonts and dromaeosaurs than they had the military.

Christine, however, was determined not to be taken easily.

As Hicks led her at gunpoint back to where ape-trio now gathered with Cameron's group, her eyes flashed with recognition as she spotted Mark.

Producing a pistol stashed in her pocket, she actually got a shot off before Hicks got his hand on it. The bullet sailed past Mark's shoulder.

Christine started to struggle, kicking and biting at Hicks, but Mark raised his own gun and shot her once in the head.

She dropped limply from Hicks' grip and spasmed lifelessly on the ground.

"That," Mark said, "was *way* too long in coming."

"Knew each other, did you?" Hicks asked.

"As crazy bitches go," Mark said, "this was one of the craziest."

"It seems to be catching," Rosa said, as she led Dawn beside her, still holding her bleeding stomach. "Sabrina did this."

Rosa explained briefly, indicating the woods where Sabrina had disappeared with the rest of the Coven.

"Are you alright?" Mark asked Dawn, who nodded mutely.

Mark frowned. They had left Luna and the others locked up but unguarded. Teresa and the rest of the surviving Coven were most likely headed back to their encampment. And Sabrina had evidently joined up.

He shook his head. Nothing to do about it but let them go, at least for now.

General Rhodes, holding his bleeding shoulder, was walking up with Jonah and Naomi. Brady and Hudson followed, and the rest of the surviving regiment of soldiers gathered behind them, dubiously regarding their unexpected benefactors.

"General Rhodes," Mark greeted. "It's been a long time."

Cameron and Maverick stepped up beside him.

"It's been a long time for us all," Cameron agreed.

Maverick offered a snappy salute.

"How ya been, sir?" he asked brightly.

Standing above him, Caesar imitated the salute. Cornelius and Zaius responded with twin grunts.

Rhodes regarded the unlikely entourage. Then with a shrug, he turned to Hicks.

"What's our damage?"

"We lost two planes, sir," Hicks replied. "And at least two-dozen men."

At that moment, the radio on Rhodes' belt barked alive.

Frowning, Rhodes pulled the radio from his waist and hit the switch.

"This is Rhodes," he said, "who is this?"

The voice on the other end was deep and full of good humor.

"General Rhodes," it said, "this is your opponent."

Rhodes frowned.

"Come again?"

This was met with a brief, rumbling chuckle.

"You may call me Draco. And I am currently residing at your former home."

Rhodes' frown deepened. He glanced at everyone gathered around.

"I got your number from your lovely former 'assistant', Michelle," Draco continued. "And I have been keeping tabs on the battle. It seems that our ground-team has dropped the ball. You are proving frustratingly hard to kill."

"You calling just to tell me that?" Rhodes replied. "What do you want?"

There was another baritone chuckle.

"We are at Endgame," Draco said. "What I want is your unconditional surrender. What I demand is for you to deliver yourself into my custody, here at the Mount, within the next twenty-four hours."

Rhodes glanced at the circle around him.

"And if I don't?"

"I have as collateral your entire population of civilians," Draco replied. "I also have access to all of your nuclear weapons. They are primed and ready to go."

"And," Draco added, "please tell all your friends there that I have Shanna here as well."

There was a murmur among the gathered crowd.

Rhodes sighed.

There was really no choice at all.

"Okay," he said. "You got it. I'll be there by midday tomorrow."

"Looking forward to it," Draco replied.

Rhodes clicked the radio off. He glanced at Hicks.

"Well," Rhodes said, "he's right. It's Endgame."

He looked around the gathered crowd.

"What do you say, people?"

Cameron glanced at Maverick, Mark and Rosa.

Standing above them, Caesar's hooting was returned by Cornelius and Dr. Zaius.

Naomi turned to Jonah who nodded back.

Rhodes smiled.

"Okay, then," he said. "We're agreed. Tomorrow we take our world back."

CHAPTER 57

Shanna and Leanne were reunited at the Mount.

Working in her lab late into the night, on what were hopefully some final calculations, Shanna had known who was coming even before Draco announced she had a visitor.

She still burst into tears at the sight of her daughter when Michelle brought her in.

Leanne had broken-up as well. Mother and daughter embraced tightly under Draco's scrutinizing eye.

"My my," he said. "How touching. The mother and child reunion."

Leanne cowered at Draco's deep rumbling voice, moving instinctively behind her mother, who stood between them like a shield.

Shanna felt Leanne's fear and it sparked an instinctive reaction of her own.

"You stay away from her," Shanna said, eyeing Draco with a mother's venom.

Draco bowed respectfully.

"Why dear mother," he said, "you wound me. Have I ever treated you with anything other than perfect consideration? The same would certainly apply to your beautiful daughter."

Draco's leathery lips pulled back in that snarling facsimile of a smile.

"Which," he said, leaning close, "would make her my sister."

Leanne shrank back.

Draco regarded them a moment longer. Then he turned abruptly away, showing his back to them. Shanna had noticed this to be his habit when he had something unpleasant to discuss – or when he was about to make an uncompromising demand.

Shanna didn't have to wonder what that might be.

"We find ourselves at a crossroads," he said. "Some rather unexpected events have unfolded. And several forces seem to be aligning."

Shanna nodded. She had felt it as well.

Draco turned to face her, now with no pretense of humor or charm. His words were flat and toneless, the charade of chivalry supplanted by the merciless eye of a predator.

The look in his eyes almost suggested that he was disturbed – something unexpected and unforeseen had been added to a carefully-calculated equation.

"The Food of the Gods must be completed," he said. "Our timetable has run out. I know you are close to a solution, and so I have decided it's time to test your chemical and see if it works."

He cocked one eye at Shanna meaningfully.

"You will test it," he said, "on my queen."

Draco leaned close.

"You see the faith I have in you?" he said. "I am willing to trust you with the life of my own mate."

The toothsome smile flashed again.

"Such faith," he said. "Not only because of your abilities, but because of that same loving heart that guides you. I know you will not willingly allow my queen to die. And if you do..."

Draco's smile widened.

"... if you fail, I will chew your daughter to pieces before your very eyes."

Leanne moaned softly.

After a long moment, Draco drew back, his smile softening, once again taking on the pretense of the polished gentleman.

"You see how much I trust you?" he said.

Shanna eyed him back squarely.

It was time, she thought.

"Alright then," she said. "Let's do it. It's ready."

CHAPTER 58

The rex queen had been indulging in a pleasant siesta and was a touch irritable at being disturbed. But when she saw her mate, and particularly Shanna beside him, her mood improved, much like a house dog perking at the sight of its family returning home.

There was also a new human female – one with a powerful aura of her own, reminiscent of Shanna herself. The queen regarded the newcomer curiously.

Of course, there was also that other human female with her entourage of sickle-claws and, worse, the annoying presence of Otto, perched upon her shoulder.

The queen detested those little lizards, and had even taken to eating a few of them before being admonished by her mate, but she would tolerate them in the presence of Shanna.

Shanna patted the queen's scaly hide, murmuring soothingly.

"Easy, girl," she whispered.

They led the queen to a prepared area up on the top deck. They couldn't test indoors, Shanna explained. With intravenous injection, growth would be quick.

Shanna glanced up at Draco.

"It will also hurt," she said.

Draco stared down at her, scrutinizing.

"I find it impossible to see into your mind," he said. "You have effectively learned to hide from me."

Draco paused, considering. He ran an affectionate claw along his mate's back.

"All I have, it seems, is trust." He gave Shanna one last lingering stare. "Very well," he said. "You may proceed."

The queen let out a low growl.

Shanna glanced over at Michelle with her sickle-clawed escort and Otto clinging to her shoulder.

"You might want to give us a little room," Shanna said. "She doesn't like you. And if this doesn't work, she might get a little temperamental."

Michelle paled slightly.

Draco nodded.

"Over by the stairwell, if you don't mind," he instructed.

Michelle immediately complied, retreating with Otto and her dromaeosaur-entourage as far as the space on the platform would allow.

Draco turned back to Shanna.

"If you please," he said.

Shanna produced a pneumatic needle. The chamber glowed green with the Food of the Gods. She paused a moment, glancing up at Draco, before pressing the needle up against the queen-rex' rough scaly skin, feeling for the pulse of a vein.

There was the soft *phut* of the air blast as she injected the chemical directly into the big female's bloodstream.

"Now," Shanna said, "we wait."

Draco turned his back.

And when he did so, Shanna pulled out a second needle – this one a simple hypodermic – and she quickly and silently administered this shot as well.

She immediately hid the second needle away, a silent prayer forming on her lips.

Leanne looked at her mother questioningly. Shanna shook her head imperceptibly.

The second shot was the counter-agent. It was the one that would keep the queen alive. The first shot had been nothing more or less than the Food of the Gods in its purist, distilled form.

In essence, the Food of the Gods was a super-stimulant, all the way down to the molecular-genetic level. Shanna had determined that it was this very quality, the stimulation of every fiber, of every neuron, within the affected creature's body, that brought upon madness and death.

It was rather like an extreme allergic reaction. And this also explained why the chemical's effect was transmissible – it was the body's own efforts to block the effect by creating similarly over-stimulated antibodies, and it was these antibodies that, in effect, transmitted the chemical itself when the tissue of the infected organism was consumed.

Shanna's approach was not to alter the Food of the Gods itself, but to moderate the side-effects by suppressing the body's reaction to it.

The counter-agent was more or less the equivalent of an anti-inflammatory.

A simple idea. But one has to be able to *have* the idea.

And if her plan was to work, Draco must not know why his queen had survived.

That was when Shanna caught Otto's eye, perched on Michelle's shoulder.

The little lizard was eyeing her curiously.

Had he seen her give the queen the second shot?

Shanna tried to look into his mind, but it was blocked as tightly as ever.

Then there came a rumble from the throat of the queen.

Sitting up, suddenly alert and aware, the big female began to growl.

Draco lay a comforting claw upon her shoulder.

The queen was growing.

It was a bizarre thing to see.

The queen stood, flexing her limbs, and with each movement seemed to morph and stretch into something larger. Shanna could actually hear the creak of expanding bones.

But in the queen's eyes, the telltale sign, the glow of green was absent.

Draco lay a restraining hand upon his mate's shoulder. Shanna had no doubt he was exerting mental dominance to keep her stable. She could feel Draco looking into his mate's mind for any spark that would begin the chain of madness.

There was none. Shanna could feel it as well.

Draco stepped back as the queen continued to grow.

He turned to Shanna.

"It would appear you have succeeded," he said, with a cautious note in his voice.

He nodded to Michelle, who stepped forward obediently.

"Please take our guests below," he said.

And then, almost to himself, he murmured, "The time has come."

Draco stood, looking down from the peak, staring pensively to the west.

Michelle, with her pack of sickle-claws and Otto perched on her shoulder, escorted Shanna and Leanne back down into the Mount.

Shanna glanced briefly at Otto, with his head perked, still looking at her oddly.

But his scaly lizard's face revealed nothing.

CHAPTER 59

It was the first glimmer of dawn when Lucas finally came to.

There was a moment of confusion and brief panic when he found he couldn't see – his scalp had bled and the drying blood had run over his eyelids like sleep crust. He picked the sticky, drying particles from his lashes until he was able to open his eyes and look around.

The embankment had not been a vertical drop, at least not immediately, but it had been quite steep enough for the truck to have rolled. Lucas had been tossed in the crash like a pair of dice, tumbling nearly fifty yards, until his descent had been halted by an outgrowth of rock.

As he peered through the smashed windshield, Lucas saw how lucky that had been. A couple more yards and the steep slope of the embankment broke off into a sheer cliff, maybe a thousand feet straight down. At the bottom, he could see the reflection of water, picking up the first snatches of dawn's early light.

The geography of the region had clearly changed. It was salty ocean air that breezed up from below.

Lucas started to move and was greeted with pain in every direction. He flexed and stretched each limb experimentally, looking for the broken bones he was certain *had* to be there. All appendages, however, seemed to be in working order.

He retrieved his bow from the backseat and then tried the door, but found it crushed shut. Cautiously, he instead climbed out through the broken window.

The embankment looked up onto the Mount, which was now framed by the early morning sunlight – a Dark Tower lit from within, like a burning pier in a forest of shadows.

Leanne was alive. Lucas knew it. He had heard her scream as she was taken.

And besides... he could *feel* it.

He didn't know how, but neither did he question.

It was her shine.

Lucas turned and kicked at the bumper to the truck. The precarious balance was compromised and the tough old rig rolled the rest of the way over the ledge.

There was a long silence followed by a satisfyingly loud crash, and then a flash of light from below as the truck ignited and exploded.

It was a small gesture, really, but Lucas felt better. It psyched him up

– the equivalent of putting on war-paint. It pushed the fear inside him to the back recesses of his mind.

And with that, he began to pick his way up the embankment.

He could feel her – somewhere up on the mountain.

"Hang in there, Leanne," he said. "Here I come."

CHAPTER 60

Shanna's voice was a soft whisper.

"They're coming," she said.

Michelle had led them below to the administration-level, leaving them in Shriver's laboratory. The front wall, which had once been outfitted with a locking door, had been torn away – part of it had fallen in the collapse when Draco had initially taken over the Mount, but the rest had been cleared out to allow his dinosaurian proportions access to the lab.

It wasn't as if a locked door was necessary anyway. Six sickle-claws lay just outside, standing guard, and an Otto sat on a console above them, like Poe's raven on the bust of Pallas, watching them like a security cam.

The sickle-claws were reclined and seemingly relaxed, but their beady, blinking eyes never wavered. Leanne could see they were hair-triggered and ready at the drop of a hat.

But Shanna seemed almost at peace.

Leanne looked at her mother questioningly.

Shanna had a distant, serene expression on her face as if listening to a tune her daughter couldn't hear. Leanne remembered her brief moment of awakening out on the road but now found herself stymied.

"Who's coming?" Leanne asked, with all the impatience of a child wanting to be grown-up. "Mother? Who's coming? Dad?"

Leanne swallowed anxiously.

"Lucas?"

Leanne almost couldn't say his name, although she had screamed it when she had seen their truck go over the edge of the ravine.

She had been sure she had lost him then, yet somehow she knew he wasn't dead.

Shanna smiled.

"Oh yes," she said. "Lucas is coming. I don't even have to be an empath to know that."

Shanna touched her daughter's hair gently.

"He loves you, Leanne."

Leanne started a little at the thought, which was, of course, something that should have been perfectly obvious all along.

"Think of what he's already gone through for you," Shanna said, smiling softly. "A man doesn't do all that just because he *likes* you. I was raised on a desert island, and I still know that.

"But," she continued with a sigh, "I suppose, in a way, you were too."

"Did Dad do things like that over you?" Leanne asked interestedly.

Shanna smiled.

"On KT-day, your father swung on a rope ladder out of a helicopter to grab me off of a two-thousand foot tower," she said.

The two of them laughed together.

"Your father's coming too," Shanna said. "But it's more than just them." She looked down at her daughter. "It's *everything*."

Leanne shut her eyes and tried to feel what her mother felt. She got nothing – not even the sensation she'd experienced in the forest.

"They're out there," Shanna said, shutting her eyes, as if listening. "Draco brought you and I together, and that was his mistake. Because together, we *shine*. And what's coming this way? He didn't prepare for this at all."

Shanna reached out and took her daughter's hand.

"You are a powerful light, Leanne."

"I can't feel *anything*," Leanne replied in frustration.

"Yes you can," Shanna told her. "A great gathering."

"I'm *trying!*"

"Yes," Shanna said. "You always did. That's *your* mistake."

The hand on her daughter's wrist became a caress.

"Stop trying so hard."

Leanne shut her eyes, trying to relax, but was aware only of the darkness behind her closed lids.

In that moment, she became certain she was a dead battery – an empathic dud. All her life, she'd been trying to live up to the ideal that had been set for her – to live up to her mother's example. And in that moment, her frustration boiling over, she at last gave up.

And in that moment, it all came to her – a torrent of sensation, pouring in like a flood.

"Oh my God," she whispered. "Mother...?"

Her mother's eyes opened and found Leanne's own.

Shanna nodded.

Together, they sensed the magnitude of the coming conflict – a battle for possession of the Earth itself – a contest to determine humanity's very right to exist.

Tears began to roll from Leanne's eyes. She looked at her mother, who was sitting there so serenely, as if she'd seen it all before.

"This isn't over us, is it?" Leanne asked.

Shanna shook her head.

"No," she said. "It never is. It's much more than that. This is happening because it's time. We could neither force it, nor prevent it."

Her hand squeezed her daughter's again.

"We're not so special really," Shanna said. "We just try to help where we can."

The two of them, mother and daughter, settled down to wait.

CHAPTER 61

Rhodes arrived at the Mount by chopper just after noon.

It was the first time he had flown in over twenty years, and he guessed it would also be his last.

As he looked down on the terrain below, he saw the gathering of giants.

Even from his vantage in the air, it went on as far as the eye could see. He had never seen anything like this – not concentrated in these numbers, not even on KT-day. They were coming from every direction – herd beasts walked in tandem with snarling carnosaurs.

And from the west, came the tyrannosaurs.

In Rhodes' experience, that was always the point where the fuse was lit. For whatever reason, the tyrant-dinosaurs just didn't seem to work and play well with all the others.

It was ironic, Rhodes thought, because that made them allies of sorts – the two most dangerous land-predators that ever evolved.

The Mount itself, however, was surrounded by the largest beasts of all. A regiment of giant sauropods was positioned around the mountain as a front-line perimeter guard, even as the rest of the titan-horde advanced towards them in a steady procession.

So far, the indomitable behemoths who guarded the Mount regarded the gathering legions impassively – in fact, all factions seemed to be operating on autopilot, almost in a trance, perhaps waiting for the first spark of aggression.

Rhodes guessed that with the arrival of the tyrannosaurs, that would not be long in coming.

As he approached the Mount, Rhodes also saw a cloud of swarming pterosaurs, and circling among them were flocks of those giant eagles that seemed to have recently encroached on the pterosaurs' aerial domain.

It was long-known that pterosaurs aggressively went after choppers. But not today. As Rhodes drew near, the flock of flying dragons – pterosaurs and giant raptors alike – actually parted, and then flew beside him in formation, almost like an escort.

Very likely, that's exactly what it was.

And standing on the precipice of the tower, overseeing it all, was Draco.

The 'Dragon Lord' stood looking down at the gathered armies in the canyons below, and seemed to pay no attention as Rhodes circled overhead and brought his chopper in, landing on the helipad atop the top-deck of the Mount.

Michelle was waiting on the tarmac, surrounded by a pack of sickle-claws. Rhodes also saw one of those damned parrot-talking lizards sitting perched upon her shoulder.

Rhodes nodded to his former paramour as he shut down the rotors and climbed out of the chopper.

"General," Michelle acknowledged, nodding back. "He's been waiting for you."

Michelle turned, and with the sickle-claws at her heel like a pack of dogs, she led him across the deck where her new lord waited.

Rhodes walked beside her, saying nothing. Michelle had been a consort of sorts for a long time, yet he found himself oddly unbothered by her utter and complete betrayal. If asked, he would have expected nothing less from her – Sally had certainly said as much many times over the years.

He felt a brief pang at the thought of Sally. He wondered if she was still alive.

Rhodes had not mentioned Sally to Mark, and even now, he was not sure why. Paternal jealousy? Or perhaps shame or guilt at having left her behind, no matter how involuntary on his part that might have been.

But for now, he pushed the thought of her completely out of his mind. He had his own job to do and he couldn't allow distractions.

Draco stood at the precipice as Rhodes and Michelle walked up behind him. His posture was one of brooding.

Rhodes could relate. He had done as much himself, on many a day, staring out from the window of his office overlooking the New Gulf – a king taking the weight of the world.

As Michelle brought Rhodes to stand in his presence, Draco spared a glance over his shoulder.

"Ah," he said. "General. Right on time. I will take this as your formal surrender."

Draco appeared preoccupied.

"Please forgive my lack of pageantry," he said. "As it turns out, I am currently pressed for time."

Now he turned, rearing to his full height, staring down.

Rhodes maintained his straight, military posture, meeting Draco's eye, even as, beside him, he was aware of a slight involuntary fade from Michelle and a brief rustling from her entourage of sickle-claws.

"As it turns out," Draco said, "you are no longer my primary concern."

As he spoke, he waved his hand, indicating the surrounding canyons and the gathered legions of beasts below.

Draco leaned forward, and for a moment, Rhodes thought he might simply crush him like a bug and be done with it.

He hoped not – that would really screw up their plans.

But instead, Draco nodded to Michelle.

"Take him down to the detention-level," he said. He glanced at Rhodes briefly. "I will deal with you formally, when I have more time."

And with that, Draco turned dismissively back to the drop-off, looking out on the bestial armies congregating at the base of his Mount.

"Let's go, General," Michelle said, putting a hand on his shoulder, glancing back at Draco, as if disturbed.

On her shoulder, Otto chittered.

CHAPTER 62

There were no battle lines being drawn – it could not even properly be said that there were sides to be taken.

Beyond the circle of infected sauropod giants that guarded the Tower, the beasts that gathered in the canyons below were a random milling crowd, each of them following one of two separate stars.

Most of the assembled giants had not even the cognitive awareness to understand what had drawn them – it was the instinctual reaction of a moth to flame.

But Big Red knew well enough why he was there.

He also understood in a dim way what had drawn the others.

On one hand, there was the combined presence of Shanna and Leanne.

And then there was the other, darker presence – the one that seemed to extinguish all light.

Both together were a beacon for the gathered hordes.

Yet, excepting the tight protective circle of sauropod guards surrounding the Mount, Draco, himself, appeared to have so far made no effort to influence any of the congregated masses either way.

On the other hand, Big Red could sense that slight, subtle, psychic stench of Otto as well.

As always, if there was manipulation to be found, that was where it would be. And if that was the case, that meant that nearly every single creature around him was a functional enemy.

The great tyrannosaur did not think about such things, so much as was simply aware.

But he also knew forces were aligning behind *him* as well.

The packs of *T. rex* had followed from the Valley – Trix' female pack, Rudy and Junior and the rest of the gang of rogue males, as well as Big Red's own juvenile and adolescent offspring.

But the tyrant-beasts had come from far and beyond just the Valley – and not just the *T. rex* – it seemed that every tyrannosaur – every gorgosaur, albertosaur, or tarbosaur – from the entirety of the surrounding regions had followed as well.

And like every other beast on the mountain, they had all grown into giants, their eyes glowing green with the fire of the Food of the Gods.

This bloom had spread far and wide.

Again, Big Red did not question how this could have happened, or how every single beast could have possibly been infected so quickly, over such a wide range – he was simply aware, and accepted.

For Big Red, his own goal was in sight.

The Mount was just ahead.

Both Shanna and Leanne lay somewhere inside.

So now, without ceremony, Big Red began to move forward.

The pack of tyrannosaurs, a regiment all their own, began to move with him.

Around them, the other beasts responded.

No manipulation was needed here, just instinctual response. The chemical madness building within them did the rest.

The ceratopsians reacted first – the equal and opposite reaction to the advance of the *T. rex* – shaking their shields and horns, the deadliest anti-tyrannosaur weaponry ever evolved.

Big Red's jaws split in an echoing roar. Junior and Rudy's bellows joined him.

Like falling dominoes, the challenge also activated the natural response from the rival predators – the snarling howls of the carnosaurs rose in kind.

And now, the sauropods surrounding the Mount suddenly seemed to snap out of their apathetic trance – they reared upright like monolithic stallions, bringing their massive hooves smashing into the ground.

The tundra began to shake.

Territorial instinct fed predatory savagery, with all of it inflamed into a brush-fire by the Food of the Gods.

And somewhere amid it all, Big Red could still sense that foul psychic-stench, egging it on.

But Big Red needed no further incentive.

The great red rex saw his goal before him, and every beast in the world was in his way.

The first of the ceratopsians lowered their shields.

His mouth agape, Big Red charged.

Rudy and Junior followed.

The packs of tyrannosaurs moved in behind.

And now the world itself seemed to shake as the battle erupted all over the entire surrounding countryside.

CHAPTER 63

Maelstrom was five miles straight ahead.

"Okay, people," Hicks said, "we're coming up on our target."

The four F-16s dropped below the cloud cover and the nuclear base came into view.

Jonah had flown exactly one jet fighter in his life – it had scared the hell out of him then – *and,* in point of fact, he had crashed and was nearly killed.

Yet, here he was again.

Hicks banked, leading them in. His wingman, Biggs, followed in formation.

Jonah looked over to his own wingman – Naomi gave him a thumbs-up from her own fighter as she took the lead, following the other two down. Jonah took a breath, keeping on her tail.

Naomi had taken to flying as naturally as a bird, and she handled the jet as casually as the old Cessna bush plane in which he'd taught her to fly.

Jonah found himself in awe of her yet again.

The truth was, she had amazed him every single day of his life, ever since they'd first met on KT-day, so long ago.

Nineteen years, and she still dazzled him – with her ability, her courage. He was often actually jealous of her. And he was yet again.

That was the difference between them, he thought – she was simply a higher-end-model human being. An eleven on a scale of one-to-ten. She was off the charts.

Even now, he couldn't believe she was going to be the mother of his child.

Although, he knew perfectly well, if not for the end of the world, that would have never happened.

Still, she *had* made him earn his keep.

And somehow he had risen to it. Something about her brought out the best possible version of himself that nature would allow.

Unfortunately, the thing about living post-Apocalypse was that you didn't get to just rest on your laurels.

Today, he had to earn it all once again.

The attack on the Maelstrom base had been the hardest part of the plan to sell to Rhodes. But the General had made the best case for it himself.

Draco had taken over the base. That meant he had control over their nuclear assets, and had already openly threatened to use them.

"A very *credible* threat," Rhodes had emphasized.

The only possible option was the obvious one. Major Hicks was the one who voiced it.

"Then we have to destroy the base," Hicks said.

Rhodes had frowned.

"That takes away our ability to deal with blooms," he objected.

"That's what Shriver was telling us for almost twenty years," Hicks replied. "Maybe it's time we stopped listening."

Hicks shook his head.

"Either way, it's all about priorities."

He was right of course, and Rhodes knew it. In the end, there was no choice.

And so, here they were.

As they dropped below the cloud cover, Hicks' voice sparked static in their headsets.

"We're sixty seconds from our target, gentlemen and lady," he said. "With any luck, this will be short and sweet. In and out."

Jonah, however, could already see that was not meant to be.

There was a battalion of giant beasts surrounding the base, but those were not the problem.

Their true obstacle was the storm cloud that seemed to hover in the sky above.

And as they drew nearer, coming in at super-sonic speed, they could clearly see that cloud was alive.

The sky was full of circling pterosaurs – infected giants.

Jonah groaned.

At their approach, the cloud began to break apart, and the first of the flying dragons veered in their direction.

Jonah glanced to Naomi on his wing.

"It looks like they knew we were coming," he said into his headset.

"Ya think?" Naomi replied.

Not a trace of fear in her, Jonah thought. A higher-end-model.

An eleven.

He would be in awe of her until the end. He himself was terrified.

Hicks' voice barked alive in their ears.

"Okay, people," he said. "Follow me in.

CHAPTER 64

Lucas had been traveling along the edge of the cliff, overlooking the New Gulf, as he approached the base of the Mount, and it was still early morning when he'd first begun his ascent up the canyon wall.

The climb had been suitably treacherous. The volcanic rock allowed for plenty of hand-holds, but years of seismic upheaval and the weathering of saltwater had left cracks. More than once, he'd grabbed for his next handhold only to have the rocks crumble and break away.

He had nearly fallen the first time, and then had made the mistake of looking over his shoulder as he caught his grip, watching the handful of rubble as it tumbled down the sheer cliff into the inland sea.

It was better than a thousand feet from the base of the mountain where he'd started, to the gulf below, and he had already scaled five-hundred feet beyond that.

When the rumbling started, threatening to shake him from his perch, at first, he thought it was his own nerves finally getting the best of him. Then he realized it was the mountain itself. Fragile rock began breaking away and tumbling past, sending sharp pieces of shrapnel and blinding dust past his unguarded face.

But it was no earthquake, Lucas realized, because the sound of thunder had now joined the rumble in the earth – thunder that was not thunder.

It was the roar of the beasts.

His path along the edge of the cliff had detoured him away from the westward canyons, but before he'd started his ascent, he had seen the gathering at the base of the Mount – a whole host of infected giants – armies of titans assembled for war – the glowing green of madness shining in every one of their eyes.

Big Red was somewhere among them.

Now, clinging to his perch as the mountain began to tremble, he knew what it must be.

As the rock wall threatened to simply crumble away, Lucas tried to imagine the conflict erupting just on the other side of the mountain.

Even now, in the gulf below, the water began to churn, as debris from the Mount broke away in avalanches, collapsing into the surf.

And as the steady roll of the waves began to break, Lucas could also see gigantic shapes breaking the surface – the fins of giant sharks and the massive jaws of giant, crocodile-toothed marine reptiles.

But now Lucas' own goal was drawing near.

Leanne was somewhere up above.

He could *feel* her, as if someone had lit a beacon in his head.

Lucas' face was cut and bloody from shards of falling rock, and the dust left him nearly blind, but he continued to climb.

CHAPTER 65

Draco stood on the top deck of the tower, watching as the battle erupted beneath him.

As far as the human contingent went, everything had played out exactly as he had anticipated. For supposedly sentient beings, they were such predicable and programmable creatures.

But as he looked out on the gathered legions below...?

This was not as he had planned.

It was as if every beast in the entire region had been infected. Draco could not put a number to them, but from his vantage on the Mount, overlooking the totality of the surrounding territory, there seemed to be no end.

It was true that he had been deliberately sprouting blooms, but they had been controlled outbreaks – tactical strikes – just enough to strain the humans' resources and gauge their responses. And while a bit of a bleed should be expected, this was more than should have reasonably been the case. A *lot* more.

Moreover, his operations had been predominately to the east.

Draco frowned.

He shut his eyes, reaching out his mind, seeing the world through every creature under his sway.

It was a matter of focus, but if he concentrated, he could look through their eyes.

Just as he had seen the failed coupe by his human followers at the air base, just as he saw the squadron of planes approaching Maelstrom, he now saw the battle through the gathered armies of beasts.

But now he was searching for a blank spot – something he *couldn't* see.

Perhaps something that might be hiding from him.

At last, he found it.

And it explained *everything*.

"Otto," he said aloud.

Draco's lips pulled back, grinding saber-spiked teeth.

That little *bastard*.

For a moment, Draco actually felt chagrined – the idea that a betrayal of this magnitude could have slipped by him.

But he supposed it was his own arrogance that was to blame. His strategy was based upon a flawed presumption – he had believed himself in total control and now he had discovered the inherent unpredictability of chaos.

He looked out on the infected legions below.

Draco sighed.

Clearly, the damage had already been done.

There was nothing for it but to adapt and move on.

The bulk of his plan was already in place. Truth to tell, he had only needed the little lizards for small details and purposes of convenience.

Within the silos at Maelstrom, the nuclear launch codes had already been prepared – mostly as a fail-safe, because he had not actually believed they would be necessary. But neither had he been bluffing – he had ICBMs targeted at a number of locations – most importantly, at the Valley itself. And since General Rhodes had so conveniently programmed the launch command to be deliverable from his own desk, all he really needed to do was push a button.

The codes and coordinates, Draco had set personally. There were, however, a few pesky details – ironically, among the most simple.

He was still working with human-based technology, which meant human-sized buttons. He needed a finger smaller than his own four-foot talon to push that button.

And, of course, the silos at Maelstrom needed to be opened manually on-site.

Details.

Adapt and overcome.

Draco shut his eyes and began to concentrate, flexing his mind.

Four-hundred miles to the north, the Ottos waiting at the Maelstrom site suddenly stiffened and dropped from their posts, twitching on the floor as blood vessels from a mass embolism burst in their brains.

Beside them, their sickle-clawed former-guards popped up alertly.

Their dexterous claws ran over the controls, finding the proper buttons, guided by Draco's own eye.

The silo containing the missile aimed at the Valley slowly slid open.

And down below, within the Mount itself, the little lizards who had been waiting to initiate the launch also dropped to the floor, quivering, their eyes rolled back in their heads.

And likewise, their own sickle-clawed entourage took up their posts.

The button was pushed.

Four-hundred miles north, the missile's code was activated, and the countdown to launch began.

Draco opened his eyes. He could sense Otto's presence being erased like computer memory throughout the Mount as they dropped dead all over the facility.

It was not every one of them – not yet, anyway. After all, he had no specific headcount as to how many of them there actually were, and the little vermin were infiltrated throughout the site like rats. But he would deal with the remainder of them when he had time.

For now, he turned to the battle below.

In his hand, he held a pneumatic needle filled with the Food of the Gods.

This was a moment he had been waiting for a long time.

He injected the glowing green chemical into his own arm.

There was a rush as he felt the energy surge through his system like a highball.

Shanna was right – it *hurt*.

Draco's jaws parted in a near-involuntary roar.

And unbeknownst to him, his eyes began to glow emerald green.

CHAPTER 66

Big Red had battled his way through the horde to the base of the Mount.

His hide was gouged and gored from the horns of Triceratops, and slashed and torn from the jaws and claws of giant carcharodonts, but nothing had slowed his relentless advance.

There were no fronts or factions in this war – once the fuse was lit, the congested masses of behemoths simply went at each other's throats, lashing out at whatever target was closest – the herd beasts locked horns and spikes with each other, as if in territorial battles, even as they charged carnosaurs and tyrannosaurs alike.

Universal aggression ignited across the entire landscape, whether provoked by dominance, or predatory and defensive instinct, all of it exacerbated by the corrosive influence of the Food of the Gods.

There was also that psychic-sulfur stench egging the violence on.

The *T. rex* actually only comprised a small percentage of the battle, but Big Red's tyrannosaur-pack cut a swath through the warring beasts as they battled their way through to the base of the Mount, leaving the bloodied, slaughtered remains of both carnosaur and herd-beast alike strewn in their wake.

Their effort had not been without cost. Junior had been badly gored by the horns of several ceratopsians and Rudy was missing an entire forearm, severed by the razor-toothed jaws of a big carcharodont. They had also lost two of the juvenile females. But now, as the rex-pack approached the sauropod guard, the other beasts fell back.

None had yet directly challenged the long-necked titans that surrounded the Mount itself, but the mountain's base was already littered with the smashed corpses of those beasts who had tarried too close.

Big Red, however, was remembering the giant brachiosaur that had rampaged through the Valley – the beast that had killed both Trix and Sue – his mother and his mate.

The big tyrannosaur did not think – he hadn't yet evolved for it – but his primitive brain retained imagery and association.

It was also possible that the influence of Shanna activated precursors of more advanced cognitive traits as well, for as he approached the giant titanosaurs, Big Red felt stirrings of personal anger.

The sauropods had no such thoughts – their tiny brains operated on stimulus and response and nothing else. As Big Red approached, they perceived a threat, and so they responded accordingly, rearing up, lashing out with their pile-driver-like forelimbs. As always, their defense was their sheer size – an advantage that had served their kind well for a hundred million years.

But it was also why their line had not lasted in tyrannosaur territory. In the predator/prey arms race, faced with the most advanced super-predator nature had ever produced, they were simply too big, cumbersome, and slow.

The impact rattled the entire battlefield as the first of the titanosaurs missed its strike, instead crashing both forefeet into the tundra, and before the massive beast could rear up a second time, Big Red had already moved in. The tyrannosaur's powerful jaws clamped onto the base of the giant sauropod's long neck, striking with power, sinking deep into the thick muscles just above the collarbone.

The giant titanosaur bellowed, its tiny brain belatedly recognizing pain, as it attempted to push forward with brute force. But Big Red's teeth cleaved through the heavy muscle all the way to the jugular, and with a powerful wrench, he bit completely through the creature's esophagus.

There was a wet-sounding gasp and the giant sauropod staggered, falling back on its heels, tripping under its own weight.

The earth shook as the first of the Mount's guardians fell.

Now the other sauropods reared, lashing out with their piston-feet and whipping tails at the usurper. Big Red, however, was not alone.

Rudy and Junior hit the first of them together, going for their legs like wolves attacking an elk, severing tendons, bringing the larger beasts down to the ground.

The rest of the rex-pack moved in, and now the sauropods started to panic. Their tight circle around the Mount began to break apart as the giant long-necks lashed out mindlessly in every direction.

Around them, the rest of the beasts quickly gave ground as the sauropods rampaged in among them, with the tyrannosaur-pack dogging at their heels.

Big Red now stood at the base of the unguarded mountain.

With his path now open before him, he erupted with a mighty challenging roar that briefly silenced the battle around him.

The other creatures faded back – even the sauropods – allowing the rex-king passage.

But as he advanced on the Mount, Big Red's challenge was met with an answering roar.

On the peak just above, at the lowest crest of the Mount, stood

Draco's mate.

The rex queen was the only beast on the mountain whose eyes were absent the green glow of chemical-induced madness, but the battle-lust had risen in her nonetheless – natural instinct was quite enough – defense of her territory – defense of her mate.

Not to mention the approach of an aggressive male.

Without hesitation, the queen advanced down the slope. In rex society, female pack-leaders were traditionally preternaturally aggressive towards males. Even a full-grown rogue only approached the female packs during mating season.

Circumstances, however, were not ordinary. The chemical flowing through Big Red's veins was just beginning to spark his simple brain into madness.

Roaring with the force of a hurricane, the giant tyrannosaur charged.

The queen met his attack head-on, her own jaws agape, but Big Red, the rogue male, was specifically built for inter-species conflict. Constructed for battling other males and rival hunters, his heavy brow was lined with bone. And today, he treated the big female accordingly, striking a heavy blow with the brunt of his skull, and his greater weight knocked her to the ground. Within moments, he was kicking and stomping the queen into submission.

He did not, however, bite with his lethal jaws – and perhaps the presence of Shanna intervened once again to save the queen's life. *T. rex* often killed each other in inter-species battles, but on this occasion, despite the chemical blood-lust coursing through his system, once the big female had lapsed into unconsciousness, Big Red left her alone.

Then he turned from the fallen queen to face his true goal.

Big Red could feel Shanna waiting in the Mount ahead. And beside her, glowing as brightly as Shanna herself, was Leanne.

And somewhere on the air, perhaps he also caught the scent of Lucas as well.

For all of it together, he was ready to raze the mountain itself to the ground.

His challenging roar echoed for miles.

And once again, it was answered.

Big Red's head craned up to the ridge just above.

Now the mighty tyrannosaur almost seemed to smile.

At last, he beheld his true rival.

Draco stood, framed against the midday sun.

The Dragon Lord reared to his full, awesome height, which was now over two-hundred feet and still growing. His jaws split with a roar every bit as powerful and mighty as Big Red's own.

At the sound, the rest of the warring beasts paused.

For a split second, the world itself seemed to watch and wait.

Then, with his jaws agape, Big Red charged.

Draco thundered down the mountain to meet him.

Their footsteps shook the earth.

And when Big Red and Draco came together, it was like a clash of continents – an impact that would shatter the foundations of the entire world.

CHAPTER 67

Rhodes sat alone in his cell.

Michelle sat watching him, Otto perched on her shoulder and two sickle-claws curled at her feet.

"Where are the other prisoners?" Rhodes asked. "Your 'Dragon Lord' said the civilians were still alive."

Michelle said nothing.

Rhodes shook his head.

"What's the matter? Are you a dog who can't speak unless your master commands it?"

Michelle's eyes narrowed.

"Don't try that," she said. "The civilians are being kept in the commons."

She tipped her head.

"Your soldiers are dead," she said.

Rhodes nodded. He had figured as much.

Now that he was here, he doubted the civilians would be needed much longer either.

He again wondered about Sally. He almost asked. But he figured if she *was* still alive, the worst thing he could do for her would be to let them know he cared.

Instead, he eyed Michelle directly, the way he had when he'd first questioned her over the Coven sisterhood's activities on the Mount so many years before.

"It must have been hard," Rhodes said, "holding in all that hate for so long."

Michelle smiled thinly.

"You have no idea," she said.

"But being on a leash suits you, does it?"

Rhodes shook his head.

"How very submissive of you," he said. "But that was always what you liked, though, wasn't it?"

He eyed her.

"And I would know, wouldn't I?" Rhodes shrugged. "I guess a bigger alpha finally came along"

Michelle frowned.

"I told you. Don't try that. You can't bait me."

Rhodes smiled benignly.

"Just clearing the air," he said. "But you're a fool if you think you won't be put down like a dog with all the rest of us," Rhodes continued. "But I guess that's what you are."

"You're the one in a cage," Michelle replied.

"And soon to be put down, I'm sure," Rhodes agreed.

He smiled.

"It is a far, far better thing I do, than I have ever done," he quoted. "And a far, far better place I go, than I have ever known."

He eyed her.

"I'm not afraid," Rhodes said. "What about you, Michelle?"

Michelle stared back, not answering.

In the momentary silence, they heard the first rumbles.

The sickle-claws popped their heads up.

"How about it, Michelle?" Rhodes said again. "Are you afraid?"

Michelle glared.

Around them, the Mount trembled again.

Rhodes thought of the beasts gathered outside – armies of infected giants that had seemed to be waiting. It sounded like they weren't waiting any longer.

He could only imagine what was going on out there.

Rhodes regarded Michelle sitting there – a sell-out to the serpent, with a lizard on her shoulder and a pair of dragons curled at her feet – and he was surprised to find himself feeling rather sorry for her.

She really was quite a beautiful woman, he thought – intelligent and capable – and dangerous in the way of a predator. That was always one of the things he'd admired about her – she was an alley-cat.

An amoral alley-cat.

Sally had been so right.

"It doesn't have to be like this, Michelle," he said.

Michelle stood, even as the rumbling in the walls began to grow louder. With a purposeful look in her eyes, she moved towards his cell.

Rhodes would never know exactly what she had in mind, for in the next moment, the lizard perched on her shoulder suddenly squawked as if in pain.

With a strangled cry, it toppled to the ground, spasming and kicking, until it finally stiffened and lay still.

And at that same moment, the two sickle-claws suddenly sprang to their feet.

Rhodes realized what was about to happen an instant before Michelle did. He actually made a move towards the bars of his cell, as if he could stop it.

The sickle-claws tore into her like a pair of tigers.

Michelle screamed.

It was perhaps merciful that there were two of them, because it only took a few seconds before she was ripped apart like a rag doll.

Rhodes saw her eyes as they faded and went blank.

Then the sickle-claws turned to him.

Rhodes fell back as they launched themselves at the cage, snarling, reaching through the bars, trying to squeeze their way through.

The cell was empty besides the bunks bolted to the wall – there was not even a chair – nothing to use as a weapon.

But then the rumbling that shook the complex was suddenly punctuated by a heavier impact directly against the walls of the detention center.

The sickle-claws turned as the wall behind them crashed in and Caesar smashed his way into the cell-block. Cornelius and Zaius were right on his heels.

With warbling shrieks, the clawed dromaeosaurs attacked, only to be swatted down and crushed like sparrows.

A moment later, a squadron of soldiers filed in behind the giant apes.

Mark was in the lead. Hudson was right behind.

Rhodes nodded.

"Your timing couldn't have been better, gentlemen."

"Those back tunnels were a little crowded in spots," Mark replied, nodding to Caesar, "but we made it through."

He glanced down at the tattered remains of Michelle on the floor – yet another face he recognized from long ago. Mark shook his head. It seemed a lot of karma was coming due these days.

Caesar grunted as he pulled the cell doors loose.

Mark handed Rhodes his radio. The General clicked the switch.

"Okay," he said, "bring them in."

Cameron's voice sparked static on the other end.

"You got it, sir," he said.

Rhodes nodded to Mark as he led them out of the cell block into the stairwell, which was just barely wide enough to accommodate the three giant apes. He pointed to the lower floors below.

"The civilians are in the commons," Rhodes said. "You need to get them to the hangar. The choppers should be landing there within minutes. You're going to need to split up.

He turned to Hudson.

"Your squad," he said, "secures the hangar."

He pointed to Cornelius and Zaius.

"You two go with them."

The pair of big apes grunted.

Rhodes turned to Mark and Caesar.

"You get to the commons."

Mark nodded. Caesar raised his hairy arm in an affirmative salute.

"What about you?" Mark asked.

Rhodes looked at Hudson.

"Do you have something for me?"

Hudson handed over a duffle bag. Rhodes looked inside and nodded. He held up the contents – timed seismic charges.

"You get everybody out," Rhodes said. "I'm going to bring this place down."

As he spoke, the Mount rumbled again. Rocks began falling from the walls and ceiling.

"Unless the monsters beat me to it, that is," he said. "Let's hurry, gentlemen. We haven't got much time."

CHAPTER 68

Down in the commons, Kathryn was already dead.

Tom had seen the little lizard on her shoulder spasm and drop, twitching to the floor, and then the sickle-claws that had been standing at her side like such disciplined guard-dogs promptly ripped her to pieces.

It had only taken a few seconds. She barely had time to scream.

And Tom had a good idea what came next.

With blood still dripping from their jaws and talons, the clawed devils turned and came sprinting for the rest of them.

"Get back!" Tom yelled, grabbing Kristie and Sally as the crowd surged for the daycare center and its locking doors.

But the sickle-claws were upon them too quickly. There were at least a dozen of them and they leaped into the crowd, claws flailing.

Birdlike hooting mixed with human screams.

As the crowd bottle-necked at the entrance to the daycare facility, Tom grabbed the fire hose off the wall. He cranked the pressure to maximum, and turned the water-stream onto their attackers, knocking them off their feet and blasting them back.

"Hurry!" he shouted over his shoulder.

But now the entire cavern was beginning to shake.

The integrity of the Caverns' interior-support architecture had already been compromised and it wasn't long before pieces of rubble began breaking loose from the walls and ceiling.

Sally looked up just in time to catch a softball-sized chunk of debris right in the forehead and she dropped to the floor, unconscious.

Kristie bent to help, struggling to pull her up over her shoulder. She looked up as Lily pushed her way through the crowd.

"Help me!" Kristie shouted at her.

Lily paused, looking back where the sickle-claws were now attempting to surround Tom, as he held them at bay with the fire hose. Then she bent next to Kristie, grabbing up Sally's other arm, and the two of them pulled her up from the ground, pushing into the milling crowd.

Tom glanced over his shoulder as his wife retreated to safety.

Or at least momentary safety – he could already feel the water pressure beginning to weaken.

There were torn bodies scattered all over the floor. Tom couldn't tell how many, but it was already at least a dozen people dead. He also wasn't sure how much protection the daycare offices would ultimately provide – the windows were Plexiglass, but they could be knocked from their frames. The area had been built for childcare, not security.

Of course, if the walls kept shaking the way they were now, it might soon be a moot point.

And as if that wasn't enough, from deeper down the corridor, at the far end of the Caverns, Tom heard the warbling hoots of more sickle-claws on their way.

But then there was an even louder caterwaul from the stairwell.

All at once, the entire wall crashed in.

Tom's jaw dropped as a twenty-foot gorilla smashed its way into the chamber.

At its heels was a battalion of soldiers.

The sickle-claws turned even as the rattle of machine-gun fire opened up within the Caverns.

The big ape leaped to the forefront, and began smashing the clawed beasts under its feet and massive fists.

Going with the moment, Tom kept the fire hose focused.

Behind him, with Sally still slumped over one shoulder, Lily's eyes widened as Mark separated from the unit of soldiers.

But Mark didn't see her as he moved to take Tom's place at point, opening up with machine-gun fire, even as another entire pack of sickle-claws appeared from the opposite end of the Caverns.

Mark turned to Tom.

"Get everybody up to the hangar!" Mark shouted. "We've got choppers waiting. We'll cover you down here!"

Mark looked up at Caesar.

"Go with them!"

Tom looked up at the big ape, who pinched two fingers together in an 'okay' signal."

"*Oooohh*-kay," Tom agreed, not questioning.

Mark turned with the rest of the soldiers, their guns blazing, as they met the onrush of attacking dromaeosaurs.

Tom looked over his shoulder. Kristie and Lily were carrying Sally over their shoulders.

"What's happening?" Kristie asked.

"I think it's a jailbreak, hon," Tom replied. "Get everybody up top."

Sally was just recovering groggy semi-consciousness, but then she abruptly blinked to attention as she spotted Mark, who was now turned and focused on the battle.

Then she was grabbed up by Caesar as the big ape led the crowd into the stairwell.

The screams of the sickle-claws mixed with the clatter of gunfire as the mountain continued to rumble around them.

CHAPTER 69

When Rosa's chopper swooped into the hangar, the cavern was already echoing with gunfire.

The three choppers ahead of them had already landed and the onboard gunmen opened fire on the swarming packs of dromaeosaurs, mowing the clawed beasts down in a torrent of bullets.

Rosa hung on tightly as Brady, their pilot, circled in the tight quarters, turning their open bay doors towards the hangar, allowing their own two gunmen, Drake and Parker, a clear shot at their sickle-clawed targets and they both opened fire.

It had been five minutes since Rhodes had given the order, but they still had not yet cleared a path through to the stairwell. Worse, the sickle-claws were bunched together right in front.

If they couldn't get the way cleared, the civilians would be running straight into them.

Rosa need not have worried.

First through the gate were two giant hairy apes. Cornelius and Zaius crashed through the stairway opening like a pair of juggernauts and immediately began smashing the clustered dromaeosaurs who were caught from the rear and taken by surprise. Hudson and his platoon of soldiers followed immediately on their heels and added a second-wave of gunfire.

Within minutes, the first of the civilians appeared behind them, now accompanied by Caesar, who joined Cornelius and Zaius trampling the dromaeosaurs under foot and fist.

With the three giant apes taking point against the sickle-claws, the on-ground troops began directing the refugees into the choppers.

Rosa hoped they had enough room to get everybody on board – they had four rescue choppers, each designed to carry twenty passengers in addition to crew, and they had come in planning to overfill. They had already been hard on the fuel transporting Caesar and his giant hairy companions.

But the presence of three eight-ton gorillas helped dramatically, allowing the soldiers to focus their attention on the rescue. Drake and Parker shouldered their rifles and began helping people on board.

But as she searched the faces, there were still two that were conspicuously absent.

Rosa picked up her radio.

"Cameron? You there?"

Cameron's voice responded immediately.

"Right here, Rosa. Talk to me."

"We're boarding the civilians now."

"Gonna be able to fit 'em all?"

"It's going to be close," Rosa replied. She looked around as the other choppers filled up rapidly. "We should be sending our first transport out within the next few minutes."

"Got it," Cameron said. "We'll be covering you."

Rosa shut her eyes. She knew what Cameron was waiting to hear.

"No sign of Shanna or Leanne yet," she said.

There was a tick of a pause.

"Understood," Cameron replied. "You let me know the very *second*."

"I will," Rosa returned. She shut off her radio.

Their chopper was already nearly full. Rosa jumped out, looking back at Parker and Drake.

"Go," she said. "I'll get the next one."

In the pilot seat, Brady nodded, and the chopper began to lift off.

Rosa turned to the crowd. Both Shanna and Leanne were here somewhere and she wasn't leaving without them.

CHAPTER 70

Cameron clicked off his radio.

Okay. *Now* he was getting worried.

If Shanna and Leanne didn't make it to the hangar, that meant they could be anywhere in the Mount.

Never mind he was riding second in an F-16 behind Maverick.

Maverick had been positively giddy when Hicks had led him up to the fighter.

Cameron, himself, had been a little nauseous just at the thought. In fact, right at that moment, he could honestly say he was more frightened than he'd ever been in his life.

To his credit, he hadn't thrown up yet.

Wedge was flying wingman, and right now, it seemed like they were currently engaged with every damned flying dragon in the whole world. Pterosaurs were bad enough, but these giant eagles were faster, more nimble, and a lot better armed.

At least this time they weren't stuck in an old clunker cargo plane – the war-bird they were flying now had supersonic speed and guns capable of fighting back.

On the other hand, that was a dubious blessing with Maverick at the controls.

Cameron had ridden shotgun with Maverick through many a hairy episode, ever since the days of joy-riding in his daddy's old crop-duster. It had scared him every single time. He'd actually lost track of how many times they'd ended up crashing.

Maverick's father, who everyone in the Valley, including Shanna, still called 'Mr. Taylor', had once remarked, "That son of mine hasn't got a brain in his head. But he's proven that he's damn hard to kill. Which makes it beneficial to be standing next to him."

Again, a somewhat dubious blessing.

And right now, they had a pterosaur on their tail and another moving in from the front.

Wedge was on the radio in their ears, shouting instructions to the first-time fighter-pilot that Maverick completely and utterly ignored as he corkscrewed wildly, ducking under the swooping pterosaur even as it lunged at them with its beak, sending the two flying dragons crashing into each other.

Maverick cackled wildly.

Cameron heard Wedge over his radio, muttering, "*Jesus,*" at the near-miss.

Maverick craned his head over his shoulder to Cameron.

"I gotta tell ya, buddy," he said, with that crazy joyful light in his eye, "this is scaring the *shit* out of me!"

Cameron nodded.

That one almost caused him to throw up.

Down below, he saw the first of the choppers emerging from the hangar like a honeybee leaving its nest.

The purpose of their air mission today was to cover their escape. They had a single squadron of six fighter jets with which to pull that off.

"Okay, people," Wedge said, "there's our first runner. We need to keep these hell-bats off of them."

"Aye, sir," Maverick said, as he turned into loose formation with the rest of the squad, banking down towards the Mount.

Cameron shut his eyes.

Rosa said Shanna hadn't shown yet.

But she and Leanne were down there somewhere – he knew that much – he could *feel* it.

On the other hand, it was entirely possible they were being sequestered somewhere away from all the rest.

So what then?

For the moment, all he could do was wait and pray.

CHAPTER 71

Leanne felt a sudden pressure in her head.

They had already been aware of the rumble as the Mount shook with the battle outside, but now Leanne felt a wave of vertigo. She wobbled slightly and Shanna held her hand to steady her.

"*Ow*. What was *that*?"

But before Shanna could answer, the Otto that had been standing sentry suddenly let out a strangled squawk and then toppled over, hitting the floor and convulsing as if it just suffered a stroke.

Shanna rubbed her temple. She had felt it too.

"What's happening?" Leanne asked, as the little lizard kicked and spat spasmodically on the ground.

Another tremor hit the Mount, shaking the laboratory walls.

It almost covered the sound of a low, cawing trill coming from out in the main chamber.

They had almost forgotten about the sickle-claws – the six of them that had been standing guard now rose to their feet.

Leanne felt a second wave of pressure and realized that this mental pulse was being aimed at the sickle-claws themselves.

It was not words – not for a simple creature like a dromaeosaur – but more of a kind of mental shorthand – initiating an impulse.

But the message was clear enough all the same.

Kill them all.

Shanna grabbed Leanne, pulling her back, as the sickle-claws advanced.

They were cornered in the lab. There was nowhere to go.

The first of the clawed-devils coiled as it prepared to spring.

Leanne looked around for anything to use as a weapon, but the only things handy were glass beakers and flat-screen computer modems. Shanna grabbed up her plastic chair.

The dromaeosaur leaped.

Leanne screamed, even as Shanna stepped in front of her, brandishing the flimsy folding chair.

But the clawed beast suddenly arched stiff in midair, letting loose a shrill screech.

Then it went limp and landed in a heap right in front of them.

Leanne saw an arrow protruding from its back, penetrating through to its heart.

There was another pair of abbreviated squawks and two more of the sickle-clawed devils dropped in quick succession.

Leanne gasped as she now saw Lucas standing behind them, already stringing another arrow into his bow.

The sickle-claws pivoted, claws spread, and the first two immediately leaped in Lucas' direction. The third, however, turned back to Leanne and Shanna.

Lucas stepped to one side, clearing his vantage, and let his arrow fly, dropping the lone dromaeosaur nearly at Leanne's feet.

The motion, however, left him briefly defenseless, as the other two were upon him in an instant.

With no time to string another arrow, Lucas shunted the first of the attacking beasts aside with his bow, and ducked the flailing claws of the second, even as he grabbed two more arrows out of his quiver.

He brought one shaft down in a stabbing motion directly into the first creature's back as its missed-strike carried it past him. The sickle-claw shrieked, and Lucas kicked it into the path of the second, tripping it up, even as he notched his second arrow.

Scrambling quickly, the remaining dromaeosaur regained its footing and immediately turned and sprang, but Lucas fired at the same moment, and his arrow caught the creature dead in the heart.

The still-kicking beast, however, landed on top of him, knocking them both to the ground.

Lucas let out a shriek of his own as the claws dug into him, and was only spared being disemboweled by his bow deflecting the brunt of the strike.

A moment later, Shanna and Leanne were pulling the dead dromaeosaur off of him.

"Lucas!" Leanne cried. "Are you alright?"

Her hands came up bloody as they helped him to his feet.

Lucas pulled up his shirt, revealing two ugly slashes across his abdomen.

"I think I'm okay," he said, even as blood ran freely, and then he shrieked again as Shanna poured a tin of alcohol over the cuts.

"It got you good," she said, attempting to wipe away the blood with a towel, "but it didn't go too deep. You could stand some stitches, though."

"Probably," Lucas agreed, pulling down his shirt, "but we have to make it out of here alive first."

As if to highlight the point, the chamber around them rumbled again, rattling the walls.

"We've got to go *now*," Lucas said, grabbing up his bow.

Shanna nodded to Leanne.

"I told you he was coming," she said, eyeing her daughter meaningfully. "And you remember why."

Leanne blushed as they followed Lucas out into the main chamber.

"Wait," Shanna said suddenly, turning back into the lab. She ran back and grabbed up several vials, emptying out a sample-bag and dropping them inside.

"This is the counter-agent to the Food of the Gods," she said. "We might just be able to save the world yet."

The three of them ran for the stairwell. Along the way, they saw several more Ottos lying scattered on the floor – a couple of them were still alive, kicking spasmodically.

"What happened to these guys?" Lucas asked as they passed by.

"I think Draco did it," Shanna replied. She shrugged. "He's got a lot of *T. rex* in him and tyrannosaurs don't much care for Otto."

"Where are we going?" Leanne asked.

"Down to the hangar," Shanna replied. "That's where they'll be."

Lucas glanced at her.

"*Who* will?"

Shanna started to answer, but then they heard the catcalls of more sickle-claws echoing from the other end of the chamber. Shanna shook her head.

"Just trust me," she said briefly.

Lucas looked back nervously over his shoulder and nodded, and the three of them ducked into the stairwell.

Leanne looked down the alternating staircases, which at this level seemed to descend into a bottomless abyss.

"How far down to the hangar?" she asked.

"It's at the base of the first peak," Shanna replied. "I'm guessing at least seven-hundred feet worth of stairway."

Even as she spoke, the Mount rumbled yet again and pieces of rubble broke away from the walls, clattering on the metal.

"We better hurry," Shanna said.

They started down the stairs but had not made even four landings before another massive tremor struck. The three of them grabbed the railing for purchase.

Leanne was thrown forward. Lucas reached out to stop her fall, but slipped in his own blood, losing balance, and instead was pulled along with her. The two of them tumbled down the flight together, piling in a heap where the landing ended forty-feet below.

Lucas cried out as they hit the bottom, landing badly on one leg.

Riding out the tremor, Shanna started down after them, when a second quake hit, and this time, the stairway itself started to fall away.

The entire landing collapsed off the wall, breaking away almost right below Shanna's feet. The cement and metal structure came apart and dropped off into the circular abyss, banging loudly off the remaining staircases as it fell.

Lucas and Leanne pulled back from the edge, looking up helplessly.

Shanna stared down at the sudden forty-foot gap that now sat between them.

"Get to the hangar," she shouted.

"What about you?" Leanne cried.

Shanna looked up, even as the rest of the staircase threatened to break loose.

"I'll head up to the top deck."

Leanne was about to say something more but the walls shook again.

"*Go!*" Shanna shouted, and she turned and began running back up the stairs.

Lucas struggled to his feet. His ankle was already swelling up purple and was probably broken.

"Let's go," he said. "We've got to hurry."

They turned and made their way down the stairwell, even as the Mount continued to shake apart all around them.

CHAPTER 72

Draco and Big Red faced each other, circling.

The warring beasts around them faded back, granting the two Generals room.

Big Red advanced more slowly now. Their initial clash had left them both bloodied and cautious.

"Well," Draco said, "*Father*. What now?"

As he spoke, Draco reached out his mind, opening up his consciousness to his fearsome sire.

Big Red's head perked, nostrils flared, and he paused.

"Yes," Draco said. "It's true. I *am* your progeny. I am what was stolen from you that day, so long ago. Your first brood. For what possible reason should we quarrel? I *am* the reason you fight.

"Mother," he continued, summoning an image of Sue from Big Red's memories, "would feel the same way."

Big Red regarded Draco with narrowed eyes.

As with Shanna, he did not so much understand the words or their meaning – it was all just sound – but the big tyrannosaur recognized the scent of his own kin.

It was twisted and corrupted, perhaps, but it was there.

"So what happens now?" Draco pressed. "Is it your intention to kill me? To slay your own hatchling? All for the sake of one tiny, smelly, little she-ape?"

Draco smiled.

"My world," he said, "will be better."

Big Red eyed Draco mistrustfully, his deteriorating faculties searching for a clear message. A rex' behavior was always determined by its senses and its actions were always a programmed response. But Big Red's senses were giving him conflicting information and his instincts were confused.

The presence of his kin was strong.

But the other part of Draco was Otto. And Otto was a clone a thousand-thousand times over, repeated so many times that his very DNA had taken on a synthetic turn.

Over generations and generations, something had been lost – the copy was never as clean as the original.

Moreover, Draco was a rival, and in traditional *T. rex* society, long before Shanna's pacifying influence, kin-slayings were common in matters of dominance.

And Big Red, having now regressed back into a full-on rogue, and already progressing into the first stages of chemical-induced madness, let his most basic instincts decide for him.

"Well?" Draco said expectantly, "Father?"

Big Red charged.

There was no display this time, no strikes with his thick, bony head. Big Red came in, teeth first. No inter-species contest, this was a killing fight. In Big Red's savage breast, the blood-lust was on.

But Draco was part rex as well, and he knew what was coming.

He met Big Red in the middle, batting the tooth-studded jaws aside, and he lunged in with a jagged, gaping maw of his own. Their skulls crashed together, jaws locked, twisting and pulling, each of them straining for the other's throat.

They grappled, wrestling for dominant position. Their muscular legs delivered powerful, stunning kicks, with ostrich-like, taloned hooves, while Draco slashed with his larger, dromaeosaur-like fore-claws at Big Red's neck.

Big Red, however, was the stronger inside. Despite Draco's greater height, the Otto-dromaeosaur influence in his DNA had left him a touch more slender in the legs and neck than a pure rex.

Draco felt the difference as Big Red now began to force him back.

If brute strength were to be the deciding factor, this was where the battle would have turned.

A pure *T. rex*, however, would never understand battle tactics. A Tyrannosaurus came forward, gave no quarter, and the stronger always won.

But Draco broke away from the lock-up and stepped back.

Big Red read it as a retreat and attempted to press the advantage, charging forward, jaws agape.

Draco sidestepped, delivering a mighty blow with his own bone-ridged skull as Big Red stumbled past.

The big rex was momentarily knocked off-balance and Draco hit him again, lashing out with a fusillade of blows.

Big Red made an attempt to regain the offensive, lunging with his teeth, but now he was kicked with a brutal, clawed hoof square across the side of his head, rocking him with stunning force, and his deadly jaws snapped shut on nothing.

The world began to dim.

Sensing victory, Draco kicked again. Big Red stumbled and went down, and Draco moved in with stomping feet, raining down blows, until finally Big Red's struggles ceased.

Draco raised his head in a guttural roar that bore no sense of charm or intellect. He was a pure beast now, raging and enjoying that rage, relishing the battle and eager for the blood of his opponent – indeed, eager for the blood of every creature around him who had so foolishly dared challenge his rule.

He poised over Big Red's helpless form and his jaws parted for the death-bite, aiming high on the neck, ready to sever the fallen tyrannosaur's head from his body.

Draco's lips drooled in anticipation, and he felt the power within him surging like nothing he'd ever imagined or dreamed of.

It was in that moment when he realized something was wrong.

Draco paused, looking down into Big Red's eyes.

In those glowing green mirrors, he saw his image reflected.

And he could see the glow in his own.

He realized then what had happened.

Draco threw Big Red aside and turned back to the Mount, looking up to the Tower.

The furious roar that erupted from his jaws was like no other sound in Creation – the sound of an erupting volcano – a neutron bomb – a killer asteroid from space.

It was a name.

"SHHHAAAANNNAAA!!"

At the sound, the world trembled.

Draco latched his claws into the wall of the cliff and began to climb.

CHAPTER 73

Shanna heard Draco's roar.

Something told her he'd figured out her little trick.

By his tone, she guessed he was taking it badly.

The stairs were shaking beneath her feet and she suspected these were the first reactionary rumblings from the mountain itself, as the relentless pounding from the battle outside finally triggered a seismic response.

The Mount, after all, was nothing but a dormant volcano, just like every mountain in the entire range. And they were actually not so dormant anymore – the New Gulf alone was evidence enough of that.

Shanna had just barely regained the administration-level they had fled from only minutes before, and she heard the screeching wails of sickle-claws echoing from the cavern within.

The mounting tremors threatened to knock her off her feet, but Shanna didn't slow as she pounded her way up the stairs.

Only moments after she passed the landing, the first inquisitive dromaeosaur-snouts poked into the stairwell, following her scent.

Shanna didn't look back, but she heard their hooting cries as they spotted her.

The top deck was maybe another hundred feet of stairs, directly above – not that she had any idea what she might do when she got there. There was no way to block the smashed-out opening to the stairwell, and once up top, she would be as cornered and trapped as anywhere.

But at the moment, it was just about immediate survival and headlong flight.

Behind her, Shanna heard the clatter of sickle-toed-claws tapping on metal as the dromaeosaurs funneled out onto the stairs in pursuit, their trilling catcalls echoing up after her.

There was another massive tremor and now the stairs under her feet began to break loose from the walls.

Shanna leaped, grabbing hold of the railing and catching the bottom steps of the next landing, pulling herself up, even as the stairway beneath her dropped away.

Behind her, the first of the sickle-claws were caught in the collapse, and went tumbling with the falling staircase down into the narrow chasm, their screeching hoots bouncing off the walls. The others paused at the broken edge of the landing, looking up, momentarily frustrated.

But as Shanna looked to the floor above, she saw part of that staircase had started to pull loose as well, and was hanging precariously from its moorings, jutting at an angle off the rock wall.

She stood for a moment, indecisive – there was still a good eighty-feet and two landings up to the top deck.

Then there came a loud and defiant screech from below.

Shanna turned as one of the sickle-claws leaped, its claws reaching out for the loose pilings dangling just beneath her feet. The creature caught hold and began to pull its way up.

Looking around frantically, Shanna grabbed a large piece of rubble, and dropped it over the edge. There was a startled squawk as the chunk caught the clinging beast face-first, just as it reached for the bottom step, knocking it loose and sending it falling down into the tunnel.

The next moment, however, another one leaped, and then one more behind it.

Shanna turned and with painstaking slowness, began to pick her way up the loosely-hanging stairway.

And echoing up from somewhere just outside the Mount, she heard Draco's enraged roar.

Calling her by name.

CHAPTER 74

Rhodes worked his way down the old elevator shaft into the deepest depths of the Mount.

This had once been the primary access route to the lower levels in the days before the collapse, more than nineteen years ago, but it had not been in use in the time since. The carrier car had crashed all the way to the bottom, and had never been recovered, but there was still an access ladder leading down.

Rhodes, however, was beginning to wonder if he would be able to make the climb.

Besides the fresh bullet-wound in his shoulder, the heat in the corridor was rapidly becoming intolerable. There was no ventilation, and the further down he went, he began to worry about the possibility of toxic gases leaking up from below. He was already becoming dizzy just from the temperature alone, and his hands were slick with sweat, threatening his grip on the ladder.

He was also starting to wonder if the mountain might not shake itself to pieces all on its own.

It was actually a tempting thought, to just let it happen, and head back to the surface, but he knew he couldn't take that chance.

On the other hand, there was a good possibility he might be cooked alive before he could set his charges. After the original collapse, he had sent crews down as far as they could manage, but they'd been outfitted in fire-suits and oxygen-masks.

At the time, it had been treated as a salvage mission. Dr. Shriver's lab had originally been located in the deepest bowels of the mountain. In retrospect, that seemed foolish, but the concern back then had been primarily security. The volcano itself had been dormant for thousands of years, with every expectation that it would remain that way – objects at rest tend to stay at rest.

But boy, once they started moving again...

His crews had never been able to access the lowest levels – the plasma from the volcanic core had risen too high. And besides the resulting heat, the way was barred by countless tons of debris that would have taken heavy-duty equipment to break through – an inconvenience at that depth, to say the least – and eventually their efforts had been abandoned.

That had been a point of concern for Shriver. There was enough of the Food of the Gods in storage in his buried lab to destroy the world several times over.

"It's inaccessible," Rhodes had pointed out.

"Inaccessible to *us*," Shriver had replied.

The doctor had not needed to elaborate on who it might *not* be inaccessible to. It had taken weeks to root the last of those damned talking lizards out of the ventilation pipes.

And so they had created a fail-safe.

Over the following months, they had planted seismic charges at various strategic areas all over the lower levels – structural points where geologic pressure was maximized.

Ideally, these charges could be activated from his office, but that wasn't an option anymore, and so what he had in his pack amounted to a makeshift fuse. He just had to get low enough to activate one of the trigger-points.

The charges he'd brought with him were attached to a timer – set up by his demolitions squad with the idea of providing him the opportunity to escape once the clock was set.

Rhodes had allowed it simply to avoid the argument.

But he'd known this was a one-way ticket, and had intended it that way all along.

He was an old warhorse who was getting on towards the end of his days, and the war still wasn't won. In fact, the enemy had solidly gained the upper-hand.

Time to put paid to it all.

There were a few things he regretted. He had never found out about Sally.

But at least he had learned the final truth about Shanna and her idyllic Valley.

It was there, alright, and had been all along – Shriver had been right about that much.

And while he'd never seen it himself, he knew it was a treasure worth preserving simply by the fact that it was the first thing Draco had threatened to destroy.

It meant there was something else for humanity other than the police-state that he had allowed to metastasize under his watch – something better.

Rhodes had held the line for the sake of the human-race here at the Mount for more than nineteen years. He didn't know if he'd made the world better, but at least they were still here.

And he could honestly say that he'd done his best. He'd fought the good fight until the bitter end, and this was the way he wanted to go out.

His hands were starting to slip on the ladder. His back was creaking and his eyelids were beginning to flicker.

Rhodes knew he would lose consciousness before he burned alive.

He paused, hanging by one hand, his wounded shoulder complaining loudly, and he pulled the pack off his back.

Reaching inside, he set the timers.

Five minutes.

He would keep climbing, get as low as he could, and hope the blast was sufficient to ignite the rest of the charges, or at least shake enough of the plasma loose to finish the job.

Rhodes continued to climb, and as he did, he started to dream awake, watching his life flash before his eyes.

He saw visions of his daughter, Kate, lost on KT-day. He also saw Sally, who had taken her place in all the years since. He even saw Michelle.

The minutes ticked-off until the end.

At the count of zero, the charges in his pack went off.

Rhodes was aware of impact, a flash of light, and then a sense of falling.

It was all in the space of a split second.

He felt no pain.

And in the bowels of the mountain, the chain reaction began.

CHAPTER 75

For just one shining moment, Jonah thought they had pulled it off.

Up to that point, the air battle had been going poorly. Hicks and Biggs' fighters had both been crippled on their very first run.

It was quickly becoming evident that these giant eagles were going to be much more of a handful than the pterosaurs – besides being more agile and powerfully-built, their clasping foot-claws were like dealing with a flying dromaeosaur – which Jonah supposed, in evolutionary terms, was exactly what a bird actually was.

On the other hand, the pterosaurs seemed a lot more brainlessly aggressive – they flew headlong right into you – even into each other. Perhaps that was how they suppressed the evolution of birds for so long – they had an initial size advantage after coming down the evolutionary-line first, combined with pure reptilian meanness.

But between them, the giant flying denizens had successfully blocked passage to the missile silos.

Naomi's jet had also taken damage on their last attempt. She seemed pretty damn mad about it too. Her fighter had been hit by one of those particularly ugly pterosaurs with teeth in their beaks, and the thing had clipped her wing.

She had actually been quite lucky, because Jonah had been right behind her and unloaded his guns directly into the creature's eye, otherwise it would have all been over.

All four jets had pulled back briefly, regrouping when Hicks' voice sounded in their headsets.

"I'm afraid we've got problems."

Naomi barked derisive laughter.

"Is he *kidding*?"

"One of those silos just opened up. They're getting ready to launch a missile."

Hicks banked back towards the site.

"Folks," he said, "this just became a do-or-die mission. Follow me in."

Biggs veered beside him, hugging close to his wing.

Jonah glanced over at Naomi on his own wing. He could see her in the cockpit. She looked over at him and he could see her face was grim. But then her voice sounded over the air.

"We're with you, Major."

She banked her fighter, following the other two planes in.

No fear.

Jonah took a breath, arcing in after her.

Hicks had taken point, arrowing low and straight, even as the pterosaurs and giant raptors circled in, converging.

Behind him, all three jets unloaded their guns, doing their best to cover him.

Unfortunately, the guns were an insufficient deterrent and they were all down to their last few missiles.

Biggs' fighter was the first to go. One of the eagles snatched him out of midair with its claws. The giant raptor shrieked as the resulting fiery explosion did more damage than any of the F-16s had managed with their guns.

A second raptor was honing in on Hicks, its talons stretched out.

Naomi pulled up behind the giant bird, opening up her guns, firing straight up its tail feathers. But if the creature even noticed, it gave no sign.

Then a pterosaur moved in on her, and she was forced to veer away. But as she turned-off, the creature's beak clipped her already-damaged wing.

Jonah felt his heart skip a beat as he saw her fighter stagger, and one of its engines starting to smoke. He opened his own guns, again aiming for the creature's eyes.

But Hicks had broken through and the silo-field lay straight ahead.

The eagle on his tail, however, was closing fast, its giant claws spreading – reaching.

Hicks fired his remaining missiles, letting go with everything he had.

The field lit up in a series of massive blasts.

Hicks had hit his target.

Jonah imagined it was the last thing the Major saw before the grasping talons reached him.

Hicks' fighter exploded in the giant raptor's claws.

But the entire silo field below went up in flames.

Naomi had one moment of exultation.

"He did it!" she shouted excitedly.

But then they saw the missile launching-up and out of the conflagration, straight into the air, before arching and turning west.

They could guess its trajectory well-enough. Draco had told them as much.

It was headed for the Valley.

"We've got to stop it," Naomi said.

But even as she said it, her damaged engine flamed-out.

Immediately, a pterosaur honed-in on the smoke from her trail.

Jonah let one of his last two missiles go, catching the flying dragon behind the neck. The creature staggered, banking away.

But Naomi's fighter was down to one engine.

"Jonah," she said, "I'm crippled."

Jonah shut his eyes.

"I know," he said. "Pull back. You can make it back to the base. I'll take care of this."

And with that, he turned, following the path of the flying warhead.

As a flock, the entire swarm of flying dragons immediately converged on his tail.

Naomi banked off to the side as they now ignored her completely.

Jonah glanced over his shoulder as the sky behind him darkened with the storm cloud of winged monsters.

He turned back. Couldn't think about that now. He had one missile – one chance.

Yet again, it seemed, the human race's future lay in his hands.

Naomi had been dreaming about the Valley, about a new and better life, for a long time. Here was his chance to give it to her – and to their child.

Naomi watched helplessly.

"Jonah," she said in his ear. "They're gaining on you."

She could see they were going to reach him if he stayed his course.

She could also see that he was holding the line.

Massive claws reached for his fighter as Jonah locked his missile-sights.

"Jonah!" Naomi shouted. "Pull up!"

Jonah shook his head.

"Naomi... *I can't.*"

Suddenly, she was crying in his ear.

"Don't you do it, Jonah. Don't you dare leave me alone. *Please...*"

"You're not alone," Jonah replied. "You've found the Valley."

He nodded affirmatively.

"For what it's worth," he said, "it was worth all the while. I'd do it all over again. Every single second with you. I loved you. I loved you *so much.*"

Naomi's voice broke.

"Jonah... I love you too. You were the best thing that ever happened to me."

Jonah smiled, even as his own eyes welled with tears.

His computer locked on his target and he fired.

He saw the streak of flaming smoke as his missile streaked out towards its target.

Impact.

His aim had been true.

There was a fiery explosion as the warhead was destroyed.

I did it, he thought – and was about to say so – but then the reaching claws caught him

His world exploded in fire and light.

And watching it all, Naomi screamed.

Nearly blinded by tears, she turned her fighter away, even as the burning debris from Jonah's jet fell from the sky like a falling star.

And although she didn't know it, she finished his words.

"You did it," she sobbed. "You did it."

He saved the world.

And her.

Again.

CHAPTER 76

Lucas didn't think the staircase was going to last.

The rest of the structure beneath their feet showed every indication of collapsing the same way the section above had. There was also the bombardment of falling debris shaking off the ceiling and walls.

As they descended to the next level, however, they discovered a more immediate problem.

Leanne suddenly stopped.

"Wait," she said, listening over the sound of the quaking mountain and collapsing rubble.

From below, they heard the distinct warbling cries of sickle-claws echoing up the stairwell.

They looked down the winding staircase, and sure enough, several flights below, a pack of four sickle-claws was making their way speedily up the stairs, on their single-minded search-and-destroy mission.

Lucas glanced at Leanne – he had three arrows left in his quiver.

With no other choice, they turned and began running back up the way they had come.

The uphill climb was a lot harder on Lucas' broken ankle and each step produced bolts of almost nauseating pain. He was also still bleeding badly from his clawed side – bad enough that the steps beneath his feet were becoming slippery.

But regardless, there wasn't much further they could go. The stairs had already fallen away just a few flights above – they were running into a dead-end.

They had to get out of the stairwell.

The next floor above was marked 'detention-level', and as they turned onto the landing, they saw that the entire front wall had been knocked out. Leanne glanced at Lucas doubtfully, but he nodded.

"Let's go," he said.

As they ducked out of the stairwell, the chamber within looked to have been the site of a battle.

Besides the smashed front wall, the jail-cells had been ripped right out of the ceiling. Beyond that, there were several dead dromaeosaurs lying about – and they all appeared to have been *crushed*, Lucas noted, not shot.

There was also the body of a woman whose body had been utterly ripped to pieces in trademarked sickle-claw style.

"My God," Leanne breathed, "what happened here?"

But they had no time to ponder. The hooting of the dromaeosaurs echoed in the stairwell right behind them.

The chamber ran parallel to the administration-level above and the corridor surrounding the cell-blocks stretched ahead for some distance. But the entire floor was sparse, with no adjoining rooms or features beyond the cells themselves.

Then Leanne grabbed Lucas' hand, pointing to what looked like a sealed doorway on the opposite wall.

"Wait," she said. "This is an elevator."

Lucas, who had never seen or heard of an 'elevator' in his life, shook his head blankly.

"It's a carrier car," Leanne explained, pointing to the lights above signifying floor levels. "If this thing is working, it can take us down. Or if we can get the doors open, we might be able to climb down the shaft."

She pushed the button and was rewarded with a loud *ding*, as the lights above the door began to count-off.

"I think it's working," Leanne said breathlessly.

But then the blinking lights stopped two levels down. Leanne cursed.

"Too much to hope for." She looked around for a lever. "Here. Help me pry the doors open."

Lucas recovered a bar from one of the torn cells and wedged it between the opening. As if designed to do so, once he got the lever between them, the doors slid open.

They looked down the shaft.

"There," Leanne said. "That's the elevator car. It looks like it's jammed."

The car was stuck two levels below, maybe eighty feet. It appeared the rails had bent, blocking the elevator's ascent.

"It doesn't matter," Leanne said. "There's an access ladder. We can climb."

At that moment, however, there was a screeching holler as the four dromaeosaurs appeared at the smashed entryway to the chamber.

Lucas already had his bow unslung and an arrow in the string as the sickle-claws charged.

Four of them, and he had three arrows. Lucas let the first shaft fly.

There was a squawk as the first of the clawed beasts dropped in its tracks. The second leaped over its fallen comrade without hesitation, only to be skewered by a second arrow.

Lucas fired the third, but the last two dromaeosaurs were already upon him. Leanne screamed as both creatures leaped, their wicked foot-claws flailing out.

The last arrow caught the lead beast in the chest, and Lucas ducked aside, swinging his bow like a bat at the second, catching the murderous foot-claw in mid-kick, even as he simultaneously lashed out with his knife.

Lucas' blade caught the villainous beast across the throat, nearly severing its head, and the creature flipped over on its back, twitching like a clubbed fish.

The dromaeosaur, however, had done its own damage. The toe claw cleaved a rift through Lucas' already-injured midsection, slashing his abdomen in a deep, ragged tear.

Lucas clutched his side, doubling over. He had narrowly missed being disemboweled.

He was hurt, though, and he stumbled, dropping to one knee, his head going dizzy.

Leanne's face was suddenly above him.

"Lucas? Are you alright?"

Lucas smiled a little as he looked down at the blood leaking over his hands. He started to reply, intending something witty and sarcastic, but instead the world swarm and went dark.

He blinked awake a moment later as Leanne was wrestling him up to his feet.

"Oh no you don't," she was saying. "You're not giving up on me now."

But then there was another cacophony of shrill squawks, as a half-dozen more sickle-claws appeared at the doorway.

"Leanne," Lucas said weakly. "Go on. You can get away."

He held up his knife, trembling weakly in one bloodied hand.

"I'll hold them off."

Instead, Leanne hiked him over one shoulder.

"Not without you," she said and stepped into the elevator shaft.

Leanne grabbed the first rung of the access ladder, but their combined weight nearly pulled them loose, and they dangled perilously over the eighty-foot drop.

"You can't carry me," Lucas protested.

"Then start *helping* me, Goddamn it!" Leanne barked.

Lucas' free hand caught a ladder rung, even as his feet scrambled for purchase. The movement caused a fresh torrent of blood from his side. His hand slipped on the rung.

He started to black out, but was brought back by a firm smack across his face.

"You better hang on," Leanne said. "You remember that damned mountain? If you fall, *I'll* fall. Don't you quit on me."

Lucas started to argue, but was met by another firm slap.

Obediently, he grabbed the next rung and began to climb.

The first of the sickle-claws appeared at the elevator opening above, looking down, hooting wildly at their retreating prey.

They were twenty feet above the stalled elevator car when Lucas finally lost his grip and fell.

He hit the top of the elevator, landing hard on his already broken foot. He screamed out loud and the sudden bolt of pain was actually enough to snap him back to full consciousness.

"*Lucas!*" Leanne cried as she dropped down next to him.

Above them, the sickle-claws were pawing at the ledge, looking for a purchase, but without opposable thumbs, they had no way of gripping the ladder, and they cackled and jeered in frustration.

Leanne pulled the access hatch from the top of the elevator and dragged them both down into the carrier car, where they landed with a thud, eliciting another painful shriek from Lucas as he struck his broken ankle.

The control switch indicated the hangar as the bottom floor and Leanne pushed the button. She waited a moment as the light flashed, but there was no response.

Cursing, she pushed the button again.

There was a sudden shift in gears and then the elevator started moving down.

"It's working," Leanne said, "it's work..."

Then there was a sudden snap as the shaking Mount finally tore the cable loose, and the elevator began to drop.

The safety brakes screamed like shrill banshees as they scraped along the bent rails, peeling away metal as they tried to slow their descent.

The shaft, however, had been spread wide by the tremors and the braking-gears were loose.

Their stomachs dropped as they plummeted.

Then there was a heavy clunk as the brakes finally caught and the elevator slowed to a stop.

"I think we're okay...," Leanne began breathlessly, and then her voice broke into a scream as the carrier-car finally broke entirely loose of its tracks and dropped in complete free-fall.

Her scream was cut short a few seconds later, morphing into a heavy grunt, as the car hit the floor some forty feet down, the shock-absorbers underneath the carrier breaking their fall.

They lay there for several moments, too stunned to move.

Then there was a ding, and the elevator door opened.

Lucas looked up at Leanne, and for a moment, he wished that he had died because he was never in his life going to be able to forget how beautiful she looked right at that moment – nor would he ever forget her dark eyes staring down at him.

It would have been better to die.

He changed his mind, a second later, when she bent her head and kissed him full on the lips.

The mountain continued to shake, the Earth roared and crumbled all around them, but for one brief moment, neither Lucas or Leanne cared.

Then there was a voice above them.

"Okay, you two."

They looked up to see Rosa standing over them. Behind her was Major Tom. The carrier-car had taken them all the way down to the hangar.

"Where's your mother?" Rosa asked, even as she and Tom moved in to help fish them out of the wreckage.

"She went up top," Leanne replied. "The stairway collapsed. We got separated. She was headed to the roof."

Rosa nodded, turning to Tom.

"Get them onto the chopper," she said. "We've got to move."

Then she pulled out her radio, hitting the switch.

"Cameron?" she said. "We've got a little problem."

CHAPTER 77

To Cameron's surprise, Maverick hadn't killed them yet, although every flying dragon in the sky was doing their level-best.

They'd already lost two planes so far, bringing them down to four, but they had managed to escort the first three choppers out of the combat zone. They were waiting on the last when he got the call from Rosa.

"Talk to me," Cameron said.

"We've got your daughter," Rosa replied.

"What about Shanna?"

"Leanne said they got separated. She says her mother was headed up to the roof. But the whole place is falling apart. There's no way we can get to her."

Cameron shut his eyes.

"Understood," he said. "Get everybody out. I'm on it."

He shut off the radio.

Maverick was looking over his shoulder

"You heard that?" Cameron said.

"I heard."

Maverick tapped his head-set.

"Wedge? You there?"

"Right here, Mav."

"The last chopper is on its way," Maverick said. "You cover them and then get the hell out of here." He glanced back at Cameron. "We've got a little something to do."

"Got it," Wedge replied. "Good luck."

Maverick turned towards the Mount. Coming in low, he pulled a flyby over the top deck.

"What do you see?" Maverick hollered back to Cameron.

"Nobody there yet," Cameron shouted back. "I see Rhodes' chopper, but other than that, the top deck looks empty." He shook his head. "There's no room to land without an anchor-line."

Maverick nodded.

"That's pretty much what I figured," he said.

But then, as they soared over the top, they got a look over the eastern face of the mountain.

Draco was scaling the cliff.

"Okay," Maverick said. "That ain't good."

"He's almost to the top," Cameron said. "We haven't got much time."

Maverick glanced back at Cameron.

"You know," he said, "it occurs to me. My whole life, I've never once been sky-diving."

Cameron eyed him dubiously.

"What does *that* mean?"

Maverick circled the fighter back towards the Mount, coming in low.

"It means there's only one thing to do."

And now he laughed – that maniacal laugh that Cameron had long-since learned to be wary of.

"*Hang on!*" Maverick shouted.

"What are you talking ab...?"

That was all he got out before Maverick hit eject.

Cameron's voice peaked into a scream as they were blown out of the cockpit into free-fall, only to be jerked upright a few seconds later as their chutes opened automatically.

Their F-16 sailed on, crashing in a fiery explosion against the cliff below.

Maverick was pulling on his chute-cord, shouting frantically, something that Cameron couldn't hear, but he was angling towards the peak of the Mount.

Looking down at the wide-open canyon beneath him, Cameron attempted to do the same.

Then the sky darkened as a winged shadow from above blocked out the sun.

One of the giant eagles was boring down on top of them.

Maverick pulled his pistol out and started shooting. Cameron almost laughed – he might as well have been firing a pellet gun.

The giant raptor closed on them, claws outstretched.

Then one of the other fighters swooped in. Wedge launched a missile, catching the giant bird broadside. There was a gale-like caw as the creature spun in midair, turning in pursuit of Wedge.

"*Thaaank* you," Maverick hollered, waving, as he guided his chute in towards the top deck.

With his feet already running, he hit the tarmac and pulled the clip on his chute, letting it loose as he landed and rolled, as if he'd done it a thousand times.

Cameron, however, seemed to be sailing over the edge.

Maverick ran beneath him, shouting up.

"Pull the clip! Release your harness!"

Cameron shut his eyes and cut loose from the chute, dropping more than twenty-feet onto the deck.

He rolled too – a good nine or ten times, bouncing like a tumbleweed.

"Ouch, ow, oof, oh-shit, ow, ow, ouch, shit, shit, shit!

His tumbling path was intercepted by a large ventilation pipe that caught him dead across the ribs, taking what was left of his wind.

Maverick came running past as Cameron lay curled on the tarmac, clutching his gut. Looking over his shoulder, Maverick climbed up into the chopper Rhodes had left docked on the helipad.

"Go get your lady," he hollered. "I'll get this thing hot-wired up!"

Cameron groaned, staggering to his feet.

He was getting too old for this shit.

"Oh, I'm gonna get you for *that* one, Mav," he muttered.

Then he turned, drawing his own pistol, as he headed for the stairway down into the Mount.

CHAPTER 78

The chain reaction had started deep in the bowels of the Mount. Seismic disruptions sent ash and smoke bursting through the crust all over the region, as deep beneath the Earth, molten pockets of lava were breaking free to the surface.

The mountain itself seemed to tremble.

Big Red was drifting back to consciousness and he became aware of a bug buzzing in his ear.

Caesar was standing on his cheek, hollering into his face.

Big Red stirred, sitting up and shaking his head, barely aware of the tiny ape clinging to the back of his neck.

Beside him, the dragon queen was stirring as well. Cornelius and Zaius were both dancing on her head, hooting and shrieking, trying to rouse her.

The two *T. rex* staggered to their feet, regarding each other briefly, then looked up at the Mount as the world began to shake itself apart.

Around them, the battle was breaking up, as the other beasts were now turning to retreat.

Caesar roared into Big Red's ear again and now the big tyrannosaur started to move, even as sparks of lava began spitting up from the ground.

The queen fell into step behind him as they left the Mount behind.

Caesar hitched a ride latched in the crook of Big Red's neck, still hooting into his ear, waving to Cornelius and Zaius mounted on the queen, as the three of them guided the two giant tyrannosaurs out of the territory.

He had never much liked the *T. rex*, but it was the least he could do.

CHAPTER 79

Shanna could hear the sickle-claws on the stairway behind her and she could feel the tremors shake the mountain as the seismic reactions began to magnify exponentially.

More than that, she could feel the approach of the Dragon Lord.

Draco's rage was palpable in her head – it was like Otto's psychic burn a thousand times over. It made her eyes water.

In a way, she felt a bit of renewed confidence. She knew that, if he could, Draco would have blasted the capillaries in her brain with an embolism just like he had Otto's, but she was stronger than that.

She made her way up past the broken section of staircase onto more solid footing, and the light of the top deck was now only one more forty-step flight above.

Behind her, however, at least four sickle-claws had already made the leap from the tattered landing below and were on her tail, gaining quickly.

The Mount itself was also working against her. A particularly violent tremor struck, and this time, she lost her balance and stumbled. Her bag, carrying the precious vials of counter-agent, slipped from her shoulder, and as she reached for it, she tripped and fell down the steps, landing in a heap at the bottom of the landing.

The first of the sickle-claws was upon her before she could gain her feet, its talons outstretched.

With a wild yell, Shanna lashed out from the ground with a vicious kick of her own, catching the creature by surprise, knocking it off the steps over the railing, and sending the startled beast tumbling down into the crumbling chasm.

The others, however, were on her in an instant. The first of them pinned her down, its wicked foot-claw already poised to strike.

Shanna started to scream, but this time it was drowned out by a gunshot that suddenly rang out in the stairwell.

The sickle-claw on top of her went stiff, a glut of blood bursting from its chest. Two more shots rang out and the creature fell, toppling right into the path of the other two and sending them all bouncing back down to the bottom of the stair-level below.

Shanna turned to see Cameron at the top of the stairs, a smoking pistol in his hand.

She nearly teared up as he came running down the steps, bending at her side. For a split-second they stared at each other, unable to find words.

The two remaining dromaeosaurs, however, quickly recovered, and with a barrage of outraged hooting caws, were already coming after them again.

Cameron started shooting and kept firing until both of the demon-beasts were down and had stopped kicking. His pistol clicked empty.

He looked down the winding staircase for any more.

"I hope that's the last of them," he said, "because I'm out of bullets."

He grabbed Shanna's hand and started back for the top, but she pulled away.

"Wait," she said, running back down the steps, "I forgot my bag!"

Cameron stared after her incredulously.

"You forgot your *bag*!?"

With a spurt of profanity, Cameron followed after her.

The sample bag was still where it had fallen.

Standing over it, staring back at them cheekily, was a certain parrot-talking lizard.

Shanna froze as Otto snatched up the bag.

It looked up at her and chittered as it turned and darted back down the stairway.

Then another shot rang out from behind them and Otto's head exploded in a spurt of blood.

They turned to see Maverick standing at the top of the stairs, his gun out and aimed.

"I *hate* those little bastards," he said. "Can we please go now?"

Shanna snatched up her bag as Cameron grabbed her hand, pulling her up the stairway.

But now the rumble of the mountain was joined by a mighty roar.

Shanna felt a sudden pressure in her head, worse than before.

It wasn't enough to knock her out, but she felt a wave of vertigo and staggered, nearly falling.

Cameron caught her as she wobbled dizzily, stumbling on the steps. Taking her weight, he grabbed her up into his arms, carrying her like a bride over the threshold, as he ran up the stairs.

On the top deck, Maverick had the chopper started and he was waving frantically.

"Let's *go!*"

At that moment, a massive claw reached over the edge of the cliff as Draco pulled himself up to the top.

His spike-fanged jaws were pulled back in a snarl and they could see his eyes glowing bright emerald green.

Cameron and Shanna scrambled aboard the chopper even as

Maverick launched them into the air.

Draco's claw smashed down a half-second later, shattering the tarmac where they had been.

Maverick took them straight up, past the circling pterosaurs, aiming for the clouds.

Beneath them, the top deck began to crumble, falling in on the Mount's hollow core.

Draco roared.

At his feet, the Mount split upon itself as the pressure from below reached its peak.

The volcano erupted.

Draco's scream rose and then was drowned out as lava and ash exploded into the air all around him. The eagles and pterosaurs circling above were either smothered in the burning plume or else turned and fled.

For a moment, Draco stood engulfed in flame.

Then the mountain crumbled beneath his feet and he disappeared, collapsing into the billowing smoke and fire.

CHAPTER 80

The Mount crumbled down to its hollow foundation as the eruption spread to the surrounding peaks. In the gulf below, the water boiled as lava emptied into the ocean – pliosaurs and Megs alike were boiled alive.

In surrounding wilds, the beasts had fled. Some stragglers were overcome by smoke, some burned in lava, but most retreated to the outskirts of the territory.

Big Red and the rex-queen paused on one of the neighboring peaks, looking back on the destruction.

Caesar rode astride Big Red's mighty back, with Cornelius and Zaius still perched upon the queen's. So far, neither of the two giant rex had even noticed their presence – no more than the birds that occasionally lit across their hides to dig insects and parasites out of their skin.

Their rivalry, it seemed, faded with scale.

Around them, the tundra continued to rumble as the seismic turbulence bubbled beneath the surface, but the entire territory now seemed oddly subdued.

The psychic pull of the region was gone.

Draco was dead – and that psychic stench of Otto had been likewise cleared out, at least in the immediate area. Caesar suspected the scaly little rats would continue to fester elsewhere – certainly in the territories to the east. They were a hard pest to eradicate.

But for most of the beasts, once they were beyond the volcanic upheaval, they simply, aimlessly went on their way. And while the Food of the Gods continued to percolate in their simple minds, the aggravating factors that had exacerbated their mental deterioration settled, for the moment, into remission.

Caesar looked up to the sky. Shanna's chopper was already out of sight, but the big ape sensed she was returning to her Valley.

Big Red obviously felt the same, as he and the queen turned from the ashes of the Mount and began moving west.

Presently, the king rex was joined by Junior and Rudy, and the rest of the surviving rex pack.

Having no further concerns, they all headed for home.

CHAPTER 81

Eight weeks later, everyone was home back in the Valley.

There had, of course, been a few significant changes.

First and foremost was a rex-pack now grown to titan-proportions – not to mention a bloom that had been spread across most of the surrounding territory.

Shanna had set about administering the counter-agent in mass quantities for weeks following the fall of the Dragon Lord, arresting the cycle of madness, minimizing the potential destruction, and saving the lives of as many of the infected beasts as possible.

The long-term effects to the ecology from a sustained population of giants throughout the region would have to wait to be seen.

Shanna had some ideas going forward, however.

Most importantly, the temperament among the Valley's *T. rex* had once again mellowed, perhaps even more than before, with the addition of Leanne's own light.

Even Junior, Shanna assured a dubious Mark, would be on his best behavior going forward, so long as the two of them were around.

Shanna and her party's return to the Valley had been met with a hero's welcome, as the community greeted her with all the love and respect due a queen.

Of course, one of the warmest receptions was perhaps reserved for Maverick, as he stood before his father with nothing but the keys to the cargo plane in his hand.

Maverick had worked out a story beforehand, but Cameron had jumped in quickly, pointing at Maverick and exclaiming loudly, "He wrecked your plane, Mr. Wilson! I saw it! Tore it right in half!"

Mr. Wilson had been happy to see his son and was glad he was alive. The first punch didn't even knock Maverick down. The second did. So did several succeeding blows.

The Valley-folk, however, were not the only ones who greeted Shanna with reverence – there was also the influx of the refugees from the Mount, almost all of whom told Shanna they had seen her in their dreams, some of them for a good portion of their lives.

Of course, not all the refugees were from the Mount.

Naomi had approached Shanna on that first day, wracked with grief, and had burst out crying at the sight of her.

"I've dreamed of you for so long," she said.

Then she had told Shanna of Jonah, and of their life together – and about how it had finally ended. She also told her about her miscarriages and how she was pregnant once again.

Shanna felt a strong shine from this woman and had touched Naomi's stomach lightly – and she felt the light growing within her as well.

"They're strong too," Shanna said.

Naomi had blinked.

"*They?*"

Shanna smiled, nodding.

"Twins," she said.

But it was Mark who received the biggest surprise on his return to the Valley that day.

As he had come walking through the jubilant crowd, Dawn had separated from the others, bouncing joyously, running up to hug Mark with both arms. She had called over her shoulder.

"Mother! This is him! He's the one who saved me!"

Sally had separated from the crowd.

Mark had stared, his heart hitching in his chest.

For a moment, he doubted his own eyes – his voice was caught firmly in his throat.

"*Sally...?*" he said.

Sally smiled back at him.

Dawn looked at the two of them, startled.

"You know each other?"

Sally had reached over and pulled Dawn close to her in the manner of introduction.

"Mark," she said, "say hello to your daughter."

Mark had much to celebrate that night, both he and Sally, well into the morning.

And then, on the day marking the eighth week after the fall of the Dragon Lord, Leanne and Lucas were married.

The entire Valley gathered for the celebration – even Caesar and the ape-tribe attended – along with a pack of giant *T. rex*, which stood presiding at the perimeter like a giant honor guard.

Rosa, a bridesmaid, had cried at the vows. Shanna, also crying, had hugged her friend, and then received an empathic surprise of her own.

She pulled back and looked at Rosa knowingly.

"When are you due?" she asked.

Their eyes both fell on Maverick, standing beside Cameron and looking uncomfortable in his tux.

"How long were you two locked up together?" Shanna asked.

"We still hate each other," Rosa assured her. "It was just sex."

"He'll be a good father," Shanna said.

"I know," Rosa said, pained. "Damn him to hell."

Maverick glanced over at the two women watching him and Shanna could see him coloring redly.

On stage, Leanne and Lucas – who was still adorned with a foot cast and numerous bandages – exchanged vows, and Mr. Wilson, who had been ordained a minister in his younger days, pronounced them husband and wife.

The young lovers kissed and their town cheered them on.

Shanna smiled up at them, pulling Cameron tightly to her side and reflected that hers was certainly not the worst of lives.

Sure, it was a wild world but hadn't it always been? And sure, Otto still lurked out there somewhere, probably cooking up some new deviltry at that very moment. And certainly, the future would bring challenges and trials anew.

But that was the future and she would deal with it as it came – as would they all.

For today, they were happy.

CHAPTER 82

There was one member of the refugees from the Mount who didn't rush up to Shanna and tell her how she'd dreamed about her.

Lily's dreams had always been of a darker persuasion, even though she had a natural shine.

As did her daughter.

And while the Valley celebrated the union of Lucas and Leanne, Lily and Sabrina sat on the hill, just above what had been Lucas' parents' house, where Allison and Bud had been murdered so many years before.

Otto sat perched on Sabrina's shoulder.

When Sabrina had made her way back to the Coven's settlement, she had found Teresa, along with Luna and Abbi and all the rest, slaughtered – torn apart in the distinctive fashion of sickle-claws.

There had been the remains of several Ottos as well, their minds blown, struck down by the Dragon Lord.

But among the Ottos, there had been one survivor. Sabrina had found the small creature struggling gimpishly, half its body paralyzed, like the victim of a stroke, and she had done her best to nurse the little lizard back to health.

Now it clung to her shoulder like a spider-monkey.

It had led her the rest of the way to the Valley.

Lily herself had separated from the crowd on the arrival of the Valley's heroes. She had seen Mark greet Sally for the first time in twenty years like a soldier on VJ-day.

She had turned and run at that point, just as she had fled from her first sight of Shanna.

Shanna might have felt her shine and understood the darkness within her.

Lily and Sabrina had found each other at the outskirts of the Valley, and now they watched as those below celebrated the destruction of everything the two of them had once held dear – all the dreams of a lifetime.

Dark dreams.

They looked on from the hill above as Leanne and Lucas completed their vows.

And anyone objecting to their union would now forevermore hold

their peace.
    So they would see.
    Sitting on Sabrina's shoulder, Otto chittered.
    In its claws, it clutched a vial of glowing-green.

CHECK OUT OTHER GREAT DINOSAUR BOOKS

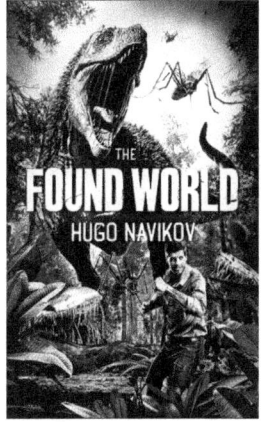

THE FOUND WORLD
by **Hugo Navikov**

A powerful global cabal wants adventurer Brett Russell to retrieve a superweapon stolen by the scientist who built it. To entice him to travel underneath one of the most dangerous volcanoes on Earth to find the scientist, this shadowy organization will pay him the only thing he cares about: information that will allow him to avenge his family's murder.

But before he can get paid, he and his team must enter an underground hellscape of killer plants, giant insects, terrifying dinosaurs, and an army of other predators never previously seen by man.

At the end of this journey awaits a revelation that could alter the fate of mankind ... if they can make it back from this horrifying found world.

HOUSE OF THE GODS
by **Davide Mana**

High above the steamy jungle of the Amazon basin, rise the flat plateaus known as the Tepui, the House of the Gods. Lost worlds of unknown beauty, a naturalistic wonder, each an ecology onto itself, shunned by the local tribes for centuries. The House of the Gods was not made for men.

But now, the crew and passengers of a small charter plane are about to find what was hidden for sixty million years.

Lost on an island in the clouds 10.000 feet above the jungle, surrounded by dinosaurs, hunted by mysterious mercenaries, the survivors of Sligo Air flight 001 will quickly learn the only rule of life on Earth: Extinction.

CHECK OUT OTHER GREAT DINOSAUR BOOKS

PRIMORDIA
by **Greig Beck**

Ben Cartwright, former soldier, home to mourn the loss of his father stumbles upon cryptic letters from the past between the author, Arthur Conan Doyle and his great, great grandfather who vanished while exploring the Amazon jungle in 1908.

Amazingly, these letters lead Ben to believe that his ancestor's expedition was the basis for Doyle's fantastical tale of a lost world inhabited by long extinct creatures. As Ben digs some more he finds clues to the whereabouts of a lost notebook that might contain a map to a place that is home to creatures that would rewrite everything known about history, biology and evolution.

But other parties now know about the notebook, and will do anything to obtain it. For Ben and his friends, it becomes a race against time and against ruthless rivals.

In the remotest corners of Venezuela, along winding river trails known only to lost tribes, and through near impenetrable jungle, Ben and his novice team find a forbidden place more terrifying and dangerous than anything they could ever have imagined.

PANGAEA EXILES
by **Jeff Brackett**

Tried and convicted for his crimes, Sean Barrow is sent into temporal exile—banished to a time so far before recorded history that there is no chance that he, or any other criminal sent back, has any chance of altering history.

Now Sean must find a way to survive more than 200 million years in the past, in a world populated by monstrous creatures that would rend him limb from limb if they got the chance. And that's just his fellow prisoners.

The dinosaurs are almost as bad.

CHECK OUT OTHER GREAT DINOSAUR BOOKS

FLIPSIDE
by JAKE BIBLE

The year is 2046 and dinosaurs are real.

Time bubbles across the world, many as large as one hundred square miles, turn like clockwork, revealing prehistoric landscapes from the Cretaceous Period.

They reveal the Flipside.

Now, thirty years after the first Turn, the clockwork is breaking down as one of the world's powers has decided to exploit the phenomenon for their own gain, possibly destroying everything then and now in the process.

A MAN OUT OF TIME
by Christopher Laflan

Five years after the Chinese Axis detonated an unknown weapon of mass destruction off the southern coast of the United States, Special Ops Sergeant John Crider and the members of Shadow Company have finally captured what they all hope will lead to the end of the war. Unfortunately, the population within the United States is no longer sustainable. In an effort to stabilize the economy, the government enacts the Cryonics Act. One hundred years in suspended animation, all debt forgiven, and a chance at a less crowded future are too good to pass up for John and his young daughter.

Except not everything always goes as planned as Sergeant John Crider finds himself pitted against a land of prehistoric monsters genetically resurrected from the fossil record, murderous inhabitants, and a future he never wanted.

www.ingramcontent.com/pod-product-compliance
Lightning Source LLC
Chambersburg PA
CBHW060406180626
46817CB00007B/2533